JOE COLTON'S JOURNAL

Well my birthday celebration sure was explosive! It's not every day that the guest of honor is the target for murder! Now I've hired the best there is—P.I. Austin McGrath—to investigate this atrocity. But I never imagined that Austin's involvement would result in a budding romance with my fragile foster daughter, Rebecca. She's had a real traumatic past and is afraid to let anyone get close. Especially a ladies' man like Austin. But he's not as cavalier as he appears. I see the pain in his eyes. He's brooding over something—but what? Maybe between the two of them, these lost souls will find solace in each other's arms. And though it won't be easy, stranger things have happened. Speaking of strange, Meredith sure is acting more bizarre with each Pacific sunset. I'm beginning to worry that there's something wrong with my wife—and that the future of the entire Colton dynasty could be in jeopardy....

About the Author

LINDA TURNER

was thrilled when she was asked to write the second book in THE COLTONS series. "I love these kinds of stories—the more complicated the better. And THE COLTONS series was of special interest because of Patsy and Meredith. I, too, have an identical twin sister, and in the not-too-distant past, we traded places, both at work and at school, and no one knew the difference until we identified ourselves. Of course, we never went so far as to trick boyfriends or husbands, and there wasn't a good twin and a bad one, but we still had fun." She says that Patsy was especially interesting to write because she's so close to the edge—sort of like Cruella DeVille, only worse. Linda loved the scenes with both her and Meredith.

As for her hero and heroine, Austin and Rebecca, what's not to love? They both had such tragic pasts. She really enjoyed helping them find happiness. She hopes you enjoy it, too.

The
Virgin
Mistress

Linda Turner

Published by Silhouette Books

America's Publisher of Contemporary Romance

Special thanks and acknowledgment are given
to Linda Turner for her contribution
to THE COLTONS series.

SILHOUETTE BOOKS
300 East 42nd St.,
New York, N. Y. 10017

ISBN 0-373-38705-9

THE VIRGIN MISTRESS

Visit Silhouette at www.eHarlequin.com

Printed in U.S.A.

The Virgin Mistress

Linda Turner

Published by Silhouette Books

America's Publisher of Contemporary Romance

Special thanks and acknowledgment are given
to Linda Turner for her contribution
to THE COLTONS series.

SILHOUETTE BOOKS
300 East 42nd St.,
New York, N. Y. 10017

ISBN 0-373-38705-9

THE VIRGIN MISTRESS

Visit Silhouette at www.eHarlequin.com

Printed in U.S.A.

THE COLTONS

*Meet the Coltons—
a California dynasty with a legacy of privilege and power.*

Austin McGrath: *The passionate detective.* Beneath his footloose facade, this bachelor would put his life on the line any day to see justice served. But did he have the courage to turn his fantasy of a wife and family into a reality?

Rebecca Powell: *The oldest living virgin.* Though the Coltons had provided a safe haven for the then-fourteen-year-old runaway, this schoolteacher is still haunted by her nightmarish childhood. Do the patient P.I.'s caresses offer more than just comfort...? Perhaps the promise of a future together?

Meredith "Pasty" Colton: *The scheming impostor.* Her nerves worn to a frazzle by the police investigation into Joe's attempted murder, the deranged sibling knows that after ten years it's time to find the real "Meredith"....

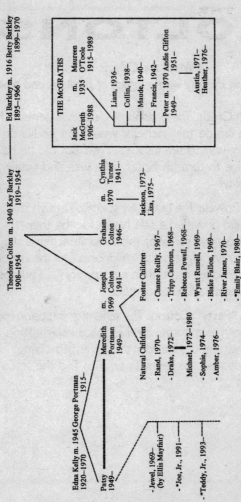

THE COLTONS

Theodore Colton m. 1940 Kay Barkley
1908–1954   1919–1954

Ed Barkley m. 1916 Betty Barkley
1895–1966   1899–1970

Joseph Colton m. 1969 Cynthia Turner
1941–   1941–

Graham Colton
1946–

Jackson, 1973–
Liza, 1975–

Edna Kelly m. 1945 George Portman
1920–1970   1915–

Meredith Portman
1949–

Patsy
1949–

Foster Children
- Chance Reilly, 1967–
- Tripp Calhoun, 1968–
- Rebecca Powell, 1968–
- Wyatt Russell, 1969–
- Blake Fallon, 1969–
- River James, 1970–
- *Emily Blair, 1980–

Natural Children
- Rand, 1970–
- Drake, 1972–
- Michael, 1972–1980
- Sophie, 1974–
- Amber, 1976–

- Jewel, 1969–
  (by Ellis Mayfair)
- *Joe, Jr., 1991–
- *Teddy, Jr., 1993–

THE McGRATHS

Jack McGrath   m. 1935   Maureen O'Toole
1906–1988   1915–1989

Liam, 1936–
Collin, 1938–
Maude, 1940–
Francis, 1942–
Peter m. 1970 Audie Clifton
1949–   1951–

Austin, 1971–
Heather, 1976–

LEGEND
— Child of Affair
━ Twins
* Adopted by Joe Colton

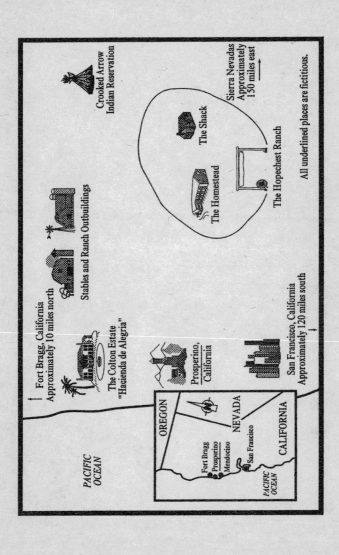

One

Someone had tried to kill him.

A week after the fact, Joe Colton still couldn't believe it. He'd been surrounded by friends and family, his champagne glass lifted in a toast in honor of his sixtieth birthday, when a bullet had ripped through the party, shattered his glass and grazed his cheek. Even now he could still feel the heat of it, the shock.

For days, he'd been trying to convince himself and the police that this was all just some terrible accident. He couldn't imagine why anyone would bring a gun to his birthday party, but it must have discharged by accident and he'd just happened to be in the line of fire. It was the only logical explanation. No one had actually meant him any harm.

Thaddeus Law and the two other detectives handling the case, however, weren't quite so sure of that. A friend didn't bring a gun to a party—it wasn't good etiquette.

And when that same gun went off and just missed the guest of honor by a hairsbreadth, there could be no misunderstanding. This was no joke. Someone wanted him dead badly enough to try to kill him in front of three hundred witnesses.

The question was...who? Who hated him that much?

Joe wasn't stupid enough to think he had no enemies. Like every successful man, he had, no doubt, stepped on a few toes over the years, but he'd never deliberately hurt anyone to get ahead. He wasn't that kind of man. He was fair and hardworking and he'd never taken anything from anyone that didn't belong to him. So who had taken that shot at him?

The police thought it was someone in his family.

Oh, they hadn't come straight out and said as much, but their suspicions were pretty obvious. And he knew the statistics. People weren't usually killed by strangers—it was someone they knew, and often loved and trusted, who did them in.

Maybe that was true in a large percentage of cases, but not in his, dammit! His family was important to him—everyone knew that! He'd left the Senate to devote more time to his children and the foster children he and Meredith had welcomed into their home. He worked closely with his brother and foster brother, not to mention the friends he'd made over the years and brought into Colton Enterprises, and he refused to believe any of them wanted him dead.

Which meant that it had to be a stranger, maybe a crazy, disgruntled constituent who read about the party in the gossip columns and decided to sneak in with the party-goers to kill him. Or a psychopath who felt like Joe deserved to die just because the price of gas was going up and he owned oil wells. There were a lot of nuts walking around free.

He'd told the police that, but no one seemed to be listening. After the shooting, the detectives had gone over the estate with a fine-tooth comb, taking statements from everyone present, but it was obvious from the beginning who the authorities suspected—his family. And it infuriated him. Idiots! They were pressuring people he loved—even Meredith, for God's sake!—and he wasn't going to stand around with his hands in his pockets while the real culprit got away with attempted murder. If the police couldn't track the bastard down, then he knew someone who could.

The decision made, he reached for the phone on his desk, punched in a number, and sighed in relief when the son of his foster brother, Peter, came on the line. "Austin McGrath, private investigator," his nephew said brusquely. "May I help you?"

"I certainly hope so," Joe growled. "Someone tried to kill me Saturday night."

Leaning back in the old leather chair he'd bought at a secondhand store when he'd first opened his own office, Austin sat up straighter with a frown. "I know," he said, recognizing his foster uncle's voice immediately. "Dad told me about it. I've been meaning to call you, but I got tied up in a case and had to make a quick trip to Vancouver. How's the investigation going? Dad said half of California was there, so there must have been plenty of witnesses. Have the police made an arrest yet?"

Joe snorted at that. "They're a bunch of bumbling idiots. It's been a week since the shooting and they still don't have a clue what they're doing. Which is why I'm calling. I need you to come down and find out who tried to kill me."

Austin wasn't crazy about going to California. It wasn't that he didn't like Joe or sympathize with his situation—he'd just never had much to do with the Colton side of the family. With their money and political clout, they were almost like the Kennedys of the West Coast. They even lived on an estate like the Hyannis Port compound, for God's sake!

Austin grimaced just at the thought of it. He had little interest in living that kind of high-profile existence and much preferred his quiet lifestyle in Portland. Unfortunately, he couldn't, in good conscience, refuse to come to Joe's aid because he didn't care for all the flash and glitter that went hand in hand with the Coltons. Joe and his father were brothers, though they shared no blood, and they'd always been there for each other. For his father's sake—and the fact that he couldn't stand by and let some bastard get away with trying to murder anyone, let alone his uncle—he, too, had to be there for him.

"I need to wrap up a few things here and arrange for a friend to take over the office for me for a couple of weeks," he replied. "If everything goes all right, I should be able to fly down late tomorrow. How does that sound?"

Relieved, Joe sighed, and it was that, more than anything, that told Austin just how rattled his uncle was. "Great," Joe said. "You don't know how much I appreciate this. You'll stay at the house, of course. I'll have Meredith prepare the guest room for you—"

"I'd rather you didn't," Austin said honestly.

He was more than willing to do whatever he could for Joe, but he drew the line at staying at the estate. From what his father had told him, there was no such thing as a quiet evening at home with the Coltons and he didn't know how Joe stood it. There were always several guests for dinner, not to mention business dinners several times a week and the socializing that never seemed to end. And while he knew he would have to endure some of that in order to conduct his investigation, Austin had no intention of suffering through any more of it than he had to. At the end of a long, hard day, he preferred the peace and quiet of his own company, not polite chitchat with a house full of strangers.

That wasn't, however, something he could tell Joe without being rude, so he said tactfully, "The investigation needs to be unbiased. It'll be easier to remain objective if I stay at a hotel."

Far from being offended, Joe saw right through his excuse and only chuckled. "I should have known you'd want to get a place of your own. You always did like to go your own way."

Grinning, Austin didn't deny it. He'd always been something of a rebel, and he made no apologies for it. Unlike the rest of the family, who all seemed to work for Joe in one capacity or another, he'd never had any desire to work for Colton Enterprises. Instead, after a stint in the Navy, he'd joined the Portland police department and worked his way up to detective. A shoot-out with drug dealers eventually ended that, but he still hadn't turned to Joe for a job. He liked police work and opened his own detective agency, instead. Like Joe, he liked being his own boss.

"Guilty as charged," he retorted. "I'm just more comfortable that way, especially when I'm working. I like to be able to move around without answering to anyone."

"Hey, you don't have to explain yourself to me or apologize," Joe said quickly. "Your dad says you're damn good at this P.I. stuff, so do whatever you have to do. You won't hear any complaints from me."

"Fair enough," Austin said. "I'll call you when I get into town."

Hanging up, he sat back in his chair and frowned down at the quick notes he'd made as Joe told him about the shooting. The details were sketchy—he'd get the rest of the facts when he got to town—but one thing was clear: Someone Joe knew and loved wanted him dead. But who?

The Colton estate near Prosperino, California, was called the Hacienda del Alegria—the House of Joy—and it gave every appearance of being just that. Situated in a beautiful valley, the large sand-colored adobe house faced the mountains in the distance and backed up to the ocean, offering spectacular views from every direction.

As a child, Austin had loved coming there. There was the ranch to explore, as well as the ocean, and then there was the house, itself. Built with two wings that jutted off the main section, it was a home, not just a house, thanks to Meredith. Back then, she'd had no interest in being a society queen, just a wife and mother, and she'd made sure the house was comfortably decorated and filled with children. She'd even done much of the gardening around the main house herself, and in the process, she'd created a lush tropical paradise that everyone had loved.

It had been years since Austin had been there, but the minute he drove down the lane to the house, he could see that it wasn't the same as he remembered from his childhood. Oh, the house was the same structurally, but the grounds were professionally landscaped now and looked just like any other rich man's estate.

And so did the house itself. The second the housekeeper, Inez, who had been with the family as long as Austin could remember, opened the door for him, he could see that this wasn't the home he'd always enjoyed visiting when he was a child. It was too formal. In a single glance, Austin noted the expensive decor that had replaced the once comfortable furnishings that had made the house so welcoming in the past. The inviting home he remembered now appeared to be just a showcase for the Colton wealth. And that was a shame.

When he greeted Inez, however, none of his thoughts were reflected in his smile. "It's been a long time, Inez. I don't have to ask if Marco's been taking care of you. You look wonderful."

At the mention of her husband, who was the head groundskeeper, her pretty black eyes twinkled merrily. "Marco's a smart man," she replied. "He knows I'm the best thing that every happened to him." Sobering, she confided, "Mr. Joe will be glad you're here. These last few days haven't been easy for him."

"No, I don't imagine they have. I'll need to talk to you later about that, okay?"

"Any time, Mr. Austin. I was just about to start supper. You're family. You know the way, right?"

It had been years, but Austin could have found Joe's study blindfolded in the dark. "Sure. Thanks."

Located down the hall from the living room, the study was decorated just as Austin remembered—with a huge oak desk and big, comfortable leather chairs, and books everywhere. Pleased that that much had stayed the same, at least, Austin grinned at the sight of his uncle scowling at his computer screen. It had been years since he'd seen him but he was still one good-looking son of a gun. At sixty, he was strong and athletic in spite of the gray that peppered his dark brown hair.

"Watch it, Unc," he teased. "Frowning like that's going to cause wrinkles. And you've hit sixty now. You have to be careful about that kind of thing."

"Austin! Thank God! Just the man I wanted to see." Grinning broadly, he jumped up from his chair and strode around his desk to envelop him in a bear hug. "I made some notes of the shooting and was just going over them. I keep thinking if I read them enough, I'll figure out who the hell tried to kill me."

That sounded good, but Austin knew better than to think it would be that easy. Someone had come damn close to pulling off a murder in full view of an entire party of birthday guests without anyone seeing him—or her. Which meant this wasn't a crime of passion. It had been plotted and planned down to the smallest detail by someone who didn't lack for cleverness or daring. Cracking it wasn't going to be easy.

Nodding at the computer screen and Joe's notes as he sank into one the chairs in front of his desk, he said, "I'd like to have a copy of that and the guest list. I'll need to talk to everyone who was here that night."

"I've got it all right here," his uncle said, handing him the information he'd already printed out for him. "The police needed the same thing, not that they did much with it," he added in disgust. "They gave the family a hard look and didn't look any further."

Not surprised, Austin said, "You can't really blame them, Joe. Think about it. Somebody tried to kill you at your own birthday party. There were no enemies here at the house that day—at least none that you were aware of when you sent out the invitations. Just friends and family—people who have the most to gain from your death. I bet everyone who's named in your will was here on Saturday night, weren't they?"

Not liking that one little bit, Joe growled, "Are you saying you agree with the police? I need to be suspicious of my own family?"

He gave him a look that had, no doubt, made lesser men quake in their shoes, but Austin didn't so much as blink. Joe had called him down to Prosperino to do a job, and he intended to do it—even when that meant telling him something he didn't want to hear.

"I won't know that until I examine the facts and talk to the witnesses," he said honestly. "Only time will tell. For your sake, I hope the shooter's not someone in the family, but if that's who it turns out to be, you'll have to deal with it. You could end up dead if you don't."

His expression grim, Joe had little choice but to agree with him. "Just find out who it is as quickly as possible. This not knowing is eating me alive."

"I'll get on it first thing in the morning," Austin promised. "After I read your accounting of the shooting and get a feel for what happened."

Satisfied, Joe couldn't ask for anything more. "Good. Do what you have to do." Pulling out the top drawer of his desk, he removed a key and slid it across the desk to him. "Here. I had you a key to the house made. I want you to feel free to come and go here as much as you like. If you need anything, all you have to do is ask. If I'm not around, Meredith should be, and I'll instruct Inez to co-operate with you in whatever way she can."

Rising to his feet, Austin held out his hand. "Thanks, Joe. That'll help a lot."

Anxious to read Joe's accounting of the shooting, he would have left then, but Meredith bustled in just then, looking flustered and more than a little put out. "Austin! I told Inez to let me know when you arrived, but as usual, she ignored me. I don't know why we keep her on. She doesn't follow orders and she's only a competent cook, at best."

"Inez is a part of the family," Joe said with a disapproving frown. "As for her cooking, I'm sure Austin would agree that she makes the best chocolate cake on the planet."

"Oh, yeah," Austin agreed with a quick grin, his mouth watering just at the memory of some of the great meals he'd had there as a kid. "And don't forget her chicken enchiladas. They're fantastic."

Far from appeased, Meredith only sniffed. "If you like that sort of thing. But she still doesn't follow orders worth a damn."

Studying his aunt, Austin frowned slightly, surprised by her attitude. From what he remembered, Meredith and Inez had never had an employer-servant type of relationship. They'd always worked together to make the house a comfortable and inviting home, so there'd been no such thing as orders between them. When had that changed?

"She said something about starting supper," he said. "Maybe she just forgot."

"She always forgets, but at least she does serve the meals on time. I suppose that's something." Dismissing the subject with a shrug of her slender shoulders, she turned a bright smile on Austin. "There won't be any chicken enchiladas for supper, but there is chocolate cake for dessert. Inez just made one yesterday. You are staying to eat with us, aren't you? It's just the family—the boys and Rebecca. I had planned to include Senator Hays—he and his wife know *everyone* who's anyone in the California social scene—but Joe wanted a quiet evening at home."

Grimacing as if she couldn't understand that, she added, "Please stay. It's been so long since we've seen you, and I'm just dying to know how you're going to find out who tried to kill Joe. Where do you even begin? Obviously, you're smarter than the police—"

"Leave the boy alone, Meredith," Joe growled. "He just got here, for God's sake! He hasn't even had time to read my notes, and when he does start investigating the case, you can be damn sure he's not going to talk about it to you or anyone else. So don't pester him. He'll let me know when he's narrowed down a suspect."

For just a second, her brown eyes snapped with fire, and Austin thought she was going to let his uncle have it with a few choice words, which was surprising. All couples had their moments when they irritated each other, but from what Austin remembered, there had always been a deep affection between Joe and Meredith that had been obvious even when they disagreed. But not today. If Austin hadn't known better, he'd have sworn they thoroughly disliked each other. What the devil was going on here?

Before he could even think about asking, Meredith smiled coolly and confided to Austin, "Don't pay any attention to him when he growls, Austin. I don't. Will you stay for dinner?"

Already on the job and intrigued by the tension that crackled between his aunt and uncle, Austin wouldn't have missed it for the world. "I'd be delighted."

The food was great, just as Austin had expected, and the best home cooking he'd had in a long time. But it was the company that held his full attention. Joe and Meredith were civil to each other, and to all appearances, they seemed to be like any other couple who'd made up after a disagreement. Austin, however, had learned a long time ago not to be taken in by appearances. Whatever was going on between his aunt and uncle went deep.

And then there were the kids—Emily, Joe Junior, and Teddy. Austin supposed he could hardly call Emily a child anymore. Adopted by Joe and Meredith when she was just a toddler, she was now eighteen and a sweet, pretty, self-possessed young woman. Her brothers, however, weren't nearly as mature. Nine and seven respectively, Joe Junior and Teddy were both good-looking boys and growing like weeds. And much to their discomfort, they were the apple of their mother's eye. She watched over their every move, fussing over them until they both squirmed. "Don't slouch, Joe. Teddy, eat your vegetables. You know you can't have cake later if you don't clean your plate."

"Geez, Mom!"

"I don't know why we have to eat broccoli. Dad doesn't."

"Because Mother knows what's best for you, and if your father doesn't want to eat properly so he'll be healthy, he's the one who'll pay the price. Teddy, you know better than to use your salad fork for the entree. Please eat correctly."

They both shot her rebellious looks when she wasn't looking, and Austin couldn't say he blamed them. He'd always hated someone picking at him when he ate when he was a kid. As far as he could remember, Meredith had never done that with the older children. She certainly wasn't with Emily—she hardly spared her a glance. Why was she so protective of the boys?

And then there was Rebecca Powell, who sat across the table from him. Where did she fit in in the family dynamics? He knew he'd met her before, when she'd first come to the ranch as a foster child after Meredith had come to her aid at the Hopechest Ranch, a shelter for children from troubled homes where she'd donated much of her time. He didn't remember—if he'd ever known—the circumstances that had brought Rebecca to the shelter, but she'd touched Meredith's heart so deeply that she and Joe had offered her a home with them, just as they had other lost children over the years. Now in her early thirties, Rebecca was still very much a part of the family.

And far more beautiful than he remembered.

Caught off guard by the direction of his thoughts, Austin stiffened. Oh, no, he told himself. He wasn't going there. Rebecca was pretty—he'd give her that. Tall and willowy, with the grace and height of a dancer, she was modestly dressed in a skirt and blouse and wore her long brown hair in a French braid that fell halfway down her back. Normally, Austin doubted he would have even noticed her because she was quiet and shy and did little to call attention to herself. But for some reason, that only made her harder to ignore. She didn't say much, but beneath her thick, dark lashes, she sneaked a peek at him, and one look at those soulful, blue-gray eyes of hers and Austin felt like he'd been kicked in the heart.

Surprised, he frowned and tried to convince himself he'd imagined his reaction to her. Since his wife, Jenny, and their baby had died years ago, he'd been the love-and-leave-'em ladies' man. He'd wanted nothing to do with commitment, with any kind of feelings that could lead to hurt, and the fast and loose women he'd gone out with hadn't had a problem with that.

He didn't have to know anything at all about Rebecca to know that there was nothing fast and loose about her. She had love and marriage written all over her, and that made her the kind of woman he avoided like the plague. The investigation would keep him busy, and once he discovered who wanted Joe dead, he'd go back to Portland, where he didn't have to worry about a quiet woman with blue-gray eyes who disturbed him far more than she should have.

Lost in his thoughts, he didn't notice that Rebecca was now openly studying him until she said softly, "Joe said you needed to interview everyone at the party. Since you don't know the city, I can help you with that if you like."

"That's a good idea, honey," Joe said, pleased. "Rebecca's a teacher at a year-round school," he told Austin. "She's usually home by three-thirty every afternoon, so she could help you after that."

"But she has a heavy schedule at school," Meredith reminded him as she shot Rebecca a worried frown. "Are you sure you want to do this, sweetheart? I thought you were going to do some extra work with the Thompson boy after school."

"I am. We start Monday, in fact. But that's only once in a while. The rest of the time, I'm free. And then, there's the weekends."

When Meredith's frown only intensified, Austin stepped in, not wanting to be the cause of a family argument, though why Meredith would care if Rebecca helped him, he didn't know. "I appreciate the offer," he said quietly, "but I'm used to working alone. It's just better that way."

For a moment, he thought he saw disappointment darken her eyes, but then she lowered her gaze to her plate. "It was just a thought," she said with a shrug. "If you change your mind, just let me know."

He wouldn't, but she didn't have to know that. There was no use hurting her feelings any more than he already had. "Thanks," he said. "I'll keep that in mind."

When he returned to his hotel room after dinner, he was sure he wouldn't call her. It just wouldn't be smart. Not when he was drawn to her in a way he hadn't been to a woman in a long time. He didn't need that kind of complication in his life.

But over the course of the next few days, he found

himself thinking of her more than he should have, and it didn't help matters that the investigation wasn't going anywhere. Using the guest list Joe had given him, he systematically began interviewing the guests, starting with the family members and friends who'd been standing near Joe when the shot rang out. But after talking to well over twenty people—and the detectives who were handling the case—he was no further along than when he'd started. None of them claimed to have seen anything. And questioning them about possible suspects hadn't helped, either. Trying to help, all they'd talked about was old slights and resentments that hadn't amounted to a hill of beans.

"This is unbelievable," Austin muttered in disgust as he left the law office of one of Joe's oldest neighbors, who'd gone on and on about another neighbor who had never forgiven Joe for some perceived transgression or another. "I don't care about petty grievances. A bullet grazed Joe's cheek, for God's sake! He's got a serious enemy out there."

The question was, who? Over three hundred people had been at Joe's party, but so far, no one had admitted seeing anything. And some of them were standing right there next to him! Someone had to be lying, but there was no way for Austin to know who, not at this point. He didn't know the dynamics of Joe's family and friends, didn't know who had old grudges and new, who could lie with a straight face and who would need to. And without that information, his job would only be that much more difficult.

So call Rebecca. She's like family, but she's not. She'll be objective, and she already offered to help you.

Irritated with the needling voice that was quick to whisper the suggestion in his ear, he scowled as he slipped behind the wheel of his rental car and told himself to forget it. He wasn't calling her. He'd spent all of an hour with her the other night and he could still see that shy, hesitant smile of hers. It was far too memorable for his peace of mind.

Knowing that, he should have never reached for his cell phone. He did it, anyway.

"Rebecca? This is Austin McGrath."

Her heart suddenly skipping in her breast, Rebecca sank down onto a stool at her kitchen counter. "Austin! H-hi. How are you?"

"Actually, I'm in a bit of a bind," he admitted. "Are you busy? I was hoping I could drop by your place and run a few things by you."

"Now?"

"If that's okay with you. I could use your help."

"Oh…yes, of course. You have the address, don't you? I just live a few miles down the road from the estate at the Ocean Bluff Apartments. I'm in 323."

"I'll be right there," he assured her, and hung up.

Rebecca knew it was foolish, but for a moment, she'd thought he was calling to tell her he wanted to see her again. Not that a man like Austin would look twice at her, she admitted wryly. She'd been in the family long enough to hear the stories about him. She knew about his wife and baby's tragic deaths in childbirth, how he hadn't let a woman get close to him since. Instead, he'd found comfort in the arms of a bevy of beauties who weren't anymore interested in a commitment than he was.

That wasn't who she was, and she supposed Austin only had to look at her to know that. And that, she acknowledged sadly, was for the best. Because the only thing he wanted from a woman was the one thing she couldn't give him.

Pain squeezed her heart, and for a moment, she couldn't

stop herself from hoping that maybe someday soon, things would be different. But even as she clung to the thought, she knew better than to let herself fall into that trap. She hadn't been able to let a man touch her since she was a teenager, and that was never going to change.

And that hurt. Why couldn't she be normal like other women? Why couldn't she feel comfort in the arms of a man she liked and cared about instead of fear?

But even as she asked, she knew the answer to that. Her childhood hadn't been an easy one. She'd never known her real father, and her mother was an alcoholic who was always bringing home all sorts of men. Then when she was fourteen, one of those men—Frank—nearly assaulted her. Frightened and feeling like she had no one to turn to for help, she ran away from home. But she'd only jumped from the frying pan into the fire. She'd lived on the streets for six months and was in constant danger. One night while she was staying in a homeless shelter, she was almost raped. That forever traumatized her, and after years of therapy, she still couldn't allow herself to share physical intimacy with a man.

And that hurt. She couldn't be normal like other women, and she'd learned to deal with that by focusing all her emotions on children. A caring policewoman had gotten her to the Hopechest Ranch after the near rape, and it was there that she'd met Meredith. After she came to live with her and Joe, Rebecca began to help her with the younger children and found great comfort in that. When she later started college, she naturally gravitated to teaching and helping children with learning disabilities.

But she still shrank away from a man's touch.

That didn't mean she hadn't tried. She had. But regardless of how much she liked a man, she could never get past her own fears from the past. After years of disappointment and dashed expectations, she'd finally accepted the fact that she was never going to be able to have a relationship with a man. So she'd stopped dating. It was just too painful.

But, oh, how Austin tempted her. There was something about him that pulled at her, an attraction she was afraid she couldn't hide, and that horrified her. He would be there any moment, and she was terribly afraid she was going to make a fool of herself.

"He just wants help with the case," she muttered to herself as she hurriedly straightened the pillows on the couch and checked the rest of the living room to make sure that it was neat and presentable. "He's not interested in you as a woman."

To make sure she remembered that, she tried to picture him with a bevy of gorgeous blondes doing things with him she could never do. It didn't help. When the doorbell rang, she was suddenly breathless.

Later, she never knew how she faced him with any degree of composure. Her heart was racing, her palms slightly damp, and she felt as giddy as a schoolgirl. But when she opened the door to him, she greeted him with a smile that was calm and serene. If her heart was thundering like a locomotive on a downhill run, no one had to know that but her. "Hi."

"Thanks for seeing me like this, with no notice," he said gruffly as he stepped into her living room. "I hope I'm not interrupting anything."

"No, not at all," she assured him. Dropping down into her favorite chair in front of the fireplace, she motioned for him to take a seat on the couch. "Now what's this you wanted to run past me? Have you tracked down a suspect?"

"Not exactly," he said in disgust. "According to

everyone I've talked to, Joe doesn't have any major enemies, but he's ticked off more than a few people over
the years. And he invited them all to his party. I was
hoping you could help me eliminate some of the names
on the list.''

"I'll try," she promised. "What do you want to
know?"

"Start with the immediate family and tell me everything you can about each person's relationship with Joe.
Who's close to him, who's not, who argues with him or
owes him money or doesn't like his business practices.
And don't worry about this going anywhere beyond this
room. Whatever you tell me is privileged information.''

He was strictly business and somber as a judge, and
Rebecca felt like a fool for thinking he might have
stopped by for any other reason than to talk about the
case. Thankful he couldn't read her mind, she deliberately
focused her thoughts on the family. If he could be all
business, so could she.

"I guess I should start with Meredith," she said quietly.
"They argue sometimes, but it's usually over minor
things—like having dinner with just the family. She likes
to entertain a lot and it drives him nuts.''

Surprised, Austin frowned. "When I was a kid, I got
the impression she didn't care much for the social scene.
When did that change?"

"I don't know," she replied, trying to remember. "I
guess it was after Joe, Jr. and Teddy were born. Once
they were in school, she had more time on her hands and
really enjoyed having people over. It just seemed to mush-
room after that.''

"And their marriage? It's okay?"

"Oh, I think so," she replied, surprised that he asked.
"It's not all lovey-dovey like it was when they were

younger, but that's pretty normal, isn't it, when people have been married as long as they have? And Meredith changed after the accident.''

The entire family knew about the car accident nine years ago when Meredith was driven off the road by a drunk driver when she was taking Emily for a visit with her natural grandmother. Shaken by the near tragedy, Meredith hadn't been quite the same since.

''She never recovered from that, did she?'' Austin asked quietly.

''She's harsher,'' Rebecca said. ''More on edge. I guess that's what happens when you come so close to death.''

Noncommittal, Austin only shrugged. ''Then what about the kids? Do all of them get along with him? I'm not just talking about now,'' he said quickly, before she could answer. ''Were there any fights or disagreements in the past? Any resentments that might have festered over the years into rage?''

Frowning, Rebecca didn't even have to think about that. ''Oh, no. Joe's always been supportive of the kids. He never missed one of Rand's football games if he could help it, and he's crazy about the girls. Drake ...'' Searching for words to describe Drake, she smiled sadly. ''I don't think Drake ever got over Michael's death. I never had a brother and can't imagine what it would be like to lose one, especially a twin. He doesn't let anyone get close to him, but I don't think he harbors any resentment against Joe. He just stays to himself.''

Unable to think of anything else, she grimaced. ''This isn't what you wanted to hear, is it? Obviously, Joe's infuriated someone but I don't see how it could be anyone in the family. They're too close-knit for that. It's got to be someone he works with. Have you talked to Graham or Emmett yet? They'd be able to help you with that more than I would. You have their numbers, don't you?''

Austin nodded. Joe's brother, Graham, and his old army buddy, Emmett Fallon, both worked closely with him at Colton Enterprises and would know better than most any enemies Joe had made in the corporate world. ''I have appointments with both of them tomorrow.''

Considering that, there was little left to say, and they both knew it. ''I guess I wasn't much help, was I?'' she said with a rueful smile. ''Sorry.''

She was no sorrier than Austin. Damn, he enjoyed talking to her! And watching her. She was so unpretentious and natural. He liked her smile, her shyness, the sincerity in her eyes. But he'd gotten what he'd come for, and there was no other reason to linger.

Disappointed, he pushed to his feet. ''Don't apologize,'' he said gruffly as she, too, stood. ''I've been out of the family so long that I really don't know anyone anymore. Your insight helped. Thanks.''

He wisely didn't make an excuse to see her again, but walking away from her wasn't nearly as easy as he'd hoped. As he thanked her again and let himself out, he found himself fighting the need to turn back and ask her out to dinner. If she'd given him the slightest encouragement, he would have been in trouble. She didn't.

Two

He wouldn't call her again.

Lying in her lonely bed that night, Rebecca stared at the ceiling in the dark and faced the fact that Austin would, in all likelihood, never call her again. She'd told him everything she could about the family and done all that she could to help him. There was little reason for him to contact her again.

She should have been relieved. By his very presence, he stirred feelings in her that had no chance of ever developing into anything but hurt and frustration, and she knew she should have been thankful to see the last of him. Instead, she'd never felt lonelier in her life.

Why, she wondered, couldn't she be like other women? Why couldn't she have a husband and children? Why couldn't she know what it was like to have a man turn to her in the middle of the night and reach for her? Make love to her?

Because you can't bear to have a man touch you, a voice in her head said flatly. *Until you find a way to come to grips with that, you'll never have anyone.*

Slow tears seeped from the corners of her eyes. She'd tried, she thought, swallowing a sob. When she'd first come to live with Joe and Meredith, she'd been shy and afraid and had just wanted to hide away from the world and be left alone. She hadn't even been able to sit at the table with the family at mealtime and eat. With time and patience and the best therapists, however, she'd started to trust again, to let people back into her life...not only Meredith and Joe, but the children, then her extended foster family and friends. Amazingly, she'd even gotten past the fear of dating. But she still hit a brick wall whenever it came to intimacy.

She'd thought she'd accepted that, but for the first time in a long time, she wanted something she couldn't have. And it hurt. Turning over, she buried her face in her pillow and gave in to the sobs she could no longer hold back.

When she woke the next morning with a thick head and swollen eyes, she would have liked nothing better than to call in sick. But she knew she'd only brood if she stayed at home, and at work, at least, her students would keep her too busy to think of anything but them. With a groan, she rolled out of bed.

From there, everything seemed to go wrong. She couldn't find the belt that went with her dress, the new shoes she wore hurt her feet, she misplaced her keys, and to make matters worse, she had to stop on the way to work and fill up her car with gas. By the time she walked through the front door of Coker Elementary, she was late, and Richard Foster, her boss, was waiting for her in the hallway outside the principal's office.

"You're late."

Taken aback by the harshness of his tone—after all, she was only *five* minutes tardy and school wouldn't start for another twenty minutes—she said breathlessly, "I know. I'm sorry. Nothing seemed to go right this morning."

"You're supposed to set an example for the students," he retorted, his blue eyes diamond-hard behind the lenses of his glasses. "If you can't be disciplined enough to be on time, how can you expect them to be?"

Technically, he had a point, and if they'd been running a boot camp, Rebecca might have agreed with him. But it was an elementary school, for heaven's sakes, and most of the students were only just now beginning to show up for school. He wasn't usually a clock watcher as long as his teachers were in their classrooms at least fifteen minutes before the first bell rang, and she still had five minutes to spare.

Surprised that he would nitpick over such a minor thing, she frowned. Something had to be wrong—this wasn't like him. Then, before she could open her mouth and put her foot in it by asking if everything was okay, she remembered that he and Sylvia, his wife, were filing for divorce later that afternoon. And she'd forgotten all about it. No wonder he was in a bear of a mood, she thought sympathetically. She was friends with both of them and hated to see their marriage break up. They were one of those couples who had seemed perfect for each other.

"I'll be more punctual next time," she said quietly. "It won't happen again."

She was trying to be understanding, but she might as well have saved her breath. He only nodded curtly, satisfied. "Good. See that it doesn't."

And it was that, more than anything, that hurt. She knew he was going through a rough time, but she hadn't done anything to him. Dismissed, her cheeks stinging, she hurried to her classroom without a backward glance.

From there, the rest of the day went downhill. She didn't know if the moon was out of alignment or if her students had been possessed by aliens from outer space, but each class was more disruptive than the last. By the time lunch rolled around, Rebecca was exhausted.

She told herself things couldn't get much worse. She was wrong. At the beginning of her first class after lunch, she'd hardly turned to write the homework assignment on the blackboard when Tabitha Long let out a bloodcurdling scream that Rebecca was sure could be heard halfway down the hall. "Hughie's got a gun!"

Startled, her heart in her throat, Rebecca whirled just in time to see the redheaded troublemaker of the class teasingly brandishing something black at Tabitha. "Hughie Bishop, you bring that here right this minute!" she ordered sternly. "*Now,* Hughie!"

"Awh, Miss Powell, it's just a toy," he grumbled, holding it up to show her that it was just a homemade slingshot carved in the shape of a gun. "I was just playing."

Her frown fierce and disapproving, Rebecca didn't say a word. She just held out her hand.

His shoulders slumped in dejection, Hughie dragged his feet as he slowly made his way to the front of the classroom. "I wasn't going to hurt anybody," he said, pouting as he dropped the slingshot into her hand. "She was making faces at me."

Rebecca didn't doubt that Tabitha was guilty of instigating a scene—she had an irritating habit of sticking her tongue out at the other students—but that didn't excuse Hughie's behavior. He knew the rules: no weapons could be brought to school for any reason. "You can't threaten someone just because you don't like what they're doing," she lectured him. "Especially with a weapon. Yes," she said quickly when he started to object, "this is a weapon and you leave me no choice but to report this to Mr. Foster after class. In the meantime, you and Tabitha will both move to the back of the room and spend the rest of the class writing a letter for your behavior."

"But I didn't do anything!" Tabitha cried.

Not surprised that she would paint herself totally innocent, Rebecca merely arched a brow at her. "Didn't you? Think about it."

Caught in the trap of her disapproving gaze, Tabitha knew better than to argue further. Hanging her head, she collected her books and moved to the back of the room. Hughie did the same, and with a sigh of relief, Rebecca placed the slingshot in the top drawer of her desk and returned her attention to the class and the homework assignment.

School policy required that any weapons brought to school be turned in to the principal's office, and she fully intended to do that. But there was a fire drill during the next class, and halfway through the last class of the day, one of the students got sick and Rebecca had to rush her to the nurse. By the time she returned to class, she barely had time to remind the students to do their homework before the dismissal bell rang.

Finally, the day was over! Harried and exhausted after too little sleep the previous night, Rebecca completely forgot about the slingshot in the top drawer of her desk. All she wanted to do was go for a nice long ride at the ranch on her favorite horse. Then she wouldn't have to think about anything. Grabbing her purse and briefcase, she hurried outside to her car.

* * *

Taking Rebecca's suggestion, Austin spent the morning and early afternoon talking to Joe's brother, Graham, and Emmett Fallon, his friend and old army buddy who had helped Joe set up his first oil well. They were both involved in Colton Enterprises and in a position to know who Joe had had business clashes with over the years. Unfortunately, the list was longer than Austin would have liked, and he couldn't take much comfort from the fact that Graham and Emmett had included people who had only minor conflicts with Joe. The shooter had tried to commit murder in front of 300 hundred witnesses. As far as Austin was concerned, that made him a loose cannon. Anyone with the slightest grudge against Joe had to be checked out.

Frustrated, trying to imagine who would have picked such a public forum to try to commit murder, Austin headed back to the ranch. He needed to get another look at the scene of the crime, but this time in private.

Armed with the key Joe had given him, he didn't bother to knock, but quietly let himself in and shut the front door behind him. Silence immediately engulfed him. It was the middle of the afternoon, and the place seemed deserted. Inez was there somewhere, no doubt, but Meredith was probably out shopping or playing the overprotective mom with the boys. If he was lucky, he had the entire house to himself. Pleased, he stepped through the formal, too-perfect living room and headed for the courtyard at the back of the house.

When he'd visited the ranch with his parents when he was a kid, the courtyard had always been everyone's favorite part of the house. It offered a spectacular view of the Pacific and was a gathering place for the family at the end of the day. It was also the perfect setting for a party.

From the patio, the guests could spill out onto the yard and have unlimited space to mingle...and hide in the dark, away from all the bright, decorative lights that had been strung near the house for the party.

Who, he wondered, had stood back from the lights and watched Joe, waiting for just the right moment to pull the trigger? Trying to imagine the scene, Austin stepped through the French doors that opened onto the courtyard and didn't realize it was already occupied until it was too late. Standing with her back to him and unaware of his presence, Meredith was in the process of chewing out Inez.

"What do you mean you didn't take the dry cleaning to the cleaners?" she said sharply. "I need my red silk dress for the Smythes' dinner party tomorrow night!"

"Sorry, ma'am," the housekeeper said. "It just slipped my mind."

"You're not getting paid for it to slip your mind! Do you understand? If you can't do the job you were hired to do, I'm sure I can find someone else who can."

Austin couldn't believe Meredith was being so harsh over such a minor case of forgetfulness. He'd always remembered her as a kind, easygoing woman who treated servants like family. When had she become so autocratic?

He didn't make a sound, but something must have alerted Meredith that she and Inez were no longer alone. Glancing over her shoulder suddenly, she immediately spied him standing in the doorway. "Austin! What a surprise!"

"I let myself in. Joe gave me a key, so I thought I'd check out the patio."

For a second, he would have sworn that infuriated her. Something flashed in her brown eyes, something that came and went so fast he couldn't be sure he hadn't imagined it, but it left him chilled to the bone. Then she gave him a mega-bright smile that was a little too forced to be sincere. "Good. I haven't slept a wink since that maniac tried to kill Joe. The sooner you catch him, the sooner we can all start sleeping at night."

Her smile abruptly fading, she glanced coldly at Inez. "Get us some coffee and make sure it's fresh brewed."

It wasn't until she turned back to Austin that she realized she'd made a mistake and nearly given herself away. The real Meredith would have never been so rude to the hired help. Oh, no, not her nicey-nice twin sister. She'd always been perfect, and Patsy had hated her for that.

Anger boiled in Patsy Portman like hot lava just at the thought of her sister, and it only enraged her more that she was going to have to watch herself with Austin, or he would start asking questions she couldn't answer. If he figured out that she wasn't really Meredith…

Paling at the thought, she stiffened. No, she *was* Meredith! She was! If she forgot sometimes, it was just because she couldn't turn around without running into someone asking questions they had no business asking. First the police, and now Austin. Damn them all, how long did they think she could keep up this act when they kept pressuring her? If someone ran her fingerprints through the police computers, her prison record was going to pop up like a piece of burnt toast.

Feeling like she was coming unraveled, she swallowed a giggle at the thought. No! She had to get control. She needed her pills. But she couldn't take them in front of Austin. Then he would know. Then everyone would know. She had to get it together. She was Meredith. Sweet, irritatingly pleasant Meredith.

Suppressing a shudder, she forced a tight smile and tried to repair the damage by saying sweetly, "Oh, and

Inez? Don't worry about the dry cleaning. I'll wear the black lace. Okay?''

''Yes, ma'am,'' she said softly. ''I'll get your coffee.''

When the housekeeper scurried away, Patsy didn't need to see Austin's frown to know that she'd done little to redeem herself. For that alone, she wanted to scream at him. For as long as she could remember, she'd never measured up to Meredith. They may have looked just alike, but it was her twin who'd always known just how to act and what to say. Everything had come to *her,* dammit! Everything! While Meredith had played it up big in Washington parties as a senator's wife, then later socialized in her fancy house with the rich and beautiful in California, Patsy had been serving time in prison for murder. Then there was that awful time she spent at the St. James Clinic for the mentally ill. It wasn't fair!

In spite of what the doctors had said, she wasn't crazy. She wasn't, dammit! She'd just wanted the charmed existence her sister led. So when she'd seen a chance to get rid of her and take over her life nine years ago, she hadn't hesitated. And no one had been the wiser.

That wasn't to say it had been easy. She'd had to keep a tight rein on her temper, and that had been a constant struggle. She hadn't been able to do it indefinitely. Gradually, she'd showed sides of her true self, always using the excuse that she was tired or stressed or just not feeling like herself. And over the years, everyone had come to accept the changes in Meredith's personality without being aware of it.

Austin, however, hadn't been around to witness those changes in Meredith. He hadn't seen her in years, and if Patsy wasn't careful, he'd start to wonder why his now sharp-tongued aunt was so different from the simpering sweet one he remembered from his childhood.

He was a huge threat to her, and not just because there was a possibility he might notice the changes in her. The man had the eyes of a wolf. She wouldn't be able to fool him the way she had Thaddeus Law and the other detectives who'd investigated the shooting. Those yo-yos never even suspected that there had been two attempts against Joe's life that night. They'd gone over the grounds with a fine-tooth comb and completely missed the fact that she'd put poison in Joe's champagne right before the birthday toast.

Poison, she thought resentfully, that he'd never gotten a chance to drink. He'd dropped the glass when the shooter took a shot at him.

Thankfully, the poisoned champagne had soaked into the ground when it spilled and there was no evidence to connect her to an attempt against Joe's life. But Patsy wasn't stupid enough to think that she was out of the woods. Not now. Not with Austin on the case. She'd heard of the cases he'd solved in Portland, cases that his co-workers had long since given up on. When he'd quit the police department after he'd been shot in a shoot-out with drug lords, his supervisors had tried everything they could to change his mind, even going so far as to promise him outrageous promotions if he'd only stay. A man like that wouldn't rest until he cracked a case and hunted down all guilty parties.

And that infuriated her. Damn Joe! When she'd found out he'd hired Austin, she'd wanted to poison his drink all over again. He'd given him a key to the house, for God's sake! He could come and go as he pleased, and just thinking about it made her break out in a cold sweat. If she hadn't already been on the patio chewing out Inez she never would have known he was there!

So what the hell was she going to do about him?

Keep a close eye on him and distract him as much as possible from his investigation without being obvious, she concluded. It was the only way. But dammit, she couldn't watch the front door every minute of the day!

Fuming, desperate for her pills, she sank down into one of the patio chairs and gave him a look of concern that could have fooled the Pope himself. "I never thought to ask the police, but do you think it's safe for us to still use the patio? What if the man who tried to kill Joe is still out there somewhere, watching us?"

Her eyes deliberately wide, she turned to look out at the magnificent view of the ocean and was proud of the little shiver of fear she was able to manufacture. "He could be in a boat, with a high-powered rifle, pretending to be fishing and waiting for a chance to kill us all..."

"What makes you think it's a man?"

Expecting him to rush to reassure her that she had no need to be afraid, Patsy blinked. "Well, because it is!"

"How do you know that? Did you see the shooter?"

"No, of course not. I didn't see anything."

"But you were standing right next to Joe, weren't you? I believe he pulled you down to the ground when the shot rang out. What happened right before that? Were you looking out at the crowd? Did you notice anyone who looked particularly angry? You must have seen something."

Furious that he was putting her on the spot, it was all she could do not to cuss him out. Damn him, who did he think he was, questioning her? She was Mrs. Joe Colton, by God, even if she wasn't the real Meredith, and she didn't have to take this from him or anyone else!

But even as the hot words sprang to her tongue, she bit them back. No, she thought furiously. She'd be damned if she'd let him push her into losing control and destroying everything. Because once she lost it, she wasn't sure she would ever get it back again, and that terrified her. She wasn't going back to the St. James Clinic! she thought fiercely. Or any other lockup for crazies. There was nothing wrong with her. She just had to remain calm and think straight.

It wasn't easy. There was a tight knot of nerves in her gut that burned like the fires of hell. "It all happened so fast, it's hard to remember what happened," she said stiffly. "Before the shooting, I was busy playing hostess and making sure there was plenty of champagne for the toasts. When the shot rang out, I was looking at Joe, just like everyone else. I didn't see anything."

That seemed to be the favorite line of everyone he talked to, Austin thought in annoyance, and that was nothing short of amazing. A man had nearly been killed in front of three hundred guests, and no one claimed to have seen anything!

Frowning, he said, "So you don't know who was standing at the edge of the crowd? You didn't see anyone sneak off into the shadows? Hell, I'd be happy if you could just tell me if anyone disappeared for a while. But I guess you didn't notice that, either."

When she gave him a look that should have dropped him in his tracks, Austin expected her to blast him with a few choice words, but he had to give her credit. Visibly holding on to her temper, she said tightly, "No, I didn't. I told you I was busy. There's nothing else I can say."

If she wasn't going to be any help to him, Austin wished she would find something else to do and leave him alone so he could work, but that, apparently wasn't going to happen. Instead of excusing herself, she settled more comfortably in her chair, as if she was prepared to stay awhile, probably as long as he was there. And there wasn't a damn thing he could do about it. This was her house, after all. He couldn't very well demand that she make herself scarce in her own home.

Resigned, he said, "According to Joe's written notes of the shooting, the two of you were standing on the stage for the band, but he doesn't say where that was."

"It was set up at the end of the patio, on the left side," she retorted. "It was so crowded, a lot of the guests had spilled from the patio out onto the lawn."

"And the shot came from out in the yard somewhere?"

She shrugged. "It's hard to say. The floodlights for the stage were blinding and it was impossible to see anything beyond the edge of the patio."

Disgusted, Austin swore softly. "I was afraid you'd say that."

Standing at the edge of the patio, he surveyed the surrounding area with a scowl and silently acknowledged that the shooter had chosen a perfect setting in which to try to commit murder. He'd waited until it was dark, and the house and patio were crawling with people. When it came time for the toast, everyone was looking at Joe, so all the shooter had to do was stand at the back of the crowd, wait for the right moment to pull the trigger, then step back into the darkness, just beyond the reach of the lights. In the chaos that followed the shooting, he could have walked around the house, entered through the front door and merged with the rest of the party-goers and no one would have suspected a thing.

"Whoever did this had to be nuts," he said half to himself. "Joe's not the kind to generate anger in people—he makes friends wherever he goes. I can't believe anyone would hate him enough to try to kill him."

"It does seem crazy," Meredith agreed. "But there's a lot of nuts walking around loose. And Joe is so easygoing that he thinks everyone is like him. But they're not. Not everyone can let bygones be bygones. Joe always got along with the parents of the foster children we raised, but deep down inside, some of them had to resent the fact that they weren't raising their own children. Who knows? Maybe one of them was the shooter.''

That was an option Austin hadn't even considered. At this point, he couldn't overlook anyone. Turning back to Meredith he pulled the guest list from the notebook he'd brought with him. ''I'll need to know which of the guests are from the foster families.''

Only too happy to direct suspicion away from herself, Patsy obligingly gave him the names.

In spite of that, however, she didn't fool herself into thinking she'd cleared herself as a suspect. There were any number of family members, not to mention so-called friends, who had probably already told Austin that her marriage to Joe had deteriorated over the years. It was only a matter of time before he asked her why. She'd lie, of course, not that it would do her any good. With those emerald-green eyes of his, he could see through a lie in a split second, damn him. If he started asking her questions she couldn't answer and really put the pressure on her and made her mad, God only knew what she'd say or do.

Her heart slamming against her ribs, she told herself she couldn't let that happen. Because if she snapped and gave herself away, she'd lose the boys and she'd get locked up again. And while she might find a way to bear prison again, she couldn't lose her boys. Not Joe and Teddy. They were hers, dammit. Hers! Joe, Jr. didn't have a drop of Colton blood in him, and Teddy was a result of a hot quickie with Joe's brother, Graham, in the guest bathroom during a dinner party. Granted, that had been a mistake—she never would have taken a chance on getting pregnant if she'd known Joe was sterile—but she couldn't regret that now. They were her babies, and she wouldn't risk losing them.

Talk! she told herself fiercely. Distract him. Do whatever you have to to keep his focus off you.

Before she could speak, the patio door opened behind them and they both turned in time to see Rebecca step out onto the patio.

"Oh, I'm sorry," Rebecca said, startled. "I didn't mean to interrupt. I was just on my way to the barn."

"For a ride?" Pleased, Patsy thought things couldn't have worked out better if she'd planned them herself. "I think that's an excellent idea. Why don't you take Austin with you? It's been years since he was here last, and he's probably forgotten how beautiful it is.

"That's okay with you, isn't it, Austin?" Patsy continued smoothly, turning her attention to him before Rebecca could say a word. "I know you're working, but everybody needs a break once in a while. It'll do you good."

Trapped, there wasn't much the two of them could do except exchange polite looks. "Company would be nice," Rebecca said.

"A ride would blow some of the cobwebs out of my head," Austin added.

Hiding her contempt—how easily manipulated they were—Patsy shooed them toward the barn. "Then go on. Get out of here and enjoy yourselves."

Left with no choice, Rebecca fell into step with Austin and they headed for the barn. For what seemed like an eternity, neither of them said a word. Rebecca had never felt so awkward in her life. "I'm sorry about that," she said finally. "I know you didn't really want to take time away from your work, but Meredith can be pretty insistent sometimes. I hope you don't mind."

"Actually," he said honestly, "the only reason I hesitated was because I didn't want to intrude on your ride. Don't feel like you have to do this. I can go back to work if you want to be alone."

"Oh, no!" How could he think that? "I'd like some company," she said shyly as they entered the barn. "It was an awful day at school today, and I'd just like to forget everything and have some fun."

His green eyes dancing, he said dryly, "I think I can manage that." And before she could guess his intentions, he had his mount saddled and had stepped into the stirrups. "Race you!" he challenged, and was off like a shot, leaving her and her horse flatfooted.

"Hey!" Vaulting into the saddle, Rebecca sent her favorite mare bounding after him, and it didn't take her long to catch him. Her smile wide and her eyes dancing, she bent low over her mare's neck and headed for the beach. The race was on.

There was no finish line. With the wind whistling through their hair and the low rolling hills of the ranch flying past them, they rode neck-and-neck, broad smiles lighting their faces. And when they reached the beach and both pulled up by unspoken agreement, they were laughing.

Rebecca couldn't remember the last time she'd had so much fun, and that should have been enough to set off alarm bells in her head. Getting to know him better was a mistake. It would only deepen her feelings of loneliness when he returned to Portland. She knew that, accepted it, but she couldn't worry about next week or next month. Not when the day had just turned wonderful. Loving the feel of the sun on her face and the wind in her hair, she wanted to laugh out loud with joy.

"That was great!" she said, grinning at him. "C'mon. I'll show you my favorite spot on the whole ranch."

Leading the way, she took him to a secluded rocky cove down on the beach. Years ago, Meredith had taken her to that same spot when she'd first come to the ranch to live. Overwhelmed—not only by the ranch, but by the Colton family and the foster children they'd welcomed into their home so easily—she'd been feeling very lost that day and Meredith had sensed it. So she'd taken her to the cove to show her *her* secret hideaway.

There'd been no other footprints but theirs that day, and Rebecca had loved it. The pounding of the surf against the shore and the cry of the gulls had given her a serenity she'd found nowhere else on earth, and to this day, whenever she was feeling low, she only had to close her eyes to feel the spray of the Pacific on her face and the damp sand under her feet.

Nothing, however, beat being there in person. Unable to resist the call of the pristine sand that had been washed clean by the waves, she dismounted and looked up with a smile when Austin joined her. "Isn't it beautiful here? When I first came to live here, Meredith and I used to have picnics on the beach here all the time."

Her tone was wistful—she could hear it in her voice— and she wasn't surprised when Austin heard it, too. Frowning, he said, "Don't you go on picnics now? You two seem so close."

"We used to be," she said. "I admired her so much. She was wonderful with the foster children, and I loved helping her with them. But after the accident, she didn't have time for picnics. Her priorities changed."

"How?"

She shrugged. "There were little changes at first. She became totally devoted to Joe Junior—then she had Teddy and was the same way with him. Later, she got wrapped up in her social schedule, and she just didn't have time to do the things we used to do."

She didn't have time for me anymore, Rebecca added silently. And she didn't know why. She just knew Meredith was different, and they weren't as close as they'd once been. And the only explanation she had for it was the accident.

The thought saddened her, and the mood was somber as they returned to the house, where they found themselves guests at a small dinner party. Feeling underdressed in riding clothes, Rebecca felt her heart sink at the sight of a former congressman and a famous Hollywood producer who had joined the family in the courtyard for before-dinner drinks. Why, she wondered in frustration, did Meredith insist on inviting the entire world to dinner? When she'd first come to the ranch, one of the things she'd loved the most about living there had been the family suppers in the eat-in kitchen. They'd been homey and fun and intimate and given everyone a chance to catch up on each other's day.

But those times were, unfortunately, long gone, and now it seemed like there were always outsiders around. Meals were much more formal and in the dining room. And Rebecca hated it. Given the chance, she would have used the excuse that she had homework to grade and left. But she'd had so much fun with Austin that she hated to see the evening end. And one look at his resigned expression and she knew he wasn't any more thrilled than she at the idea of attending a dinner party. The least she could do was stick around and help him through it.

Fortunately, it didn't turn out to be as bad as Rebecca

had anticipated. The conversation shifted back and forth between politics and the movie industry, and the discussions on the future of both were lively and sometimes more than a little intense. But Joe was in his element, his blue eyes sparkling with interest, and for the first time since the shooting, he seemed like his old self. Rebecca could have sat there for hours, just listening to him talk.

Meredith, however, changed the entire mood with just a few carelessly chosen words. The meal was almost over—Inez was serving her fabulous praline cheesecake— when Meredith took advantage of a sudden lull in the conversation to turn her attention on Austin. "So, Austin," she said brightly, "how is the investigation going now that you've had time to check out the guest list? You must have narrowed down some suspects."

Just that easily, silence fell like a rock. For a moment, Austin didn't say a word. A muscle clenched in his jaw, and he just looked at her. But everyone at the table was waiting for his answer, and he finally said quietly, "I can't discuss that at this point. The investigation is ongoing, and I still have a lot of leads to follow up."

"But what about suspects?" she pressed. "You must have some idea of who the shooter is by now. You've been talking to people all week."

"This kind of case takes time to solve," he retorted. "You don't do it overnight."

"But—"

"That's enough, Meredith," Joe growled. Glaring at her from the opposite end of the dining room table, he gave her a hard look that anyone who knew him well was familiar with. Without saying a word, he told her to shut up. Glancing at his guests, he smiled wryly. "I don't know about the rest of you, but I don't want to talk about violence at the dinner table. It doesn't do a lot for the digestive system.''

Far from intimidated by his warning look, Patsy just barely resisted the urge to scream at him. How dare he correct her in front of guests! She could talk about anything she wanted to, and there wasn't a damn thing he could do about it!

"I would have thought you'd want to know who your enemies are," she said coldly. "But if you want to live in a fairy tale and pretend everything is hunky-dory, go ahead. I know where you want to be buried."

Urged on by that voice in her head that always seemed to get her in trouble, Patsy knew she may have gone too far, but she didn't care. He could be such a jackass sometimes. She didn't know what Meredith had ever seen in him. If he hadn't been so damn rich, she, herself, would have walked away from him years ago. But she'd been alone and poor before, and rich was better—even if that meant she did have to put up with Joe Colton.

Not, she silently amended with a secret smile, that she might have to do that for much longer. Somebody else out there wanted him dead. They'd tried to kill him once. They were bound to try to do it again. And next time they just might succeed. Then she'd have all that lovely money to herself, and she'd never have to deal with Joe Colton again.

Three

The nightmare came out of the darkness like a thief in the night, grabbing her before she even thought to note the danger. Coming awake with a startled cry of horror, Louise Smith bolted up in bed, her brown eyes wide and unfocused, her heart slamming against her ribs. In her subconscious, vague, shadowy images rose up before her, terrifying her, and for a moment, she couldn't even have said where she was. Then she blinked, and the neat feminine decor of her bedroom came into focus and she realized she was safe and sound in her modest little home in Jackson, Mississippi.

It was then that the tears started.

Suddenly cold all the way to the bone in spite of the fact that it was a warm summer night, Louise wrapped her arms around herself and rocked back and forth in her bed. The nightmares had become more frequent over the course of the last few months—and more terrifying. She'd had them for years, ever since she'd woken up one morning at the St. James Clinic with no memory of who she was, but they'd never been so bad before. Every night for the past week, she'd hardly closed her eyes when she went to bed before the nightmares began. And they were always the same—a little girl crying out for her mommy in the dark. And *she* was the mommy the little girl cried out for.

A sob welled up from deep inside her, and she could no more hold it back than she could change the fact that she was Patsy Portman, a woman with a prison record and a history of mental disability, a woman who'd had a baby girl taken from her soon after her birth that was still, to this day, lost to her. Just thinking about that still made her cringe. What kind of monster was she?

When the hospital staff at the St. James Clinic had told her about her past, she was sure that there had to be some mistake. She wasn't that kind of person. She couldn't be! She might not remember who she was, but surely she would know if she'd killed a man! But then her doctor had shown her her prison record, and there was no denying that she was as amoral as she'd been told she was. Horrified, she'd vowed to change her life right then and there.

The first thing she'd done was return to Mississippi and her last known address, where she'd changed her name to Louise Smith so she could start her new life with a clean slate. But putting the past behind her hadn't been that easy. She'd had no references to get a job, no education that she knew of, no skills. Finally she'd gotten a job at the University of Mississippi. She'd worked hard, and with time, she'd eventually risen through the ranks to become the head of administration services.

She was proud of that and all that she'd accomplished, but there were some things she couldn't change regardless of how hard she tried. Her past was still lost to her. And then there were the nightmares that haunted her nights. Inexplicably, they'd first started nearly five years ago, and had never gone away. Losing weight and sleep, she'd finally sought out Dr. Martha Wilkes, a therapist who specialized in repressed memory, and for a while, she'd felt like she was making real progress. Then she'd started having migraines, and her nightmares had gotten progressively worse. Even with Martha's continued help, she still couldn't say what her dreams were about. She just knew she was scared to death, and she didn't know why.

The dreams had to be related to her past—she and Martha both agreed on that. But what had she done that was so awful that she couldn't face it? After all, she'd murdered a man, for heaven's sake, and had a baby stolen from her arms. What could be more terrible than that? What had Patsy Portman done?

Scared, her heart aching with a hurt she couldn't put a name to, she huddled under the covers and told herself whatever it was, she couldn't keep running from it. With Martha's help, she had to find a way to face and accept whatever was haunting her dreams. Because if she didn't, it was going to slowly destroy her, and she was determined not to let that happen.

But when she lay back down and closed her eyes, the specter of her nightmare was right there beside her in the dark, towering over her like the devil himself. Her eyes flew open, and in the deep silence of the night, she would have sworn she could hear the thundering of her heart. With the covers pulled tight around her, she stared at the darkness. It was a long time before she fell asleep.

Rebecca woke with a smile on her face the next morning and didn't have to ask herself who put it there. Austin.

She couldn't remember the last time she'd enjoyed herself so much with a man. He was just so easy to be around. There'd been no pressure like there was on a date, no expectations of anything romantic. They'd just gone riding like two friends who'd known each other forever, then had dinner with the family and a few guests. It couldn't have been more perfect.

A kiss on the cheek wouldn't have hurt, she thought with a smile, but then again, she'd accepted the fact that there wasn't going to be any romance in her life. If friendship was all she could have with Austin, then she'd take it.

Happier than she'd been in a long time, she pulled on one of her favorite dresses, a white cotton sheath with an embroidered neckline, and stepped into flat white sandals. Feeling very feminine, she French-braided her hair in a single braid that hung down her back, then applied a minimum of makeup and a spritz of perfume. And when she looked in the mirror, she couldn't stop smiling. She felt pretty this morning and it showed.

The glow of the morning stayed with her all the way to work and well into her first class. There must have been something in the air, because her students were all alert and eager, and everything seemed to flow as smooth as silk. Then there was a knock at her classroom door and she turned to find Mildred Henderson, an aide from the school office, hesitating at the threshold with a note from the principal.

Surprised, Rebecca took the note and arched a brow at the curtly written message instructing her to report to the office immediately. "Mr. Foster wants to see me now?" she asked Mildred. "During the middle of class?"

The elderly, grandmotherly woman nodded somberly. "I don't know what happened, dear, but he seemed very upset. Run along now. I'll stay with the class while you're gone."

"Yes, of course. Thank you." Shaken, Rebecca hurried down the hall to the office, worry eating at her stomach. Had the shooter gotten to Joe? Was that what this was about? Was he hurt? Dead?

The blood draining from her face, Rebecca gave a perfunctory knock at the principal's door and hardly waited from him to respond before she barged inside. "Is something wrong with my family?"

Richard Foster knew all about the shooting at Joe's birthday party—the story had been all over the newspapers and covered extensively on both the local and national news programs on TV—so he knew what she was really asking. "As far as I know, Joe Colton is fine, Ms. Powell," he said stiffly. "You've been called here on school business."

It wasn't until he gave her a pointed look that Rebecca realized they weren't alone. Standing to the right of Richard's massive oak desk was a tall blond man who was glaring at her with intense dislike. "Oh, I'm sorry," she said quickly. "I didn't realize I was interrupting."

She would have excused herself, but the principal stopped her in her tracks. "This is Mr. Bishop, Rebecca," he said coldly, introducing her to the other man. "His son, Hughie, is in your fifth period class."

"Oh, yes, of course," she replied. "I've talked to your wife several times at our parent-teacher conferences. It's nice to meet you."

She would have held out her hand, but nothing in Mr. Bishop's hostile demeanor encouraged that kind of courtesy. When both men just glared at her, she looked at Richard Foster hesitantly. "I presume this is about Hughie. Is something wrong?"

"You tell us," the principal retorted. "Did you take a slingshot away from Hughie yesterday?"

Until that moment, Rebecca had completely forgotten about it. "As a matter of fact, I did. It was a carved wooden gun, and he was threatening Tabitha Long with it. I took it away and put it in my desk. I know I should have turned it in to the office, Mr. Foster, but yesterday was so hectic, I forgot."

Not the least impressed with her explanation, Hugh Bishop snapped, "Go get it. I want it back."

Confiscated weapons were never returned to the students or their families. That was standard school policy, and Rebecca expected Richard to tell Mr. Bishop that. Instead, he just looked at her with steely blue eyes and said, "You heard the man. Go get it."

Rebecca couldn't have been more surprised if he'd slapped her. "But that's against school policy—"

"When I want your advice on how to run this school, Ms. Powell, I'll ask for it. In the meantime, I suggest you do as you're told."

If you value your job. The words weren't spoken, but Rebecca heard them, nonetheless, and had never felt more like a chastised schoolgirl. And it hurt. She was a good teacher and she'd done the right thing by taking that gun away from Hughie. And Richard knew that. Aside from the fact that it was school policy, it was her duty as a teacher to take away anything from a student that could be used to hurt or intimidate someone. So why hadn't he backed her up? Didn't he realize that *he* could get in trouble with the school board for not carrying out his duty as a principal? What was going on here?

She wanted to ask, but he had that look on his face, the one that he always wore whenever he was thinking of his impending divorce, the one that she and the other teachers had learned to avoid like the plague. There was no point in arguing further.

"I'll be right back," she said stiffly, and turned and marched out of the office without saying another word.

Later, she didn't know how she did it. She'd never been so humiliated in all her life, but she walked down the hall to her classroom with her head held high and even managed a smile for Mildred Henderson when she quietly stepped into the classroom to find her reading to the class. "If you could stay just a little longer, Mrs. Henderson, I'd appreciate it. The meeting with Mr. Foster isn't quite over."

"Of course," the older woman replied easily. "Take as long as you need."

Rebecca would have loved to make both men wait the rest of the afternoon, but she'd never blatantly defied an authority figure. And in spite of the fact that she considered Richard a friend, he was, first and foremost, her boss. Insubordination of any kind wasn't tolerated, so she was left with no choice but to hurry back to the office once she retrieved the slingshot from her drawer.

Even then, she hadn't moved fast enough for Hugh Bishop. The second she stepped into the office, he growled, "You took your time getting back here, didn't you? Are you always this slow? No wonder Junior's having trouble in school."

Outraged, Rebecca almost told him off, but she bit the words back just in time. No, she thought, dragging in a calming breath. She wouldn't stoop to Hugh Bishop's behavior. And surely this time Richard would defend her. After all, as the principal, any slander of the teachers was a direct reflection on him and the school.

She looked at him expectantly, only to drop her jaw

when he said, "I'm sorry for this unfortunate incident, Hugh. I promise you it won't happen again."

Far from satisfied, the obnoxious man said, "See that it doesn't." And with one last look of dislike for Rebecca, he stormed out, making sure he slammed the door behind him.

He'd actually apologized for her behavior! Furious, Rebecca hardly noticed the silence left by Hugh Bishop's leavetaking. How dare he! she fumed. She hadn't done anything wrong, and she damn sure intended to tell him that.

But before she could even open her mouth, he turned to her with the same degree of hostility Mr. Bishop had and coldly lifted a dark brow at her. "Well? What do you have to say for yourself?"

Taken aback, she couldn't believe he was serious. At the very least, *he* owed *her* an explanation! "I beg your pardon?"

"You heard me," he retorted. "Why did you blatantly ignore the school weapons policy?"

"Me?" she gasped. "I didn't ignore anything. I took the weapon away from Hughie, just as I was supposed to. You're the one who gave it back to that awful man just so he can bring it right back to school!"

"Because you didn't do what you were supposed to do!" Enraged, he glared at her with intense dislike. "*You* did this! You didn't do your job. You didn't turn that weapon in, so I was left with no choice but to take Mr. Bishop's side."

"But that makes no sense—"

That was the wrong thing to say. If he'd been angry before, he was absolutely livid now. "I don't have to explain myself to you, Ms. Powell. Do you understand that? I'm in charge around here, and I can do whatever I damn

well please. You, on the other hand, are on very thin ice.
One more episode like this and you may find yourself
looking for another job. Do I make myself clear?''

She wanted to tell him no. She didn't understand why
she was the bad guy for taking the weapon away when
he'd been the one who'd given it back! But she knew he
was looking for someone to blame, and she was obviously
it.

''Perfectly,'' she said coolly. ''This is an argument I
can't win. If we're finished here, I need to get back to my
classroom.''

His curt nod was her dismissal, and with a sigh of relief,
Rebecca hurried out of the office and down the hall, her
cheeks stinging with embarrassment and her eyes hot with
tears she refused to shed. She would not take this personally, she told herself fiercely. He was just going through
a rough time. He needed her understanding now, not her
anger. With time, he'd be back to his old, likable self. She
just had to be patient...and pray that it would be soon.

With so many of Joe's friends and family pointing the
finger at everyone else, Austin decided the best way to
discover the truth about what really happened the night
of the party was to talk to the non-guests that had been
hired for the evening—caterers, decorators, entertainers,
security personnel. As disinterested third parties, they in-
evitably blended into the woodwork at such a large affair,
and in the process, usually saw and heard much more than
the guests realized.

Armed with a list of everyone who had access to the
estate that night, Austin paid a visit to John Roberts, the
caterer, and wasn't surprised when no one wanted to talk
to him. In a business that catered in many cases to the
rich and famous, a caterer's reputation often depended not

only on the food he served, but his discretion. If word got out that he was talking about his clients and their private lives to a private investigator, he could kiss his business goodbye.

And no one, apparently, knew that better than John Roberts. When Austin told him what he wanted, John just looked at him. "The police have already questioned me and my staff. We didn't see anything."

"I understand," Austin said easily. "But I'd still like to talk to everyone that worked the party that night. Someone may have seen more than they realized."

"They don't get paid to watch the guests, only the food," he retorted. "You're wasting your time."

Starting to get irritated, Austin shot him a narrow-eyed look that warned him he was pushing his luck. "No, you're wasting my time. Have you got something to hide? Is that why you don't want me to talk to your employees? Are you afraid the word will get out that you were somehow involved?"

"No, of course not!"

"Then there's no reason why your people can't talk to me, is there?"

Neatly cornered, there was nothing John could do but look down his thin nose at him and seethe. "You're welcome to talk to anyone you like, but my staff is small. Most of the wait staff hired for the party was contract labor."

"But they're people you've worked with before?"

"Most of them, yes. For a party the size of the Colton affair, you take what you can get."

"You have their names and addresses?"

"Naturally."

Turning to the file cabinet behind his desk, he dug out a list and stiffly handed it over. "Everyone was questioned directly after the shooting."

That was standard procedure, but Austin doubted anyone at the police department had yet done any follow-up interviews after the shock of the shooting had worn off. *That* was when people remembered vital tidbits of information that might not seem important to them.

Pocketing the list, he said, "That's okay. I'd still like to talk to them. What do you remember about the party? Did you notice anyone acting suspicious? You must have slipped in and out of the crowd. I'm sure you saw things the family didn't."

If he did, he wasn't admitting it. "It was my duty to make sure that the food stayed hot and never ran out and the champagne flowed freely. When I wasn't in the kitchen, I was making sure my people were doing their job—and trying to satisfy Mrs. Colton. I didn't have time to notice anything else."

Usually a sharp judge of people, Austin wasn't surprised by his response. The man was so caught up in his work that he probably wouldn't have seen the shooter if he'd tripped over him...unless he'd had an empty champagne glass in his hand. "Then I guess we have nothing else to talk about," he replied. "Thanks for your help."

From the caterers, he checked out the list of waiters and servers and cleanup crew and soon found himself driving all over Prosperino. He ran out nearly a full tank of gas, but had little to show for it. The catering staff that did intermingle with the crowd only knew the more famous guests. Most of the family were strangers to them and they could offer little information.

Still, Austin had no intention of giving up so easily. There was still security to check, as well as the band. Someone must have seen something!

"The band was about to break into 'For He's a Jolly

Good Fellow,' weren't you?'' he asked Ramon, the band's drummer, when he finally tracked him down at Tucker's Grocery, where he worked as a stock boy during the day. "You were just waiting for everyone to finish the toasts. Right?"

"No!" The long-haired drummer frowned. "Mrs. Colton had told us she'd warn us when the toasts were going to start, but she didn't, and we'd taken a break. Suddenly, the toasts were starting, and we were all over the place. I'd just rushed up on stage when Mr. Colton lifted his glass for the toast. The next thing I knew, a shot rang out and everybody was screaming."

"Did you see where the shot came from?"

"Are you kidding? I was looking for my drumsticks!"

"And your buddies? Where were they?"

"Grabbing something to eat and drink," he answered promptly. "Or in the bathroom. I went for a smoke. I don't know what the others did."

"Then I guess I'll have to check with them." Pulling out the list Joe had given him his first day in town, Austin quickly checked to make sure he had the rest of the band members' names and addresses, then offered his hand. "Thanks for your help. I appreciate it."

"No problem," he said with a shrug. "I didn't do anything."

He had to get back to work or Austin would have told him that every person he eliminated from the list of possible suspects led him that much closer to the shooter. It was part of the job, and, unfortunately, the most tedious part. Still, it had to be done. Resigned, he checked the list again and headed for the opposite side of town.

The address was classy. There was no other way to describe the gated condominium on the beach where

Chester Phillips lived. Conservative and sophisticated, in an area of town that appealed to old money, it wasn't the kind of place Austin had expected the bass player of a rock band to be living.

"I'm looking for Chester Phillips," he told the security guard at the gate. "I need to talk to him about a party he worked last weekend."

"He's not home."

"I could wait."

When the guard just looked at him, Austin sighed. He should have known it wasn't going to be that easy. "Never mind. I'll come back later."

Disgusted, he went looking for Luke and Greg, the two other band members, but he didn't get very far there, either. It took most of the afternoon to track down Luke on the golf course at a nearby country club. Unfortunately, he didn't have much to offer about the night of the shooting. He was inside at the buffet line when the shot rang out. By the time he made his way outside, all he saw was most of the crowd on the ground with their heads covered.

And Greg didn't see much, either. He'd been taking a glass of champagne from one of the waiters when a gray-haired man brushed past him and knocked him into the waiter, whose tray of filled champagne glasses went flying onto the other guests. He was still apologizing when Joe was nearly killed. Like everyone else, he'd hit the ground when he heard the shot.

Not surprised that the investigation was once again going in circles, Austin headed back to the high-dollar condominium where Chester lived. Only this time, he straightened his tie and put on his sport coat before approaching the guard again, this time on foot after parking next to the guard's serviceable Ford.

"Look," he said, dragging out his ID to flash it at him. "I'm a private investigator. I need to talk to Mr. Phillips about a crime he may have witnessed. Do you know when he's expected home?"

"You'll have to talk to Mr. Phillips about that," the other man said coolly.

"And how would I do that when I can't get past the front gate?" Austin tossed back.

"I wouldn't know, sir."

Grinding his teeth on a curse, Austin struggled for patience. He really hated it when anyone called him sir in that particularly snotty tone of voice. "Let's try this again," he suggested. "Would you have any idea where I might find Mr. Phillips? It's imperative I talk to him."

"You're not going to get any information out of that stiff," a gravelly voice drawled from the opposite side of the gate that barred his way. "What do you want with Chester?"

Startled, Austin turned just in time to see a tall, distinguished older woman walking her very fat bulldog. "I beg your pardon?"

"You heard me," the old lady snapped. "Don't waste my time. I'm old—I may not have much left."

Austin had to fight a smile at that. The lady might have gray hair, but she was a long way from having one foot in the grave. "I need to talk to Chester about a shooting he may have witnessed last weekend," he said, deciding to trust her. "He's not a suspect. He just may have seen more than he realized."

"So that's why the cops have been swarming around here all week," the woman replied, amused. "Chester thinks they're after the marijuana he bought for his grandmother. She's got arthritis, and he takes care of her. She owns the condominium."

That explained a lot. "I see. So how do I get in touch with Chester?"

For a moment, Austin didn't think she was going to tell him. She considered him, then nodded, satisfied. "He likes to sit in with the bands that play down out at the Silver Slipper, down on Fifth Street. A friend of his owns the place, so don't expect anyone there to point him out to you," she warned. "You start asking around for him down there like you did here and all you'll get is the cold shoulder."

Appreciating the warning, Austin said, "Thanks. I'll make a note of that."

She turned toward her own condominium, leaving Austin alone with his thoughts and not sure how to proceed. Chester might not know anything and could just be hiding out because of the marijuana he bought for his grandmother. But what if he'd really seen something and he was afraid the shooter was coming after him next? He'd be suspicious of anyone who came sniffing around asking questions, and Austin couldn't say he blamed him. He'd have felt the same way.

Which meant Chester wasn't going to let a stranger anywhere near him. He had friends to protect him and conceal his identity, and that gave him the decided advantage. Austin didn't know him from Adam. Oh, he had a general description, but there would probably be any number of men in that club who could be described as a thirty-year-old white male with blue eyes and brown hair. Chester could stand right next to him, Austin thought with a scowl, and he'd never know it. So what the hell was he supposed to do now?

If you need any help, just call me.

With no effort whatsoever, Austin could see the shy smile Rebecca had given him when she'd offered to help him the first night he was in town. She'd looked so sweet and innocent, and he had no business even thinking of bothering her again. Not after he'd had so much fun with her yesterday. She made him forget the past, what it was like to lose someone he loved, and that was a lesson he didn't dare let himself forget. He'd given his heart to one woman and lost her. He wouldn't risk that kind of heartache again with Rebecca or anyone else.

That decision made, he should have driven to the Silver Slipper and tried to track down Chester on his own, in spite of the old lady's words of caution. It would have been the wise thing to do. Instead, he found himself heading for Rebecca's, and there didn't seem to be a damn thing he could do about it. His rental car had developed a mind of its own.

He was the last person Rebecca expected to find on her doorstep—and the only person, she realized, she really wanted to see after the horrendous run-in she'd had with Richard Foster at work.

Flashing a happy smile at him, she pulled the door wider. "Hi! This is a nice surprise. C'mon in."

"I should have called—"

"Don't be ridiculous. I was just about to have some cookies and a glass of milk. There's plenty for both of us." And not waiting to see if he followed, she turned and headed for the kitchen. "How'd the investigation go today?" she asked over her shoulder. "Find out anything interesting?"

He hesitated at the front door, and for a moment, she thought he was going to make an excuse to leave, but he obviously thought better of it and stepped across the threshold. "Actually, I've run into a dead end unless I can

track down a guy who bought marijuana for his grandmother.''

Her lips twitching, she couldn't help but smile at his
disgusted tone. ''Well, that certainly sounds intriguing.
What does that have to do with the shooting? Or did I
miss something?''

''I've been trying to interview the band members at
Joe's birthday party. I've talked to all of them but one.
And he lives with his grandmother and buys marijuana
for her.'' Giving her a short rundown of what he'd discovered, he added, ''I don't know if he thinks he's on the
most-wanted list, or he really is just hanging out on Fifth
Street to sit in with the band, but if I go in there and start
asking for him, the jackass'll probably run.''

''I could go with you,'' she offered. ''I might recognize
him.''

Even as she made the suggestion, Rebecca couldn't believe the words came out of her mouth. Fifth Street was
lined with clubs and bars, not to mention an occasional
tattoo parlor, and when she was a child, her mother had
frequented the establishments there. She'd always hated
it, and as an adult, she'd always avoided the place because
it reminded her too much of her mother and her own
unhappy childhood.

She readily admitted to herself that she didn't want to
go there, didn't want to go anywhere near those memories, but there was just something about Austin that inspired trust. She knew she could go anywhere with him
and he would get her there and back safely.

But while she had no doubts about going to Fifth Street
or anywhere else with him, she'd apparently shocked him
with her suggestion. ''Oh, no,'' he said with an immediate
frown. ''I couldn't ask you to go into that neighborhood,
especially after dark.''

Rebecca had to smile at that. "You didn't ask, Austin. I volunteered."

"But—"

"No buts," she cut in. "I want to do this—for you and Joe. Let me."

Put that way, there was no way he could deny her, especially when she looked at him with such trust in her eyes. At that moment she could have asked him for anything, and he'd have found a way to get it for her, God help him. What had she done to him?

Confused, questions swirling in his head, he said the only thing he could: "Go change. I'm not taking you to a club in that part of town in shorts."

He didn't have to tell her twice. A small smile playing about her mouth, she hurried to her bedroom to change.

There was a time when the Silver Slipper had been a sophisticated place. But that was long ago, before most of the clubs on the street turned into bars, and the businesses in search of a more affluent clientele had moved to another part of the city. Now, with its graffiti on the side of the building and its painted black windows, it just looked like a run-down dive.

Reading her mind, Austin took her hand and squeezed it reassuringly as they waited at the corner for the traffic light to change. "Maybe it's not as bad as it looks."

"Yeah, and I'm Cinderella."

"Well, you do have the look about you," he teased, only to sober almost instantly. "We can call this off right now. All you have to do is say the word."

He meant it. He'd find another way to track down Chester. He never should have brought her here in the first place. It wasn't the kind of place she belonged, and they both knew it. But she was, he was discovering, nothing if not stubborn when she set her mind to something. "No, we're here," she said, squaring her shoulders. "Let's do it."

When she headed across the street to the Silver Slipper, Austin knew he should have stopped her. But there was a glint in her eyes that warned him and anyone else who cared to look not to get in her way, and he liked to think he wasn't a stupid man. Without a word, he fell into step beside her.

Inside, it wasn't quite as bad as he'd feared. Granted, cigarette smoke hovered like a thick, choking haze in the air, and the band was so loud, you could hardly hear yourself think. But the band was fairly decent, and most of the crowd seated at the tables in front of the small stage was there for the music, not the booze.

Reassured, he took her arm and led her to an empty table near the back of the club. With the music blaring, she couldn't hear anything without him talking right in her ear, so he pulled his chair over and put his head close to hers. "Do you see anyone you recognize?"

Her heart pounding, her eyes skipping over the sweaty band members who were banging out a heavy metal song up on the stage, Rebecca frowned through the smoke that stung her eyes and didn't see anyone who looked the vaguest bit familiar. Not that that surprised her. She hadn't paid much attention to the band the night of the party, and too late, she discovered that one musician looked much like another.

Bending his head to hers like they were lovers sharing an intimate secret, Austin murmured, "Well? What do you think?"

His breath, warm and moist, caressed her ear, sending a shiver dancing down her body, and for a moment, she was so surprised, she couldn't even think, let alone look for a guitar player she hadn't looked twice at on the night of the party. Then her gaze locked with that of the slender, dark-haired man at the end of the bar who was just lifting a mug of beer to his mouth, and shock stopped her in her tracks. "My God, I think that's him!" she said loudly.

Four

The words popped out just as the band took a break, and at the bar, Chester Phillips looked up in surprise. Recognizing her almost at the same time she did him, he set his beer down with a thump and headed straight for her. "Hey, you're one of the Coltons, aren't you?" he said with a frown, trying to place her. "One of the daughters, right? I saw you at the old man's party."

Rebecca exchanged a look with Austin and didn't have to ask if he wanted her to tell Chester why they were there. If he was as skittish of the cops as they'd been led to believe, he'd probably run for cover if he thought he was being questioned about the shooting.

So acting as if their meeting was a chance one and it wasn't the least unusual for her to frequent bars, she moved to join him and was thankful Austin was beside her as he joined them.

"Actually, I'm a foster daughter," she said easily, offering her hand as she introduced herself. "Rebecca Powell. And this is Joe's nephew, Austin. You were in the band, weren't you?"

"Yeah, that's right," he said. "I play bass. So how's the old man? Did the cops ever find out who tried to kill him?"

"You know, Austin and I were just talking about that," she replied, and surprised herself with the way she stepped into the role of friendly confidante without the slightest hesitation. If this was what it was like to play P.I., she could really enjoy it! "It's really bizarre the way the police haven't been able to come up with a suspect. With so many people standing right there when the shot was fired, you'd think somebody, somewhere, would have seen something."

"I know, man. It was weird. People were packed onto the patio like sardines. I didn't realize how bad it was until we took a break and I tried to make it to the back of the crowd for a cigarette. I couldn't move without bumping into someone with a glass of champagne. Every time I turned around, I got soaked."

Beside her, Rebecca felt Austin stiffen, but his tone was casual as he said, "So where were you when the shot was fired? Did you make it to the back of the crowd for your cigarette?"

He grinned crookedly. "Actually, I ran into this beautiful blonde with the most bodacious..." Suddenly remembering Rebecca's presence, he swallowed whatever he was going to say next and shot her a sheepish smile. "Sorry. Anyway, the next thing I knew, she screamed and threw herself into my arms and we hit the ground, just like everybody else. It was wild."

"So you didn't see where the shot came from?"

"Are you kidding? With a blonde plastered all over me? I don't think so."

There was no doubt in Austin's mind that he was telling the truth. Not only was there an honest appreciation in his eyes when he talked about the blonde, but if Austin remembered correctly, he had interviewed the daughter of one of Joe's neighbors who claimed she hadn't seen anything because she'd run into a slender, dark-haired man with blue eyes and a crooked smile. Now he knew who that man was.

Damn! Once again he'd hit a dead end.

He looked at Rebecca and saw that she, too, realized Chester wasn't going to be any help to them. But he had to try one more time. "What about before the shooting? Did you see anyone acting odd earlier in the evening? I know you were busy playing, but since you were up on stage, you have a full view of everyone outside. Did you see anyone hanging back by themselves or acting jittery or nervous?"

"No one but Mrs. Colton, and she was just worried about the party—that everything would be perfect."

"She's always like that," Rebecca said with a smile. "Fancy parties make her a nervous wreck, but she won't stop giving them. I don't understand it."

"Everybody seemed to be having a great time," Chester said with a shrug. "Sorry I can't be any more help than that."

"You tried," Austin said with a shrug. "Thanks."

Disappointed, he escorted Rebecca outside, then had to smile when she drew in a deep breath of fresh air. "It was kind of rank in there, wasn't it?"

"It was awful," she said, grimacing at the scent that clung to her clothes. "I don't know how those people in there can stand it. My eyes were starting to water!"

Chuckling, Austin had to admit that he hadn't even noticed. "Actually, that was pretty tame compared to some of the places I've been, but it can get to you if you're not used to it. Thanks for coming with me."

"I just wish I could have helped you more," she said. "I feel like I didn't do anything."

"Oh, but you did," he assured her as he unlocked his car and opened the passenger door for her. "Without you, I wouldn't have known Chester from the lowest barfly."

"But he didn't tell you anything!"

"True, but he could have just as easily been the one who cracked the case wide open. There was no way to know until we talked to him. That's the nature of the business," he added as he slipped behind the wheel and headed for her apartment. "I shouldn't admit this, but sometimes, it's just a matter of dumb luck that solves a case. That and a lot of hard work."

He told her about several cases he'd solved on a fluke, how he'd just happened to be at the right spot at the right time and everything had just come together, but then they arrived at her apartment, and the last thing he wanted to talk about was work. He wanted to see her again. The strength of that want hit him right in the chest, shaking him to the core. Scowling, he tried to convince himself that he just enjoyed working with her on the case, but deep down inside, he knew that wasn't it at all. He wanted to take her out to dinner, to a movie. Hell, he'd settle for an evening at the bowling alley. Anything so he could spend some time with her.

He was asking for trouble. He knew it, but it didn't make a bit of difference. The minute he walked her to her door, he said, "Have dinner with me tomorrow night."

In the process of digging her house key out of her purse, Rebecca glanced up, her eyes wide with surprise.

"To talk over the case? All right. But we've already gone over the guest list—"

"I'm asking you out on a date, Rebecca. This has nothing to do with the case."

She couldn't have been more surprised if he'd told her he was an alien from outer space who'd taken possession of the real Austin McGrath's body. Dazed, she just looked at him. "It doesn't?"

"I like you," he said huskily. "I want to spend some time with you. Why do you look so surprised?"

Her heart pounding crazily in her breast, she wanted to tell him that she hadn't let herself consider the possibility that he might be as attracted to her as she was to him. Because then he might want her. And she couldn't...she wouldn't be able to...

A fist tightened in her stomach and she couldn't even complete the thought. She just knew she couldn't let him or any other man touch her. Which was why she should turn him down, she told herself sternly. Any further contact with him was only going to lead to frustration and bitterness. She knew that, accepted it.

Still, she couldn't remember the last time she'd enjoyed a man's company so much, and she couldn't deny herself a little more time with him. He just wanted to take her out to dinner. What could it hurt?

"All right," she said softly. "I'd like that."

It wasn't until then that Austin realized just how badly he'd wanted her to say yes. That alone should have been enough to send him running for cover. By inviting her out, inviting her into his life on a personal level, he was in danger of opening himself up to all sorts of possibilities, including heartache, but he couldn't bring himself to worry about that now. She'd said yes. Nothing else mattered.

Suddenly unable to stop smiling, he said, "Good. I'll pick you up tomorrow at seven. We'll go get a hamburger or something."

One eye on the clock on the nightstand and the other on the contents of her closet, Rebecca stood half-naked in her bedroom early the following evening and told herself not to act like a ninny. They were just going somewhere for hamburgers, so this obviously wasn't a fancy-schmancy dinner date. Jeans and a T-shirt would probably do.

"So pick something," she muttered. "He's going to be here in ten minutes and you still haven't put on your makeup!"

Her eyes skipping to the clock, she felt her heart stop in her breast. Blindly, she reached in the closet and pulled out a baby-blue sundress with spaghetti straps that she seldom wore. Hesitating, she considered it. It was just a simple cotton dress...that was ultra feminine. Butterflies swirling in her stomach, she pulled it on.

When the doorbell rang a few minutes later, her stomach lurched and she had to ask herself whom she thought she was kidding. If this was just a casual date, why was she a nervous wreck? Her pulse was throbbing, and when she stared at herself in her dresser mirror, she saw a woman nearly glowing with anticipation, and that scared her to death. She couldn't let herself start to hope that this time it would be different. That could only lead to frustration and heartache, and she wouldn't, couldn't, do that to herself again. It was just too painful.

So call it off, a voice in her head suggested. A woman has a right to change her mind.

But even as the practical side of her brain tried to convince her that cancelling at this late date was the only wise thing to do, she knew she couldn't. This was all she was ever going to have of him, and she couldn't deny herself that. Just this once, she was going to pretend she was like every other woman and go out with a man she was attracted to.

Her mind made up, she dabbed on her favorite perfume, checked to make sure her lipstick wasn't smeared, and hurried to the front door. Suddenly breathless, her heart in her throat, she pulled open the door and couldn't seem to stop smiling. Dressed in jeans and a polo shirt, he looked absolutely wonderful. "Hi," she said softly.

Up until then, Austin had convinced himself that this was just an ordinary date with an ordinary woman. But too late, he realized that there was nothing ordinary about Rebecca or his reaction to her. That quiet, shy beauty of hers hit him right in the heart every time he saw her. And that beauty went soul deep. He'd heard about how good she was with children, especially children with problems, and for a man who regularly encountered the darker side of society, she was like a breath of fresh air. He found her innocence, her sweetness, incredibly seductive.

And that had him worried. She was practically family in spite of the fact that she was no blood relation, and he had to be very, very careful with her. Because once he'd solved this case and returned to Portland, there would be times when he saw Joe and the rest of the Coltons. Those times would be extremely awkward if he got involved with Rebecca, then just walked away. Over the years, he'd deliberately distanced himself from his family, but that didn't mean he wanted to be an outcast. He very well could be if he hurt Rebecca.

He should have found an excuse to call things off, but he just couldn't. Wearing white sandals and a sundress that turned her eyes as blue as a summer sky, she looked cool and comfortable and incredibly pretty. Always before, she'd worn her hair confined in either a braid or ponytail, but not tonight. Her long brown tresses cascaded down her slender back in a waterfall of gold and chestnut highlights that glistened in the late afternoon sunlight, and all he could think about was touching her. Did she have any idea how soft and feminine she was? How touchable?

He told himself not to go there, but it was already too late for that. In his mind, he was already running his hands through her hair. "Ready?" he asked huskily.

She nodded shyly. "Just let me get my purse."

He took her to a small mom-and-pop hamburger joint down by the beach. He'd never eaten there before, but he'd driven by one day while he was tracking down witnesses, and he'd liked the looks of the place. There was nothing the least bit pretentious about it. The building was small, about the size of a two-car garage, and only had a tiny eating area inside. But it was the outdoor patio that he'd found incredibly appealing. Picnic tables and benches overlooked the ocean and were positioned under a natural awning of flowering, brilliant bougainvillea.

Rebecca took one look at it as he pulled into the minuscule parking lot next to the restaurant and gasped. "It's beautiful! How did you find this place? I've lived here all my life and never knew it was here."

"I got lost one day and there it was." Grinning, he cut the engine. "I can't make any promises for the food, but I can guarantee the view is hard to beat. So what do you say? Are you game?"

For an answer, she reached for the handle to the passenger door and pushed it open.

* * *

The food turned out to be as incredible as the view, but they could have both been eating sawdust for all either of them noticed. Rebecca had never been at ease in the past when she'd dated, even though she'd always liked the men she'd gone out with. She'd never been able to get past the horror of her past, though God knows she'd tried. But with Austin, she didn't have to try—it just came naturally. They talked about everything from movies to books to politics, and it was wonderful. He'd read everything Stephen King had ever written, and so had she. And if he had his choice of movies to watch, he'd pick *Psycho* every time. How could he have known that it was her favorite, too? That blew her away. Could anything have been more perfect?

Time flew by and neither of them could have said where it went. Long after they'd finished their hamburgers and the sun had slipped beyond the western rim of the Pacific, they sat talking and laughing. Before they knew it, it was ten o'clock.

Glancing at her watch, Rebecca gasped. "We've been here three hours!"

Austin grinned. It could have been three days and he didn't think that would have been long enough for him, but she had to work tomorrow and he'd kept her out late enough. Rising to his feet, he held out his hand. "I guess I'd better get you home, then. Let's go."

Her heart thumping, Rebecca hesitated. It was such an innocent thing, holding hands, and so very sweet and intimate. She knew she shouldn't, simply because that was the first step that would eventually lead to something she couldn't handle. But she could no more resist the chance to touch him than she'd been able to resist his invitation to dinner. A tentative smile curling the corners of her mouth, she took his hand.

Later, she couldn't remember the drive home. She just knew that except when he needed both hands on the wheel, he held her hand the entire way. It was wonderful.

All too soon, however, they reached her apartment and it was time to say good-night. Still, Rebecca didn't want the evening to end. It had been so long since she'd gone out with anyone, and she'd never felt as safe and comfortable with anyone as she did with Austin. Impulsively, she turned to him as they reached her front door. "Would you like to come in for dessert and coffee? All I've got is chocolate chip cookies, but they're homemade."

It was a tempting offer, but regretfully, he shook his head. "I think I'd better pass this time. You've got to work tomorrow, and it's getting late." Taking her key from her, he unlocked the door for her, then handed it back to her, his smile fading as his eyes met hers in the bright glow of her porch light. "I had a great time tonight."

"Me, too," she said softly. "Thank you for asking me."

"We'll have to do it again."

She wanted to, more than anything—which was why she should have told him good-night right then and stepped inside and shut the door behind her. It would have been the smart thing to do. She was too attracted to him and didn't seem to have any common sense where he was concerned. If she needed any proof of that, she got it when he reached for her. She knew he was going to kiss her, and like an idiot, what did she do? She stepped into his arms.

It should have been wonderful, everything her dreams were made of. In her mind's eye, she could see herself melting against him and lifting her mouth to his for a magical kiss that set every nerve ending in her body humming with pleasure. That was the way it was supposed to be, the way she longed for it to be.

But when his arms closed around hers and his mouth covered hers, she suddenly found herself caught up in a nightmare of the distant past. Her heart slamming against her ribs and the very real taste of fear on her tongue, she forgot that it was Austin holding her, kissing her. In her panic, it was another man who grabbed at her, trying to steal something from her she didn't want to give. Terrified, her only thought to get away, she fought wildly to free herself. "No!"

It wasn't until she heard her own desperate scream and she saw the shock on Austin's face—dear God, it was Austin, not the monster who still haunted her dreams!—that she realized what she'd done. "Oh, God, Austin, I'm sorry! I didn't mean...I didn't realize—"

He'd never had a woman react quite that way to his kiss before, but that wasn't what concerned Austin at the moment. It was the very real fear on her face when she'd fought her way out of his arms. Worried, he took a step toward her. "What is it, Rebecca? Let's talk about it."

Her eyes still wide with panic, she turned quickly toward the door. "No!" she sobbed. "Talking won't do any good. I can't see you anymore."

Stunned, Austin watched her slam the door in his face and couldn't for the life of him understand what had just happened. He'd thought she was just as attracted to him as he was to her. In fact, he'd have sworn she was. So what the devil went wrong? He hadn't forced her, he hadn't even held her tightly. He wasn't the kind of man who rushed a woman into a physical relationship. He'd just kissed her.

Worried, he almost pounded on the door and demanded an explanation, but that, he knew, would be a mistake.

She wouldn't talk to him now, not when she was so shaken up. He had to give her some time. Once she settled down and realized she had nothing to fear from him, she'd be more willing to tell him what was going on.

Resigned, he left, but giving her the time she needed wasn't nearly as easy as he'd thought it would be. For that night and all the next day, she was all he could think of. What had put that look of fear in her eyes? *Who?*

Worried about her, he finally gave in to temptation and called her the following evening. "Hi," he said the minute she came on the line. "Are you busy? I was hoping we could talk."

"Actually, I was in the middle of making a test for tomorrow," she retorted stiffly. "Sorry."

"That's okay," he said easily. "I'll catch you another time."

But when he called the following evening, there was no answer, and he suspected she was avoiding him. He knew it for sure when he left a cheerful message on her answering machine, and she didn't call him back.

Another man might have taken the hint and let it go. After all, he didn't want to get involved with her or any other woman, so why did he care if she avoided him? This just made it easier for him to leave when his work in Prosperino was finished and he returned to Portland.

But every time he thought about that moment on her doorstep when she fought her way out of his arms, he couldn't forget the horror he'd seen in her eyes. It wasn't him she was afraid of, it was someone else, and that infuriated him. How had he hurt her? He wouldn't rest until he found out.

The decision made, he decided the only way he was going to get close enough to her to talk to her was to catch her by surprise. So the next day, he drove to the school at noon and found her at lunch with some of the other teachers on the patio outside the cafeteria. In the middle of eating a sack lunch she'd brought from home, she took one look at him and nearly choked. "Austin! What are you doing here?"

"I was hoping we could talk," he said quietly. "Have you got a minute?"

When she hesitated, he was afraid she was going to find another excuse to avoid him, but then something flickered in her eyes, a silent cry for help that struck him right in the heart. Then she was making an excuse to her co-workers and rising to her feet. "We can talk over here," she said quietly, and led him away from the patio to a flourishing rose garden at the far end of the school's administrative wing.

"This is Mr. Foster's pride and joy," she said with a faint smile, "so be careful. He's been known to suspend anyone who so much as touches one of his roses."

"Then I'll be careful to keep my hands to myself," he replied, and hoped she realized she had nothing to fear from him. He would never hurt her. Surely she knew that. His eyes searching hers, he watched her struggle to keep a smile on her mouth, and it broke his heart. "What is it, Rebecca?" he asked huskily. "What's wrong? What happened the other night? I never meant to scare you."

"Oh, but you didn't! I mean, you did, but it wasn't because of anything you did…at least not directly. I just…"

Unable to find the right words, she looked up at him with tears streaming down her cheeks, and it was all Austin could do not to reach for her. He'd never seen so much pain in her eyes before and it tore him apart. "Tell me, honey," he rasped. "Whatever it is, just tell me."

This wasn't where she'd wanted to have this conversation. Even though she had her back to the patio and the other teachers couldn't see her distress, she couldn't help but be aware of the fact that they were watching every move she and Austin made. There would be questions later, speculation, and she dreaded it. But Austin had the look of a man who wasn't going anywhere until he got some answers, and she couldn't blame him. After the way she'd reacted to his kiss the other night, he was entitled to an explanation.

It was just so hard. Tears clogged her throat, and after all these years, it still hurt to talk about that time in her life. But she wanted him to know so he wouldn't blame himself. He'd been so nice to her and he didn't deserve that. So she brushed away her tears and struggled to explain.

"I think it's fair to say that I didn't grow up in a home like you did. My father wasn't in the picture—I don't even know who he was—and my mother wasn't exactly Betty Crocker. She was an alcoholic and wasn't particular about the men she brought home with her. When I was fourteen, one of them tried to assault me."

"Son of a bitch!"

"That's not the worst of it," she replied quietly. "I knew my mother wouldn't do anything to protect me, so I ran away and lived on the streets for a while."

"My God, you were just a kid!"

"I managed to get by, but it wasn't easy. I survived by my wits, ate out of trash cans when I had to, and lied about my age at homeless shelters when I was so hungry, I was desperate. Then one night when I was sleeping in a shelter, I was almost raped."

He swore like the sailor he'd once been, but now that she'd come this far, Rebecca knew she had to say it all, or she'd never get it out. "I managed to get away and eventually ended up at Hopechest Ranch. That's where I met Meredith, and everything changed. But I never got over the attacks. I haven't been able to let a man touch me since.

"I've tried," she said before he could ask her the question she knew was coming next. "Meredith and Joe spent a fortune on therapists for me. I've seen doctors all over the country, but nothing worked. The minute a man touches me, even one that I trust and respect like you, I freeze. That's what happened the other night when you kissed me. I knew you wouldn't hurt me, but there's nothing logical about panic. Before I could do anything but blink, I was scared. All I wanted to do was get away."

"Honey, I'm so sorry. I didn't know."

"I should have told you. I knew you were attracted to me…and I feel the same way about you. But it's just so hard to talk about." Tears flooded her eyes and turned her voice thick with pain. "I enjoy your company so much, and I was hoping this time it would be different. But it's not, and there's nothing I can say or do to change that. We can't have a relationship—"

"You don't know that for sure," he argued, his eyes dark with concern as he tried to reason with her. "We rushed into this. Maybe we just need to take things at a slower pace."

If she'd let herself, she could have fallen in love with him right then and there. How could he have known that she needed him to say that? Or how desperately she wanted to believe that this was a problem that could be fixed that easily? But even though she wanted to cling to that hope, she knew better. She'd tried everything in the past, and nothing had helped. To think otherwise would only lead to more heartache, and she'd put herself through enough of that already.

"I wish that was all it took," she said huskily. "But you'd only end up hating me, and I can't do that to you."

"I could never hate you," he said with a frown. "And don't worry about me. I can take care of myself. It's you I'm concerned about."

"Then trust my judgment, and let me end this now. It has to be this way." Her heart breaking, she turned away because she had to. Because if she hadn't, she would have dissolved in tears again, and that was the last thing she wanted to do in full view of her co-workers. She'd have to save her pain for later, when she was alone and could cry her heart out in the privacy of her apartment.

"Thank you for understanding," she said thickly. "Goodbye."

Later, Austin never knew how he let her go. She was the best thing that had happened to him since he'd lost Jenny and the baby, and every instinct he had told him he'd be a fool to let her walk away from him. But for now, he had no choice. She was hurting, and all he wanted to do was wrap his arms around her. Thanks to the bastard who'd nearly raped her, however, that was the last thing he could do.

Frustrated, aching for her, he drove away from the school, resigned to the fact that he had to respect her wishes and cut her out of his life. It was the only decent thing to do.

But, Lord, she didn't make it easy for him. He poured himself into his work over the course of the next few days, but every time he let his guard down the least little bit, he found himself thinking of her, wondering what she was doing, worrying about her. But it was the nights that were the worst.

When he was asleep and his defenses were down, he dreamed of the man who'd tried to force himself on her, and it ripped him apart. All too clearly, he could imagine the terror on her face when she'd realized what was happening, and he wanted to kill the monster for daring to lay so much as a finger on her. But in the nightmare, there was nothing he could do but stand helplessly by and watch.

Swearing, he woke in a sweat night after night, until he couldn't stand it one minute more. Switching on the bedside light, he reached for the phone and called her. It wasn't until he heard her sleepy hello that he glanced at the clock and realized it was after midnight.

"I'm sorry," he said huskily. "I didn't realize it was so late."

"Austin, is that you? What's wrong?"

"Nothing. I was just worried about you. Are you okay?"

When she hesitated, he wanted to believe that she'd missed him as much as he had her, but all she said was, "I'm fine. Work's been keeping me busy. How's the case coming?"

"Slow," he said flatly. "But that's not why I called. I've been thinking about what you said the other day at school."

"Austin—"

"Wait," he said quickly, stopping the protest he could already hear in her voice. "I know you don't want to talk about it. I don't blame you. That had to be a horrible experience for you, and I can understand why you don't want to dredge up the past again. But you can't let that bastard ruin the rest of your life. If we stop seeing each other because of something he did to you when you were fourteen, he's still raping you."

"No!"

"Yes, he is," he insisted. "Think about it. Every time

you withdraw from me or any other man, he's hurting you all over again. And you're letting him."

"No, I'm not!"

"Yes, you are, honey. Can't you see how the past is controlling your life today? It doesn't have to be that way. You don't have to fight this thing alone."

Lying in the dark with the phone pressed to her ear, Rebecca blinked back sudden, stinging tears. She *did* feel alone—she had for a long time now. How had he known? "It's not that easy," she said thickly. "I've tried…"

"That's what I'm talking about, sweetheart. *You've* tried. Now let's try it together."

He made it sound so easy. "How?"

"By not withdrawing into yourself. You've done that in the past, and it hasn't helped. So why can't we still be friends? Why can't we still see each other? Now that I know everything, you don't have to worry about me scaring you again. I would never force you into a physical relationship."

"Of course you wouldn't. I know that."

"Then I don't see any reason why we can't start over and try this again. If you don't want me to ever touch or kiss you again, I'll accept that. It's your call. Give us a chance, honey. Give yourself a chance."

She wanted to—more than anything. But she'd tried so many times in the past, only to endure more disappointment and heartache. How could she put herself through that again?

"I don't know," she said softly. "I don't know if you realize what you're asking."

"A chance," he repeated. "Just a chance. That's all I'm asking. And you don't have to make a decision tonight," he added quickly. "It's late and I woke you up out of a sound sleep. You need to think about this when you're more alert and can consider all the pros and cons. So go back to sleep. We'll talk later in the week. Okay?''

Caught off guard by the swiftness with which he ended the conversation, she said, "Yeah...I guess. But I can't make any promises.''

"That's okay,'' he assured her. "All I want you to do right now is think about it.''

Long after he hung up, Rebecca found it impossible to go back to sleep. Lying in the dark, her mind working overtime, she couldn't help but consider his suggestion. What if he was right? What if he wasn't?

Torn, she didn't know what to do. She couldn't remember the last time she'd been so drawn to a man. She only had to think of him to smile, and she readily admitted that she didn't want to let him go. She'd thought of nothing but him since the moment she'd sat down to dinner with him at Joe and Meredith's his first night in town, but she didn't see how any kind of relationship between the two of them could possibly work. How could it? If she couldn't tolerate a simple kiss, she'd never be able to tolerate sex. And while Austin might think that might not be a problem now, with time, he would come to resent such a situation. And she couldn't blame him. She would, too.

But what if he was right? she wondered. What if, instead of running from her fears from the past, she faced them...with him. Could he help her? Was she willing to take a chance and find out?

Her heart pounding against her ribs, she replayed in her mind every date she'd ever had and cringed at the memories that flashed like one long continuous nightmare before her eyes. She didn't want to live that way for the rest of her life, she thought, swallowing a sob. She couldn't. Austin was right. He was offering her a chance she couldn't pass up.

Five

Two days came and went, and Austin didn't hear a word from Rebecca. They were the longest two days of his life. He had plenty of work to keep him busy, but every time he dropped his guard the least little bit, his thoughts invariably wandered to her. What was she doing? Had she given any thought to his suggestion? Was her silence his answer?

Frustrated, he almost called her a half dozen times, and more than once, he drove by her apartment before he even realized what he was doing. But he'd told her to take whatever time she needed to make a decision, and he promised himself he wouldn't push her. She'd call him when she'd made up her mind. For now, all he could do was wait.

In the past, he'd always thought he was a patient man. He'd never rushed an investigation or, for that matter, a woman. But then again, he'd never met anyone quite like

Rebecca Powell before. She had a peacefulness about her that called to his troubled soul and a vulnerability that made him just want to wrap his arms around her and hold her.

But that was something she couldn't tolerate right now and might never be able to accept from him. And that was the reason he waited. This had to be totally and completely her decision, with no pressure from him whatsoever.

So he waited, and tried not to watch the clock. But when the phone rang two nights later, he pounced on it like a teenager waiting for a call from the first girl he'd ever had a crush on. "Hello?"

"Hi," she said huskily. "Have you had dinner?"

"Actually, I ordered a pizza. It should be here any minute."

"Why don't you bring it over?" she suggested. "I'll make a salad to go with it. Then we can talk."

"Give me ten minutes, max," he said, and hung up just as the delivery boy knocked at the door.

Hurriedly paying for the pizza, he reminded himself that just because she wanted to talk didn't mean she was going to give him the answer he wanted. She was the type of woman who would let a man down face-to-face. And if that was why she'd invited him over, he would have to accept it, like it or not. After all that she'd been through, the last thing she needed was any kind of pressure from him.

Standing at her front door a few minutes later, he couldn't remember the last time he'd been so nervous. Then she opened the door at his knock, and he forgot all about the pizza he carried. He hadn't eaten in nearly seven hours, but the only thing he was interested in was her.

It wasn't that she'd dressed up for him—she hadn't.

She was dressed casually, in red capris and a white T-shirt, and was barefoot. She'd twisted her hair up and secured it on top of her head, and with only a minimum of makeup on, she looked like she was sixteen. He took one look at her and her shy smile and had to fight from falling in love with her right there on the spot.

"I hope this is okay," she said, motioning to her casual attire when she pulled the door wide for him. "It was so hot today, and when I came home, I just wanted to get into something comfortable."

"No problem," he replied, and hoped she didn't notice the huskiness in his voice. If she'd guessed what she did to him with just a smile, she probably would have shown him the door immediately. "Work going okay?"

"Same as always," she said as she led him into the kitchen, where she already had plates set out and the salad on her small table. "Summers are always hard. The kids want to be outside, and the three weeks they get off in June just never seem to be enough. Especially for my students. They're easily distracted."

"I can understand that. We had nearly three months off in the summer when I was a kid, and I was never ready to go back."

"I was just the opposite," she said as they took seats across from each other at the table. "I couldn't wait for school to start again in the fall."

She'd hated the summers—and her mother's boyfriends, who never seemed to work. With no effort whatsoever, she could remember the touch of their eyes on her, the way they'd made her feel awkward and self-conscious in her shorts and skimpy summer tops, and all she'd wanted to do was go back to school, where she'd felt safe. But every year, the summers seemed to get longer and longer.

Pushing the awful memories away, she deliberately brought the conversation around to the reason they both knew he was there. "I've been thinking about what you said the other night," she said as she served herself a piece of pizza.

In the process of pouring dressing on his salad, he looked up and arched a brow at her. "And?"

"I think you're right. Running away isn't helping. I have to try something else."

When he didn't push her, but let her tell him in her own time, she was grateful. "This isn't going to be easy," she warned. "You have to know that. You could end up hating me."

"That's never going to happen," he assured her. "We can do this, Rebecca."

"Only if we set some ground rules and stick to them. That's the only way this is going to work."

"Name them," he retorted, "and I'll agree to them. Just say the word."

There was no doubting his sincerity, and that touched her heart as nothing else could. "Thank you," she whispered, blinking back the sudden tears that stung her eyes. "I just want to make sure that neither one of us has to go through what we did the other night. It wasn't fun for me, and I'm sure it wasn't for you, either. So there can be no unexpected hugs or kisses. Surprises scare me."

His expression grim, he nodded. "I can see how they would. It won't happen again." Studying her reflectively, he asked, "What would have happened if I'd told you beforehand that I wanted to kiss you? Would that have made it less traumatic for you?"

Surprised, she blinked. "I don't know. No one's ever given me fair warning before."

"Next time I will. Not that you have to worry that I'm

going to try anything like that soon," he quickly assured her. "And never without discussing it with you first. That might destroy the spontaneity of the moment, but what good is that if you're terrified? It's much more important that you feel comfortable."

He was so understanding that Rebecca couldn't stop the tears from filling her eyes all over again. Did he know how special he was? "That might help," she said huskily, "but I can't make any promises that any of this is ever going to work."

"So, we'll still be friends," he promised her. "You will still go out with me, won't you?"

"Well, yes, I suppose so."

"And you won't be afraid to hold hands? I do like to hold hands with a woman I'm attracted to. But if the idea of that makes you nervous..."

Surprised, she had to smile. She wouldn't have thought he was the type to want to hold hands like teenagers, but she found the idea very appealing. "No, I don't think I would have a problem holding hands."

"Good," he said, his smile pleased. "Then we'll take it from there. I can tell you right now, I'd like to kiss you on the cheek at the end of the evening, but I'll never do it without your permission. From there, we'll take it one step at a time. Okay?"

He was a man of his word. Rebecca only had to look in his eyes to know that she could trust him. He wouldn't push or hem her in or take more than she was willing to give. And for that, she sent up a silent prayer of thanks. Maybe he was right. Maybe they could get through this together.

"Okay," she said with a smile, and held out her hand to shake on the deal.

When his fingers closed around hers, Rebecca couldn't

explain the feeling that came over her. It was almost like coming home. And for the first time in a very long time, she actually looked forward to the future.

They watched "Who Wants to be a Millionaire" on TV after dinner and Austin was amazed at the questions that she could answer. "How did you know dipsomania was an insatiable craving for alcohol? And that Fillmore was the thirteenth president of the United States? That's not the kind of stuff you pick up reading *Newsweek*."

"I like to do crossword puzzles," she said with a twinkle in her eyes. "It stretches the mind."

"Remind me not to play Trivial Pursuit with you," he laughed. "You'd kick my butt."

"Not if we played the sports edition," she retorted. "I probably shouldn't admit this, but I don't know a home run from a touchdown. I was never interested in sports."

That didn't surprise Austin. She'd grown up without a father, and the only men she'd encountered before Joe came into her life as a foster father were alcoholics and lechers who weren't interested in anything but where the next drink and woman were coming from.

"So we can take care of that by going to a baseball game sometime and I'll teach you all about home runs," he said easily. "In the meantime, I've got to go. It's getting late, and I imagine you have to be at school early in the morning."

"Yeah, I do," she admitted, following him to the front door. "But I had a really good time tonight. I'm glad you came over."

"Me, too."

Standing in her foyer, Austin stared down at her pretty, upturned face and wondered if she had a clue what she did to him. She was so sweet and natural and totally without artifice. He didn't doubt for a second that her students adored her, and he could see why. She didn't seem to realize how attractive she was. After everything she'd been through in her life, she was still open and friendly and giving.

And he wanted to kiss her. Much, much more than he'd expected.

Need tightening in his gut, he got a grip on his control and sternly reminded himself that tonight and all the other times he and Rebecca were together weren't about him. She was counting on him to help her, and by God, that was what he was going to do. So he could just forget about what he wanted. Her needs were the only ones that mattered for now.

But Lord, it wasn't easy. Even though the kiss he'd given her the other night had been over almost before it began, he hadn't forgotten what it felt like to hold her in his arms. Or how soft and enticing her mouth was. Images teased and tempted him, and with a silent curse, he drew himself up sharply. No! He wouldn't go there. Not now, maybe not ever.

Forcing a rueful smile that cost him far more than she realized, he said hoarsely, "Thanks again for supper."

"You brought the pizza," she reminded him with a grin. "I should be thanking you. I didn't have to cook or eat alone. It was fun."

"For me, too."

There was nothing left to say. A wise man would have gotten out of there while he could, with his promise ringing virtually in his ears. Instead, he lingered and couldn't stop himself from asking, "Would you mind if I kissed you on the cheek?"

Her heart thumping crazily, Rebecca knew she should have said no. It was too soon for even such an innocent kiss; she wasn't ready. But as she looked up at him with wide, searching eyes, she wanted more than anything to be normal, to know what it was like to end a wonderful evening with a kiss—even if it was only on the cheek.

"All right," she said, and braced herself.

His eyes met hers, and in the sudden hushed stillness that fell between them, they both knew just how important the moment was. If she couldn't handle a simple kiss on the cheek, the agreement they'd had earlier in the evening was all for naught.

"This isn't something you need to worry about," he said huskily as he stepped toward her. "My hands are behind my back, and you're perfectly safe. All I'm going to do is brush my lips against your cheek. That's all." And suiting his actions to his words, he did just that.

It happened so fast, it was over almost immediately, and all Rebecca had time to do was drag in a quick, soundless breath before he stepped back, giving her plenty of room. "Okay?" he asked. "I didn't scare you, did I?"

Her cheek tingling from the soft kiss, Rebecca couldn't have told him what she was feeling, but she knew it wasn't fear. Not when she was tempted to ask him to do it again.

"No," she said shakily, unconsciously cradling her hand to her cheek to hold the magical sensation close. "I-I'm fine."

"Good." Making no attempt to hide his satisfaction, he grinned. "This is going to work, honey. You'll see. We just have to be patient and give it some time."

She wanted desperately to believe him, but long after he left, she couldn't stop thinking of all the times she'd tried in the past to get past her fears. Every time she'd thought she was getting somewhere, the terror rose up before her like the devil himself, frightening her all over again.

But not this time, she told herself fiercely. This time she had Austin to help her. This time there would be no surprises, just slow, steady progress that would eventually banish all her fears for good. All she had to do was be patient.

Feeling more optimistic than she had in a long time, she went to bed and dreamed of him almost immediately. And it was wonderful. With a magic that was only possible in dreams, the kiss he gave her on the cheek turned into one on the mouth, then another and another, until they were making love before the fireplace in the living room, and it was everything she'd always dreamed it would be. There was no fear, no trepidation, not the slightest hesitation. It was just her and Austin, together, loving each other, and it was beautiful.

When she woke, there were tears in her eyes and a longing in her heart unlike anything she'd ever felt before. Curling in on herself, she held the emotions close and wished with all her heart that the day would soon come when her dream would come true. But even as she sent up a silent prayer to her angels, she knew deep down inside that she and Austin would never, in all likelihood, have more than they had right now. If years of therapy couldn't heal the hurts of the past, then some things just weren't meant to be.

When he showed up at Rebecca's apartment bright and early Saturday morning with fresh croissants, Austin told himself that he was just being friendly. He had his feelings under strict control and there was nothing to worry about. If he was thinking about her more than he should and he'd found an excuse to see her every other night since they'd agreed on how to proceed with a limited physical relationship, it was just because he liked her and enjoyed her company. He readily admitted that his attraction to her was stronger than ever, but he wasn't stupid enough to let things get out of hand. Everything was fine.

When she opened the door to him, it was obvious she wasn't expecting company. Dressed in jeans and an old T-shirt that was splattered with paint, she'd tied her hair back with a piece of yarn and hadn't bothered with makeup. And in her hand was a glue gun, and it was pointed right at him.

Grinning, he held up his hands...and the bakery bag of croissants. "Don't shoot. I've come bearing gifts."

"Austin! Just the man I wanted to see." And with no more warning than that, she grabbed his arm and dragged him inside. "I need some help."

"With a glue gun? Oh, no," he grimaced. "That's not my thing. I'm not into crafts."

"Neither am I," she retorted. "I'm making a project for school. Oh, no, you don't," she said quickly, grabbing his arm again when he started to sink down into one of her kitchen chairs. "Glue," she said with a nod toward the seat. "I wouldn't if I were you."

He jumped up like a jack-in-the-box, drawing a laugh from her. "Sorry," she giggled. "Did I mention that I'm not very good with a glue gun? I have a tendency to get it all over everything."

That, Austin discovered with a quick look around, was an understatement of gargantuan proportions. He couldn't tell exactly *what* she was making, but there was construction paper, poster boards and Styrofoam all over the kitchen. It was the glue, however, that really raised his eyebrows. It was everywhere.

Glancing up, he directed her gaze to the spot over her

head, where a Styrofoam ball was stuck to the ceiling with a huge glob of glue. "How did you manage that?"

Far from embarrassed, she just grinned. "I accidentally tripped over one of the kitchen chairs just after I put some glue on the ball, and when I stumbled, it just sort of flew out of my hand."

"Straight up to the ceiling, huh?" Amused, he had to laugh. "Well, at least it wasn't the cat."

She gave him a chiding look. "I don't have a cat."

"Now I know why," he teased, grinning. "What *are* you making, anyway?"

"It's a game for my students," she explained. "I saw it on the Internet, and it looked like so much fun that I thought I'd make it for class Monday. But it's not as easy as it looked."

A wise man would have made an excuse and gotten out of there before she glued the door shut, but his common sense had been in short supply from the moment he'd met her that first evening at Joe's. Before he could stop himself, he set down the bag of croissants on the kitchen counter and said, "Here, let me look at the instructions. Maybe I can help."

An hour and a half later, the croissants still sat untouched on the counter, they were both covered in glue, and the project was still in pieces. But Austin couldn't remember the last time he'd laughed so much. "I think whoever designed this damn thing left out a few pieces on purpose just to drive us crazy," he said. "Are you sure it's supposed to look like the space shuttle?"

"It's right there in the picture," she pointed out. "See? The shuttle and the space station, complete with loading dock. According to the instructions, a six-year-old can make it in about twenty minutes."

His gaze followed hers to the directions she'd printed

out, then shifted to the shuttle they'd constructed. For a moment, neither one of them said a word. Then their eyes met, and they both burst into laughter.

"It's awful, isn't it?" she chuckled, wiping her eyes. "It looks just like a—"

"Penguin," he finished for her. "A fat, slightly lopsided, drunk penguin."

In response to his comment, the penguin chose that moment to fall over on the table, face-first, and that sent Rebecca into gales of laughter. "I'm sorry," she laughed. "It's just so pathetic. I'm usually a better teacher than this."

"Hey, this has nothing to do with your teaching abilities. Somebody just screwed up with the directions. So let's change the game into something with penguins. At least the kids will laugh."

He had a point. Her mind working, she studied the pathetic Styrofoam and paper penguins, and all of a sudden, she could see all sorts of possibilities. "You know, that just might work! Here, let's try this."

By lunchtime, they had constructed what appeared to be an entire army of penguins, and even though more than a few of them didn't stand up straight and had a tendency to lean, Rebecca was thrilled. She knew her students were going to love them.

Her eyes shining as she and Austin both stood at the kitchen sink and scrubbed the glue from their hands, she looked up at him and said, "You don't know how thankful I am that you dropped by this morning. I probably would have spent the rest of the day trying to construct that crazy shuttle and ended up with nothing to show for it but frustration. Thanks."

"My pleasure," he said with twinkling eyes. "It was fun."

Standing hip to hip, he was so close, Rebecca could have been in his arms just by leaning a little to her left. It would have been so simple...and so right. At that moment she wanted to feel his arms around her more than she wanted anything in the world, but she couldn't tell him, couldn't ask. They'd seen each other just about every day over the past week, and he'd ended each evening with a kiss on the cheek—after asking her permission, of course. But this time, she ached for more...just this once.

Her fear wouldn't let her say a word, but something in her eyes must have given her away. The smile on his face slowly faded and his hands stilled under the running water of the faucet. For what seemed like an eternity, time seemed to stop.

"Did I ever tell you how pretty I think you are?" he asked huskily.

Her heart thumping in her chest, Rebecca could only shake her head.

"You've just got this natural prettiness that you're not even aware of. Every time you laugh, I just want to grab you and kiss you. I'm not, though," he assured her quickly, then qualified that statement with, "going to grab you. I will kiss you, though."

This time, he didn't ask, but he knew he didn't have to. He had to see her permission in her eyes. Her heart wanted nothing more than for him to draw her into his arms and kiss her on the mouth like he would never let her go. It was what she'd dreamed of, what she ached for with all of her being.

But her head still wasn't ready to trust him or any other man. Try though she might, she couldn't stop herself from tensing.

But he was, this time, as always, a man of his word. He leaned over to kiss her on the cheek, just as he had so many times before over the last week. Only this time it was different. He didn't just brush his lips to her cheek and quickly draw back so as not to scare her. Instead, he lingered for the span of a heartbeat, his mouth pressed warmly to the curve of her cheek, and just that easily, he set her body temperature spiralling upward. Entranced, she gasped softly, wishing the moment could last forever.

She wasn't the only one. Given the chance, Austin would have slowly folded his arms around her and drawn her against his heart, where she belonged. Just for a moment, the temptation of that was almost more than he could bear. What harm could it do? She had to know now that he was never going to hurt her. She had to let go of her fear sometime, and this was perfect. It was broad daylight, they were both still sticky with glue, and there was nothing the least romantic about the situation.

But even as he went over all the reasons why he should have been able to give her more than just a kiss on the cheek, he suddenly realized what he was doing and swore silently. What the devil was wrong with him? Rebecca was still suffering years after she'd nearly been raped. After everything she'd been through, only she could decide when she'd be ready for something more satisfying than a kiss on the cheek.

And that was a decision she might not ever be able to make, he acknowledged. Only time would tell. In the meantime, however, she was calling the shots, and he didn't have a problem with that. Women had been calling the shots since the beginning of time, anyway, he thought wryly. They just let the men think it was all their idea.

When he grinned suddenly, Rebecca lifted a soapy finger to her face. "What? Have I got glue on my nose or what?"

"Not at all," he chuckled. "I was just thinking about something else. Are you hungry? We never did eat those croissants. Why don't we go pick up some chicken and have a picnic in the park? We've worked enough for one day."

For an answer, she dried her hands and grabbed her purse from where it hung from a kitchen chair. "Last one out locks up," she said with a grin.

Laughing, they both rushed to the front door.

"All right, Tommy! Way to go!"

"My penguin made it to the North Pole before his did, Miss Powell. Does that mean I win?"

"This isn't about winning, Lucy," Rebecca told Lucy Meadows, one of her favorite students in her second period class. "There are all sorts of ways to get to the North Pole. The point of the game is to have fun and explore."

She could tell by her frown that Lucy didn't quite understand that concept, but the rest of the students didn't care. They were more concerned with playing with the penguins and learning about the way they lived than winning. And Rebecca was thrilled. All of the students had learning disabilities, which was why they were in her class, and getting them all involved in a game or activity at the same time wasn't always easy. But they'd taken one look at the penguins she and Austin had constructed Saturday morning, and they'd been instantly captivated.

"Hey, we need some fish to feed these penguins. Can we make some out of construction paper, Miss Powell? What do the fish they eat look like?"

Pleased, Rebecca smiled down at Josh Kitchen and just barely resisted the urge to hug him. She'd had a soft spot where Josh was concerned. He'd been abused by his parents and put into the foster care program by the state, and he'd been quiet and withdrawn from the moment he was first assigned to her class two months ago. Yet here he was, not only asking a question in front of the entire class, but wanting to learn more.

Touched, she smiled and prayed he didn't see the sudden tears glistening in her eyes. "Of course you can make some fish. I've got a picture right here in a book I checked out of the library that you can copy."

He and the other students gathered around her desk, exclaiming over not only the pictures of the fish, but those of an Eskimo village. Moments later, the classroom was a beehive of activity as everyone scrambled to make a school of fish for the penguins and an Eskimo village.

"Miss Powell, come and look at my fish."

"Mine's awesome!"

"I made an igloo. A real one!"

Laughing, Rebecca hurried from desk to desk, praising everyone for their efforts and offering help when asked for. This was why she'd gone into teaching, why, even when she didn't know how to get through to a student, she kept trying. Because when everything came together, it was magic.

Caught up in her students and the fun they were having, she never noticed that Richard Foster had appeared in the doorway to her classroom until Lucy tugged on her skirt and said, wide-eyed, "Mr. Foster wants to talk to you, Miss Powell. Is he mad? His face is all red."

Whirling, Rebecca felt her heart sink at the sight of the principal's sour expression. His face was, indeed, red, and he had that look in his eye that every teacher in the school knew spelled trouble. Once again, he was obviously having a bad day.

She didn't, however, want Lucy to worry about that, so she just smiled and said reassuringly, "He's not mad, sweetie. He was just out in the sun over the weekend and got a little sunburned. Go back to your penguins, and I'll go see what he wants."

Dread pooling in her stomach, she kept her smile firmly in place as she strode over to the doorway to greet her boss. "Good morning, Mr. Foster. How are you today?"

Ignoring her greeting, he glared at her and said in a low, cold voice, "What is the meaning of this, Miss Powell?"

Confused, she blinked. "I beg your pardon?"

"And well you should," he snapped. "Do you know I can't even talk on the phone in my office because I can't hear myself think for you and your students? What the devil is going on here?"

"We're playing a game—"

"I don't care if you're talking to the president of the United States. You will cease and desist immediately!"

She couldn't believe he was serious. "But—"

"There is no discussion on this, Miss Powell," he cut coldly. "Your classroom is out of control. I don't know when or why you've gotten so lax in discipline, but I can't allow this to continue. You will end the game and restore order to your classroom. *Now!*"

Rebecca had never liked confrontations. As far as she was concerned, anger was just one letter away from danger and she wanted nothing to do with it if she could find a way to avoid it. But it was her job to see that her students got the best education she could give them, and she couldn't just stand there and let Mr. Foster destroy the breakthrough she'd finally made with some of her most troubled students.

"Please don't ask me to do that, Mr. Foster," she

pleaded. "Look at Josh Kitchen and Tara Sears and David Hernandez. None of them have ever participated in any kind of classroom activity before. They're so excited, I just hate to discourage them."

If she'd hoped to touch his heart, she'd wasted her breath. His blue eyes were as cold as stone behind the lenses of his glasses. "This isn't about the students, Miss Powell. It's about the parents and what one of them would think if they walked through the front door and heard the raucous noise coming from your classroom. *I* would be questioned about what kind of school *I* was running, and that, by God, isn't going to happen. And do you know why, Miss Powell? Because you're going to shut that damn game down immediately, or I'm going to do it for you. Do I make myself understood?"

He left her no choice. Fighting tears, she nodded stiffly. "Yes, sir."

Watching the light go out of Josh Kitchen's eyes was the most difficult thing Rebecca had ever done in her life. Hours later, she still wanted to cry just at the thought of it. Under the watchful eye of Mr. Foster, she'd been left with no choice but to tell her students that they had to put the penguins away because it was time to study something else. The collective look of betrayal they'd sent her would go with her to her grave.

Sick at heart, she placed the chicken salad she'd made for supper in the refrigerator, unable to eat a bite of it. And it was all Richard Foster's fault. She'd thought she knew him, but she'd never seen him act so cold and unfeeling. Okay, so he was having a rough time with the divorce. She sympathized with that, but once he walked through the front door of the school, he was an educator, and that took precedence over his private life. How could he care so little about the students?

After school, she'd wanted nothing more than to storm into his office to tell him exactly what she thought of him, but she hadn't, of course. How could she? They might be friends, but he wouldn't take that from anyone. So she'd bitten her tongue, instead, and now her silence was eating at her like a cancer. She should have done something!

Lost in her misery, she didn't hear the soft knock at her front door. Then the doorbell rang. The last thing she wanted was company, but she couldn't pretend she wasn't home, not when the lights were on and her car was parked in front of her apartment. Resigned, she went to answer the door. When she spied Austin through the peephole, she almost cried. How had he known she needed to see him?

A wobbly smile springing to her mouth, she pulled open the door. "Austin! I didn't expect to see you tonight."

"I was just in the neighborhood and thought I'd drop by and see how the kids liked the penguins," he said easily as he stepped inside. Then his eyes met hers and he frowned. "What's wrong?"

She hadn't meant to tell him—Richard was her problem and she'd find a way to deal with him—but he'd caught her at a vulnerable moment. Her eyes stung with tears. "The kids loved them," she said huskily. "Mr. Foster didn't."

She told him what happened then, and even though she hated what her boss had done, she bent over backward to be understanding. "He's having a rough time right now. He and his wife are divorcing after seventeen years of marriage, and he's not handling it well. I guess it was just dumb luck that he was having a bad day the same day my students wanted to have a good time.''

''I don't know that I'd call it dumb luck,'' Austin retorted. ''The man sounds like a jackass. He's a professional. He should know better than to take his rotten mood out on others, especially kids. And I bet the school board would agree with me.''

''You're not going to call and report this, are you?'' she asked, alarmed. ''Please, Austin, don't. Everyone's entitled to a mistake. And I did let things get out of hand. The kids can have a good time without getting loud. I should have quieted them.''

Austin sincerely doubted that she'd been negligent in keeping her classroom under control. She obviously didn't want to get Foster in trouble, and he supposed he couldn't blame her. The worst the principal would receive was a slap on the wrist if he was turned in, and he would know who to blame for that—Rebecca. And paybacks could be hell. If he wanted to, he could make her life at work miserable.

''I think you're being too hard on yourself,'' he retorted, ''but I'm not going to turn the bastard in. That would just create more problems for you. Just avoid him when you can, and try to be polite when you can't. As soon as his divorce is over, things are bound to get better.''

Nodding, Rebecca hoped so, but she wasn't holding her breath. He had always been so devoted to Sylvia—losing her wasn't something he was going to get over anytime soon. If she was lucky, he might be acting like a decent human being again by *next* summer. Just thinking about it made her groan. How was she going to stand another year of this? Unless she wanted to look for another job— which she didn't—she didn't have much choice.

Six

Over the course of the next week, Rebecca tried to put the incident with Richard behind her, but it wasn't easy. The students kept asking her when they were going to play the penguin game again, and she had a difficult time coming up with an excuse that made sense even to her own ears. She put it away in her classroom closet, but one of the girls found it, and in self-defense, she finally took it home and destroyed it.

That should have made things easier—once it was out of sight, the children eventually let the subject drop. But that didn't help her forget the incident. Every time she saw Richard in the hall, every time she was forced to speak to him, the scene replayed itself in her mind and she got angry all over again.

There had been a time when she'd considered him one of the best administrators she'd ever worked with. He'd always been a strong advocate of discipline, but he'd had a soft spot where the students were concerned, and they'd loved him. Not anymore. They kept their distance, and behind his back, they'd started to refer to him as the old goat. Rebecca couldn't blame them. He walked around the school with a scowl on his face and growled at anyone who showed the least spark of life. The students had begun to scurry for cover whenever they saw him walking down the hall.

It wasn't just the students he was having a difficult time with. The tension between him and the staff was so thick, you could cut it with a knife. But Rebecca couldn't help noticing that it was his animosity toward her that seemed to be particularly strong. And she didn't know why. They'd always been friends, and before he and Sylvia started divorce proceedings, Rebecca had frequently been invited to their home for dinner. But now, he looked at her like he couldn't stand her, and every time he turned his hard gaze on her, she wanted to disappear right into the woodwork.

Although she tried to keep her distance from him, the situation was getting worse, not better. He'd started coming into the teachers' lounge in the morning before school started, and she couldn't seem to say good morning to him without drawing some kind of criticism from him.

"You're not a child anymore, Miss Powell," he said the second he spied her pouring herself a cup of coffee. "From now on, confine your hair or get it cut so it doesn't hang down your back like a first grader's. You're a professional. Dress like it."

Caught off guard in front of a dozen or more other teachers, Rebecca wanted to sink through the floor. She'd been running late that morning and hadn't had time to do anything with her hair except pull on a headband and comb it down her back. That wasn't, however, a violation of any dress code that she knew about. Three other teachers in the room had their hair styled exactly the same way, and Richard hadn't said a word to them.

Resentful color stinging her cheeks, she almost asked him if this new rule applied to just her or everyone, but she didn't want to get into an argument with him in front of the rest of the staff. Considering the mood he was in, he'd probably fire her on the spot. So she held her tongue instead and said stiffly, "I have a clip in my purse. I'll put it up before I go to class."

"See that you do." Not sparing her or anyone else another glance, he walked out, leaving behind a silence that echoed with mortification.

Embarrassed, Rebecca fought back tears and told herself she wasn't going to cry. Then Penny Taylor, a fifth-grade teacher, stepped over to the coffee machine and said quietly, "You okay?"

Unable to look her in the eye, she sniffed, "Yeah. I'll be fine."

Far from convinced, Penny merely arched a brow. "Really? You don't look fine. What's going on, Rebecca? You used to be Tricky Dick's golden girl. Has something happened between the two of you?"

Surprised by the less than flattering description of the principal and herself she frowned. "What do you mean I used to be his 'golden girl'? And when did you start calling him Tricky Dick? I thought you liked him."

"Are you kidding? I've tolerated him all these years because he's the boss and I need my job. He may have been nice to you, but he's treated the rest of like we were just here to make him look good. Everything's about him. And since his wife left him, he's been a real jerk. Haven't you noticed?"

"I thought it was just me," she replied honestly.

"Every time I turn around, I seem to be doing something wrong."

Sympathetic, Penny smiled. "It's not you," she assured her. "It's him. He's got a bee up his patootie because of this divorce and he lashes out at everyone who so much as looks at him wrong. Personally, I'm surprised that he turned on you, though. He's always talking about what a good teacher you are. Didn't you just do something with penguins?"

Surprised, Rebecca blinked. "You must have misunderstood. I did develop a game with penguins, but Richard hated it. He made me shut it down."

"He told everyone who would listen that it was brilliant," her friend said dryly. "I tell you, the man's losing it. He doesn't know if he's coming or going, and we're the ones paying the price. I think he needs therapy."

Rebecca didn't know what to think. "I can't believe he liked the penguins after he made such a stink. You should have heard him," she told her, disgusted. "He didn't care about the game or that the kids were having fun and actually participating. He just wanted them to be quiet in case a parent walked in."

"So he wouldn't look bad," Penny concluded, rolling her eyes. "Once you realize that his behavior is all generated to make himself look good, you can deal with the man. It's when he starts pulling this weird stuff—like attacking you for no reason—that I get nervous. I just want things to go back to normal. Maybe then, he'll just be his regular obnoxious self instead of a son of a bitch."

Rebecca had to agree, but she wasn't holding her breath that that would happen any time soon. From what she had heard, he and Sylvia couldn't agree on anything and the lawyers were expecting a long, drawn-out court battle. It could be months, possibly a year or longer, before the dust settled.

Rebecca groaned at the thought of it, but told herself she'd withstood worse things in the past. She'd get through this, too. She just had to keep a stiff upper lip and remember that she wasn't the only one who'd come under fire. Resigned, she pinned up her hair and went back to work.

Things should have been easier after that. She kept her distance from Richard whenever she could, and when that proved impossible, she tried not to take his fault-finding to heart. It wasn't easy. He seemed to know just what to say to hurt her, and he always found a way to do it in front of other people.

The next three days were a nightmare. Still, she didn't so much as wince whenever he criticized her clothes or teaching methods, and she was proud of herself for that. If he verbally attacked her because he wanted her and everyone else to be as miserable as he was, he was sadly disappointed. She continued to laugh and smile with her students and the other teachers whenever she got the opportunity.

And every afternoon when she went home, she cried her eyes out in the shower, where no one could see.

She didn't doubt that Austin would have been outraged if he'd known how unhappy she was and why, but she found excuses for him not to come over so he wouldn't see her puffy eyes. And whenever they talked on the phone, she kept her voice deliberately upbeat and cheerful. He didn't have a clue that she was still having problems with Richard, and that was just the way she wanted it. For most of her life, she'd run away from conflict and depended on others to deal with the bullies who'd tormented her. She couldn't do that anymore. She was no longer a little girl at the Hopechest Ranch looking for someone to protect her. She had to take care of her own problems.

But the strain of pretending that nothing was wrong took its toll. After a particularly difficult day, she came home and stepped right into the shower and burst into tears. The sad thing was, it didn't help. Nothing did. When she dragged herself out of the shower thirty minutes later, all she had to show for all her tears were red eyes and a runny nose. Wearily, she pulled on her nightgown and robe and dragged herself into the kitchen to heat some canned soup.

When the doorbell rang just as she sat down at her small kitchen table, her heart jumped into her throat. Oh, no! she thought, panicking. That was probably Austin and she looked like death warmed over. He couldn't see her this way. She'd just talk to him through the door and tell him she was sick. She hated to lie to him, but she just couldn't face him. Not tonight.

Hurrying to the front door, she didn't even check the peephole, but laid her cheek against the wooden panel of the door and said hoarsely, "I can't see you tonight, Austin. I'm sick—"

"It's not Austin, sweetheart," Joe called back. "Open up. What do you mean, you're sick? What's wrong? Let's have a look."

Swallowing a groan, Rebecca closed her eyes and just barely resisted the urge to cry again. As much as she loved Joe, he was the last person she wanted to see right now. He knew her too well. He would take one look at her and know that something was wrong.

But she couldn't send him away, especially after she'd just claimed to be sick. He would be hurt—and worried—and would probably just come back with Meredith later and insist on seeing her. She'd do better to let him in now, calm his fears and send him on his way.

That sounded simple enough, but she should have known she couldn't deal with Joe that handily. The minute she opened the door to him, he gave her a stern look, pressed his hand to her forehead to check for fever and frowned worriedly into her eyes. "All right, what's wrong? You've been crying."

"It's just my allergies," she replied. "My throat's scratchy and my eyes have been itchy all day. I took some medicine. It just takes it a while to kick in."

Someone else might have bought that story and never questioned it, but Joe had raised a whole houseful of kids, and he knew malarkey when he heard it. "Nice try," he said dryly. "But if I remember correctly, we've got the same allergies, and I'm just fine. So let's try this again. What's wrong, sweetheart? Is it Austin? Obviously you were expecting him. Did he do something to hurt you? I'll talk to him—"

"No!" Alarmed, she pleaded, "Please, don't involve him. I can handle this."

"Handle what? What's going on?"

She hadn't meant to tell him. He had done so much for her over the years, she just hated to drag him into another one of her problems. But she loved him like a father, and just knowing he was there for her in a way her birth father, whoever he was, never had been, sent tears spilling over her lashes.

"Oh, honey, don't," he said gruffly, and slipped his arms around her for a brief, fatherly hug. He was the only man who could touch her so, the only one whose touch she trusted to be totally nonsexual and loving. "Whatever it is, it can't be that bad. Tell me, and I'll make it better."

Once, this was the kind of thing she would have discussed with Meredith long before she reached the point of being reduced to tears, but with her busy social schedule and her involvement with Joe, Jr. and Teddy, Meredith didn't have time for her anymore. She hadn't for a long time now. And Rebecca missed that. Plus, she missed the old Meredith, the way she was before she'd changed, hardened. If she couldn't talk to Meredith, Joe was the next best thing. He could be hard as nails in business and politics when the occasion called for it, but he had a soft spot when it came to people he cared about.

Taking the handkerchief he handed her, she sank down onto the couch and sniffed, "It's just Richard…my boss. He's going through a nasty divorce, and he's a bear to work with. He's angry all the time, and is constantly criticizing me and everyone else. I just can't take it anymore."

"But I thought he was a friend," he said, surprised.

"He is. But for the past couple of weeks, he's been awful. He walks around the school like a dictator, throwing out orders, telling people how to walk and talk and teach, and everybody's afraid of standing up to him for fear of losing their jobs."

"Is that what he's done? Threatened to fire you?"

"Yes, but—"

Indignant, Joe pulled his cell phone from his pocket. "I'll just speak to Gary Sinclair and take care of this little problem right now. He's still the president of the school board, isn't he?"

Rebecca winced. She should have known Joe would go straight to the top. He might not be a U.S. Senator any longer, but he was still a powerful man. One call from him, and Richard would find himself not only called on the carpet before the school board, but in danger of losing his job.

"I don't want to get him fired," she said quickly, taking the phone from him before he could complete the call. "That wasn't why I told you."

"Then I'll go talk to him in the morning," he said promptly, undaunted. "What time does school start?"

He was so determined to take care of this for her that Rebecca had to smile. Not for the first time, she thanked God for the day he and Meredith had come into her life. She didn't know what she would have done without them.

Impulsively, she reached for his hand and squeezed it. "Thank you for the offer," she said, smiling through the tears that welled in her eyes. "You don't know what having you in my corner means to me. But this is something I have to handle myself."

"You always say that," he retorted. "Why won't you let me do this for you?"

"Because you've done so much for me already," she said simply. "And because I still consider him a friend, even though he's not acting like one. And friends don't get friends fired."

"I agree. But friends don't do what he's doing, either."

"*I'll* talk to him," she said. "I should have done it before now. I didn't want to interfere, but he's spiralling out of control. He needs some help."

Joe didn't agree, but Rebecca had to give him credit. He respected her decision. "All right, if that's what you want, we'll do this your way. Personally, I think the only kind of help he needs is a good swift kick where it'll do the most good, but if you think talking to him will do the trick, you won't get any argument from me. If that doesn't work, though, I want to know about it."

Rebecca hoped that wouldn't be necessary. Because it wasn't her nature to turn her back on someone in trouble, especially a friend. She may have already given him more chances than any reasonable person would have, but she had to try one more time.

"You will," she promised, hugging him. "Thanks."

Rebecca knew she was doing the right thing, but facing Richard the next day was one of the hardest things she'd ever done. She put it off as long as she could, deciding it was best to approach him after school, after all of the students and most of the teachers were gone for the day. Considering his mood over the last few weeks, she wasn't sure how he was going to react and she didn't mind admitting that she was nervous. But this discussion had been put off for too long.

So taking her courage in hand, she approached his office and saw through the window of his closed door that he was at his desk. Knocking softly on the glass, she opened the door a crack and poked her head inside. "Are you busy?" she asked with a forced smile. "I was hoping we could talk."

For a moment, she thought he was going to send her packing. He gave her a hard look that wasn't the least receptive, but she kept her smile in place and refused to take the hint that he really didn't want company. Left with little choice, he rose from his desk to open the door further for her.

"Come in," he said shortly. "I was just finishing up some paperwork. What can I do for you?"

Her stomach tied in knots, she didn't know where to begin. How did you tell a friend that he was acting like a jackass when he had the power to fire you? Nervously stepping farther into his office, she clasped her hands together in front of her as she turned to face him. "I don't know how to say this except to blurt it out. I know people lose friends sometimes when there's a divorce, and I just want you to know that that's not going to happen to us. I still consider you a very good friend, and lately, I've been really concerned about you. These last few weeks have been really hard for you, and I just wanted you to know that I'm here for you.''

She would have said the same thing to any other friend in trouble and gladly shed a tear or two with them in sympathy. But Richard never gave her a chance to cry for him. Before she could begin to guess his intentions, he grabbed her.

"Richard! What are you doing? Let me go!''

Snatching her close, he groaned when he yanked her flush against him. "Don't be ridiculous. Don't you know how long I've wanted you? I never thought you might feel the same way.''

Horrified, she pushed against the hard wall of his chest. "I don't! Let go! You misunderstood.''

He just laughed. "Don't play coy. I know when a woman wants me. You've wanted this as long as I have.'' And with no more warning than that, he dragged her up on her toes and kissed her fiercely.

Whimpering, the dark clouds of her own personal nightmare pressing in on her, she tried to fight free, but he was as strong as a bull. Panicking, she jerked her mouth free of his and tried to reason with him. "It isn't me you want,'' she panted. "It's Sylvia. She's the one you love. Ever since she left, you've been growling and snapping at me—''

"Because I wanted you,'' he rasped against her neck, "and I was afraid someone would notice and turn me in to the school board for playing favorites. But no one's here now. We can do what we want.''

"No!''

Ignoring her, he buried his hands in her hair and covered her mouth with his in a hot, ruthless kiss that went on and on and on. Trapped, repulsed, unable to do anything but shrink in on herself, Rebecca couldn't have said who held her or where she was. The past merged with the present, the walls of Richard's office shifted, then changed—first, into those of the homeless shelter where she'd nearly been raped, then into the flimsy walls of her mother's rundown apartment when she was fourteen. One attacker blended into another, rough hands pulled at her, hurting her, sickening her. And all she could think of was that she had to get away.

Later, she didn't remember fighting. The monster who held her was bigger than her, stronger, but fear gave her power. Working her arms free, she struck out wildly, pummelling his head and shoulders. "No!" she cried. "I won't let you do this to me again! No!"

Her fist connected with his jaw, snapping him out of the lust that held him in its viselike grip. Abruptly jerked back to awareness, he pulled back. Then he saw her face.

He'd never seen such a look of terror on a woman's face in his life. Her pupils dilated with fear and her face as white as a ghost's, she hammered at him again and again with clenched fists, but it was the total lack of recognition in her eyes that scared him the most. She didn't even know who he was.

"Rebecca?"

"You won't do this to me again!" she said fiercely. "I won't let you! Do you hear me? *I won't let you!*"

Worried, he tried to catch her fists before she could hit him again. "Rebecca, it's me…Richard. It's okay. I'm not going to hurt you. Calm down."

Caught up in whatever nightmare gripped her, she didn't hear him. When his hands nearly closed around her wrists to subdue her, she cried out in rage and something in her just seemed to snap. With a strength that came from sheer terror, she shoved him with all her might and sent him flying backward into his desk. Off-balance, he bounced off it and hit the floor hard. A split second later, Rebecca whirled and ran out of the office like the devil himself was after her.

Swearing, Richard scrambled to his feet and took off after her, but it was too late. He ran outside just in time to see the taillights of her Toyota Camry disappear around the corner.

Sitting at the small table in his hotel room, Austin stared down at the map he'd made of where the guests were standing during the shooting. He'd lost count of the number of times he'd gone over the damn thing trying to figure out who the shooter was, and every time he thought he was close to cracking the case, he hit a brick wall. The irritating thing was he knew he had the bastard somewhere on that map. He was so close, Austin could smell him. Who the devil was he, dammit?! And why did he keep missing him?

He'd spent days trying to figure out the answer to that. He'd even gone over his notes with the detectives handling the case, and they were just as lost as he was, and still focusing on the family. Maybe it was time to get a third opinion. Making a snap decision, he folded up the map and shoved it into the briefcase where he kept his notes. Five seconds later, he grabbed his keys and headed for Rebecca's.

She was home—her car was parked in the parking space directly in front of her apartment—but when he rang the doorbell, there was no answer. Surprised, he waited a few minutes, then knocked firmly on the door. Still, there was no answer.

His common sense told him she wasn't home. She'd either gone for a walk or gone somewhere with a friend in their car. He'd have to catch her another time. But even as he turned away and headed for his rental car, something told him not to leave. Not yet.

Frowning, he returned to her front door, and this time he didn't just knock. He banged. "Rebecca? It's me. Austin. Are you in there?"

When silence was his only answer, he felt like an idiot. "Of course she's not there, fool," he muttered. "She's not home." Then he heard the sound of her dead bolt lock sliding free, and he started to grin. "I had a feeling you were home—"

Whatever he was going to say next died unspoken on his tongue at the sight of her. There wasn't a drop of color in her face. Pale as parchment, she looked like she would blow away in the slightest breeze.

It wasn't that, however, that had him reaching for her in concern. It was the stark terror in her eyes. "Honey, my God, what is it? What's wrong?"

She never gave him the chance to touch her. Lightning quick, she pulled back, nearly knocking over the small table in her entrance hall in an effort to get away. It was only when she saw the shock on his face that she was horrified by her own reaction. Stricken, she burst into tears. "Oh, God!"

He wanted to hold her then more than he'd ever wanted anything in his life, but he didn't dare. Afraid she would shatter if he so much as moved wrong, he cautiously stepped inside and shut the door behind him. "Let's go in the kitchen and I'll fix you something to drink," he said quietly. "How about some hot tea with lemon? My mother swears a good cup of tea can make the worst day look brighter."

Not giving her a chance to argue, he guided her into the kitchen without ever touching her, then began to search her cabinets for tea bags. Touched by his caring, Rebecca only cried harder when he finally set a steaming cup of tea in front of her at the kitchen table. "Oh, Austin," she sobbed.

If she could have had anything in the world at that moment, she would have stepped into his arms and cried her eyes out on his shoulder. Just this once, she needed to be normal, needed to know the security of a good man's arms around her and what it felt like to be truly safe from harm. But she couldn't have that, and it broke her heart.

Tears streaming from her eyes, all she could do was reach across the table, cover his hand with hers, and hang on for dear life. It wasn't enough, but it was better than nothing. "Thank you," she sniffled. "I—I'm sorry about what happened at the d-door."

"Don't try to talk just yet," he soothed. "And don't give a second thought about me. I'm just fine. You're the one I'm worried about. Drink your tea. Then you can tell me what happened."

She didn't want to go back to that scene, didn't want to even think about how Richard had forced his tongue down her throat and put his hands all over her. But after years of therapy, she knew if she didn't discuss it and get it out of her system now, it would eat at her until it eventually destroyed all the progress she had made. And she couldn't let that happen.

So she drank her tea, first one cup, than another, and prayed it would warm the coldness that seemed to come from her very soul. It didn't.

How long she sat there without saying a word, she couldn't have said. Austin silently rose to refill her teacup, then took his seat across from her, patiently waiting. She could have loved him for that, but when she finally began to speak, she couldn't even look at him.

"I stopped by Richard's office after school," she said in a faint whisper that he had to strain to hear. "You know how critical he's been of me lately. I thought it was time we talked about it."

From the corner of her eye, she saw Austin frown and said, "I tried avoiding him, but it wasn't working. He's been awful. I'm sorry I didn't tell you about it, but I didn't want to drag you into my problems. You've got your hands full with the investigation and everything, and I thought I could take care of the situation myself."

"You don't have to apologize," he said gruffly. "You're not under any obligation to tell me everything that goes on in your life."

"But things might have been different if I *had* told you. You might have seen…might have realized—"

When she broke off abruptly, he frowned in concern. "What? What would I have seen that you didn't?"

"That he was attracted to me!"

She hadn't meant to blurt it out like that, but suddenly her hurt and anger were spilling out in a spate of hostile words. "I thought he was a friend, someone I could trust! And all the while, he just…he—"

"What?" he prompted gently. "He what?"

Tears pooled in her eyes. "He told me he wanted me." Even now the memory still chilled her blood. "That's why he's been so mean to me—because he didn't want the other teachers to think he was playing favorites. He was afraid someone would guess and go to the school board. But this afternoon, there was no one around. The others had left, and I stupidly walked into his office and told him I cared about him."

Austin's mouth compressed in a hard, flat line. "And

he took that as an invitation and was all over you like stink on a monkey.''

Numbly, she nodded. "If I'd known, I never would have gone near him, but it was too late for that. He grabbed me and kissed me. I don't remember much after that. I know I told him to let me go, but then everything got confused. I thought I was at the shelter—"

"Where you were almost raped?"

"It was like I was in a flashback and I couldn't find my way out," she said tearfully. "I was so scared. I think I shoved him—I can't be sure. The next thing I knew, I was running into my apartment, and I didn't even know how I got here."

And Richard Foster had driven her to that, Austin thought furiously. He'd terrorized her to the point that she didn't even know where she was, and all because the insensitive bastard had the hots for her and couldn't control himself. Five minutes, he promised himself. That was all he needed to teach the jackass how to treat a lady. And if it took him longer than that to learn the lesson, Austin would thrash him within an inch of his life.

But right now he couldn't do either of those things. Rebecca needed him, and nothing else mattered.

"You didn't do anything wrong, Rebecca," he said quietly. "You know that, don't you?"

"I trusted him."

"Yes, you did. But that doesn't mean you did anything wrong, honey. You were just trying to help a friend you thought was in trouble and he took advantage of that. That's a reflection on *him*, not you. Don't beat yourself up over this."

He might as well have saved his breath. "You know what bothers me the most?" she continued as if he hadn't spoken. "Just imagining what was going on in his head every time I caught him watching me." Revulsion flickering in her eyes, she shivered. "I feel so dirty."

Just that easily, she made him understand so many things he hadn't understood before. And he ached for her in ways he'd never imagined he could. She'd been through hell, not just today, but in the past, and he'd have done anything to take those memories away from her. But he couldn't. No one could. They were as much a part of her as the color of her eyes, and all he could do was help her deal with them whenever they reared their ugly head and intruded on the present.

"Why don't you take a bath?" he suggested huskily. "A nice long soak in a hot tub? It'll relax you and make you feel better."

"But I don't want you to leave."

"I won't," he promised. "Go on."

When she hesitated, he could almost see the wheels spinning in her head. She wanted to trust him, to know that she could take a bath without fear of him walking in on her, but she just couldn't. All her trust had been destroyed by another man.

"It's okay," he said quietly, wishing he could hug her but knowing better than to even try. "You're safe. I would never do anything to make you feel the way that bastard did this afternoon. You have my word on that."

For a long moment, she didn't move. Her eyes searched his, probing deep, and he welcomed the scrutiny. Staring steadily back, he didn't try to hide anything. His caring was there in his eyes for her to see, and somehow, that must have finally reassured her. "Thanks," she choked. "I'll try to hurry."

"Take your time," he returned easily. "I don't care how long it takes. I'll still be here when you get out."

Seven

Forty minutes later, when Rebecca returned to the living room, she looked much more relaxed. She'd changed into faded jeans and an oversized T-shirt and hadn't bothered with shoes. With her hair still damp from her bath and hanging in ringlets halfway down her back, she looked like a six-year-old.

His green eyes twinkling, Austin grinned. "I didn't know your hair was naturally curly."

She wrinkled her nose and self-consciously lifted her hand to her hair to smooth out the wayward curls. "Whenever it gets wet, it has a mind of its own. I always hated it when I was a kid—until I learned how to straighten it."

"It's beautiful," he assured her, and spoke nothing less than the truth. In the late afternoon sunlight that spilled through the west windows, the dark curls were streaked with gold and chestnut highlights. "So how are you feeling?"

"Better," she replied. "I'm trying not to think about it."

There was some color back in her cheeks, and her eyes weren't as haunted as they had been, but they both knew memories of the attack would remain in her system like a virus that sickened with no warning. If she didn't want it to sneak up on her, she had to keep as busy as possible.

"It might help if you got out of the apartment for a while," he suggested. "Why don't we grab something to eat somewhere?"

"Oh, I don't know," she hedged, glancing down at her clothes. "I'm not really dressed to go out."

"Trust me, you'll fit in perfectly where we're going," he assured her with a grin. "C'mon. Let's go."

He didn't give her time to argue, but simply grabbed her purse from where she'd dumped it on the couch when she ran in from school, then hustled her out the door to his car. Ten minutes later, he pulled into the parking lot of a pizza place that catered to kids. Judging from the number of vans in the parking lot, it was the most popular spot in town for families with children.

"I know you deal with kids all day and you might want a break from all that," he told her, "but if you want a place where you don't have to think, this is it. The noise level's got to be through the roof."

It was. Stepping inside, Rebecca winced as a cacophony of sound hit her right in the face. But Austin was right. She couldn't hear herself think. Pleased, she grinned and let him lead her to one of the picnic tables that overlooked the game area.

She would have sworn she was still too upset to eat, but Austin kept going back to the buffet line, bringing her

(P-BB3-01)

GET 2

HOW TO GET YOUR 2 FREE BOOKS AND FREE GIFT!

1. Peel off the **MIRA** sticker on the front cover. Place it in the space provided at right. This automatically entitles you to receive two free books and an exciting mystery gift.

2. Send back this card and you'll get 2 "The Best of the Best™" novels. These books have a combined cover price of $11.00 or more in the U.S. and $13.00 or more in Canada, but they are yours to keep absolutely FREE!

3. There's <u>no</u> catch. You're under <u>no</u> obligation to buy anything. We charge nothing — ZERO — for your first shipment. And you don't have to make any minimum number of purchases — not even one!

4. We call this line "The Best of the Best" because each month you'll receive the best books by some of today's hottest authors. These authors show up time and time again on all the major bestseller lists and their books sell out as soon as they hit the stores. You'll like the convenience of getting them delivered to your home at our special discount prices . . . and you'll love your *Heart to Heart* subscriber newsletter featuring author news, horoscopes, recipes, book reviews and much more!

5. We hope that after receiving your free books you'll want to remain a subscriber. But the choice is yours — to continue or cancel, anytime at all! So why not take us up on our invitation, with no risk of any kind. You'll be glad you did!

6. And remember...we'll send you a mystery gift ABSOLUTELY FREE just for giving "The Best of the Best" a try.

SPECIAL FREE GIFT!

We'll send you a fabulous surprise gift, absolutely FREE, simply for accepting our no-risk offer!

Visit us online at
www.mirabooks.com

BOOKS FREE!

Hurry!

Return this card promptly to GET 2 FREE BOOKS & A FREE GIFT!

The Best of the Best ™

YES! Please send me the 2 FREE "The Best of the Best" novels and FREE gift for which I qualify. I understand that I am under no obligation to purchase anything further, as explained on the opposite page.

385 MDL C6PQ

(P-BB3-01)
185 MDL C6PP

NAME (PLEASE PRINT CLEARLY)

ADDRESS

APT.#   CITY

STATE/PROV.   ZIP/POSTAL CODE

◄ DETACH AND MAIL CARD TODAY! ▼

The Best of the Best™ — Here's How it Works:

Accepting your 2 free books and gift places you under no obligation to buy anything. You may keep the books and gift and return the shipping statement marked "cancel." If you do not cancel, about a month later we will send you 4 additional novels and bill you just $4.24 each in the U.S., or $4.74 each in Canada, plus 25¢ shipping & handling per book and applicable taxes if any.* That's the complete price and — compared to cover prices of $5.50 or more each in the U.S. and $6.50 or more each in Canada — it's quite a bargain! You may cancel at any time, but if you choose to continue, every month we'll send you 4 more books, which you may either purchase at the discount price or return to us and cancel your subscription.

*Terms and prices subject to change without notice. Sales tax applicable in N.Y. Canadian residents will be charged applicable provincial taxes and GST.

If offer card is missing write to: The Best of the Best, 3010 Walden Ave., P.O. Box 1867, Buffalo, NY 14240-1867

BUSINESS REPLY MAIL
FIRST-CLASS MAIL   PERMIT NO. 717   BUFFALO, NY

POSTAGE WILL BE PAID BY ADDRESSEE

THE BEST OF THE BEST
3010 WALDEN AVE
PO BOX 1867
BUFFALO NY 14240-9952

NO POSTAGE
NECESSARY
IF MAILED
IN THE
UNITED STATES

every conceivable type of pizza known to man, and it was all delicious. Without quite knowing how it happened, she was sure she ate enough to feed an army.

She couldn't remember the last time she laughed so much. And it was all because of the kids that roamed the place like a bunch of monkeys that had just been released from the zoo. Running and jumping and playing, they were everywhere.

"This was a great idea," she yelled at Austin, grinning as a group of three-year-olds tackled the clown that management had hired to help entertain the younger kids. "Look at the little redhead. She pulled off his nose."

"That's something I would have done," he yelled back. "One time when my mother took me to see Santa, I pulled off his beard. I thought it was Dad in disguise."

"Uh-oh. I bet that didn't go over too well."

"The store manager was pretty ticked, especially when all the kids in line started crying and didn't want their pictures taken with a fake Santa. He didn't make much money that day."

Watching the laughter dance in his eyes, Rebecca could just imagine him as a little boy full of mischief. "I bet you drove your mother nuts when you were a little boy."

He didn't deny it. "She has gray hair today because of me."

She just grinned at that. They both knew his mother, Andie, had beautiful blond hair that she invariably wore up in a neat, timeless chignon. Her blue-gray eyes twinkling, she lifted a delicately arched brow at him. "And your dad?"

"Oh, he pulled his out years ago. He's bald as a billiard ball."

Since Peter McGrath had a full head of brown hair, just like his son, Rebecca couldn't help but laugh. "No kidding? So he wears a wig, does he? And all this time, I thought that was his real hair.''

"Hey, he got that rug from the best wigmaker in Europe. The Queen gets all her stuff from the same guy. Nothing but the best for Dad.''

When it came to rugs, he could lie like one. For the rest of the meal—and during the drive back to her apartment afterwards—he told one outrageous story after another. By the time they reached her front door, she was in tears again, but this time from laughter. And she could have kissed him for it. Thanks to him, she'd been able to forget, at least for a little while, the kisses Richard had forced on her, and she would always be grateful to Austin for that.

But as he unlocked her front door for her, she knew the frightening memories would start pushing in on her the second she was once again alone with her own thoughts. And she dreaded it.

Lost in her own musings, she didn't realize he was watching her until he said quietly, "I can stay for a while, if you like. I was just going to go back to the hotel and write up my weekly report for Joe. I can do that later if you want me to stay.''

He made the offer casually, as if it were no big deal, but Rebecca knew he'd noticed how uneasy she was. He really was a sweet man, she thought. And she'd have liked nothing better than for him to stay another couple of hours, just until it was time for her to go to bed. But he'd done so much for her already. She couldn't continue to accept his help. Sooner or later, she was going to have to be alone with her own thoughts, and the longer she put it off, the harder it would be.

"I would love for you to stay," she told him candidly as she turned to face him, "but I can't. I have to deal with this, and I have to do it alone. But you don't know how much I appreciate everything you did for me this evening.'' Sudden tears welling in her eyes, she smiled mistily. "I'd hug you if I could, but I don't think that's a very good idea right now.''

"It's not always going to be this way,'' he promised her. "Just give yourself time. And even though I understand why you don't want me to stay, you're not alone. If you need someone to talk to, call me. Even if it's the middle of the night. Okay?''

Touched, she nodded. "I will,'' she said huskily. "Thanks.''

Leaving her was the hardest thing Austin had ever done. She had no business being alone after what she'd been through, but he couldn't very well demand that she let him stay. Men had made too many demands of her as it was. On this, at least, she was calling the shots. And it wasn't as if he was abandoning her. He would call her later to see how she was doing. In the meantime, he had something else to take care of.

His face grim, he stopped at the first convenience store and went inside to borrow the phone book to look up an address. Two minutes later, he was on his way to Richard Foster's house. It was time the two of them had a talk.

Steaming, he told himself that was all he was going to do—talk to the man. He wasn't a Neanderthal who let his temper control his common sense, he intended to be civilized. He'd knock on the door, say what he had to say, and leave. And if Richard Foster had a single brain cell in his head, he'd never touch Rebecca again or so much as look at her wrong. Because if he did, and Austin heard about it, he'd make him wish he'd never been born.

A muscle ticked at his jaw as he thought of the terror

Rebecca had suffered because of the jackass's insensitivity and selfishness. He turned down Foster's street and easily found the small bungalow where he lived. Located on a corner in a quiet, older neighborhood that had become trendy again, it was set well back from the street and had a red Explorer in the drive.

"Good," Austin said in satisfaction as he parked at the curb. The lights were on in the front window. He'd make this short and sweet, then get back to his hotel so he'd be there if Rebecca called. Before the night was through, he had a feeling she was going to need him, and he intended to be there for her.

All his good intentions flew right out the window, however, the second Foster answered his knock. Austin had never met him before, but there was no question in his mind that this was Rebecca's boss and the same man who had grabbed her and forced her to accept his kisses. There were scratch marks all over his face.

His eyes narrowing on those scratches, Austin hung on to his self-control just long enough to growl, "Richard Foster?"

Behind the lenses of his glasses, the other man's beady little eyes were wary. "Yes?"

"You son of a bitch!" Rage temporarily consuming his common sense, he moved lightning-quick and grabbed him by the throat. A split second later, he shoved him up against the door to his own house and couldn't have cared less that they were in full view of the neighbors or anyone who chose to drive by. All he could think of was that this snivelling little piece of nothing had not only forced his kisses on Rebecca, but he'd scared her so badly that she'd had to fight her way out of his arms. And by God, Austin was going to make him admit it!

"What did you do to Rebecca?"

"Nothing!"

"Wrong answer," he snarled, shaking him like a rag doll. "Try again."

"I thought she wanted it—"

"Oh, really?" he sneered. "That's why she nearly scratched your eyes out? Because she *wanted* you?"

Obviously not a stupid man, Foster realized he'd gone too far and quickly tried to backpedal. "No! I—I misunderstood. She said she c-cared about me, and I thought she m-meant…"

"That she wanted you to scare her to death?" Austin finished for him when he hesitated. "Is that how you show a woman you're attracted to her? By forcing yourself on her?"

They both knew that was exactly what he'd done, so there was nothing he could do but admit that he was totally and completely in the wrong. Pale and shaken, he swallowed and said hoarsely, "I screwed up. Okay? I never meant to scare her. I just lost my head."

And because of his lack of control, Rebecca was the one who had suffered. And that suffering wouldn't end any time soon, Austin thought bitterly. This was not only a friend who had betrayed her, but her boss, a man she had to face and work with every day, whether she wanted to or not. And that sickened him.

His hands tightening ever so slightly on Foster, Austin leaned in close and glared at him nose to nose. "Any man who hurts a woman is a chicken-livered coward," he said coldly. "You took advantage of your position as her boss and her friend, and you terrorized her. And I'd like to beat the hell out of you for that."

His eyes huge behind the lenses of his glasses, he blanched. "I'll apologize. I swear I will."

"No, what you're going to do is stay as far away from

her as your job allows,'' he retorted. "When you do have to talk to her, you're going to be pleasant and keep your remarks impersonal. And if you ever lay a finger on her again, you're going to get another visit from me. Next time I won't be nearly as nice. Do I make myself understood?''

Foster nodded numbly. "Y-yes. Perfectly. There's no reason for another visit.''

Releasing him, Austin dusted his hands as if he'd just touched something distasteful. "Let's keep it that way.'' Satisfied he'd made his point, he turned and walked back to his car.

The second Rebecca was alone, the silence of the apartment closed around her, and all she could hear was the echo of her own thoughts. And that was one place she was determined not to go. Her heart pounding, she rushed into the kitchen and began to pull everything out of her cabinets. For some time now she hadn't been happy with where she had things stored and had been thinking about rearranging the entire kitchen. Now was as good a time as any to get started.

Working furiously, she piled pots and pans and dishes on the table and counter, then turned her attention to unloading the shelves of the small pantry next to the refrigerator. Soon, the kitchen chairs were straining under their load, and by eleven, she had a true mess on her hands. But, she couldn't have been happier. It would take her hours to set everything straight again.

Humming one of the kiddie songs she'd heard at the pizza parlor, she took her time deciding where she wanted things and didn't look at the clock again. The next time she looked up, there was nothing left on the tabletop and counters to put away, and it was nearly two o'clock in the morning.

For all of ten seconds, she seriously considered moving from the kitchen to the hall closet and starting the procedure all over again, but she was physically and emotionally exhausted. Flipping off the lights, she headed for her bedroom. It was time to go to bed. She'd put it off long enough.

She should have fallen asleep the second her head hit the pillow. She was certainly tired enough. Every bone in her body ached, and she just wanted to go to sleep and forget the whole day. Unfortunately, it wasn't that easy. The minute she turned off the lights and closed her eyes, Richard reached out of the darkness of her memory to grab her.

Her heart in her throat, she bolted upright in bed, gasping. "Oh, God!"

Shuddering, she couldn't have said how long she sat there, cursing her tears and the night and the stupid fear that wouldn't let her lie back down even though she knew she was perfectly safe. She wouldn't do this! she told herself fiercely. She wouldn't let another horrible man haunt her nights. Not again. She had to find a way to put it behind her.

When the phone rang suddenly, she nearly jumped out of her skin. Horrified, she stared at it in the darkness. Richard. It had to be Richard. Somehow he'd known she was thinking about him and what he'd done, and he'd decided to torture her for rejecting him by calling her in the middle of the night.

"Don't answer it!"

It wasn't until she heard herself speak sharply in the dark that she realized she was cowering in her bed as if she expected him to reach through the phone and grab her. And that infuriated her. What was he doing to her? What was she *letting* him do to her?

Furious with him and herself, she snatched up the phone. "Hello?"

"Rebecca? Are you all right?"

For a moment, nothing registered except that her caller was a man, just as she'd feared. Then she recognized Austin's voice. "Austin!" Wilting, she swallowed a shaky sob. "I'm sorry. Yes, I'm fine. The phone just startled me."

"I know it's late, but I just wanted to make sure you were okay. I was afraid you wouldn't be able to sleep, but I guess I woke you. I'm sorry."

"Oh, no," she assured him, "don't apologize. Trust me, I was awake."

"I was afraid of that. Would you like to talk about it?"

After avoiding the subject all evening, she would have sworn she didn't. But as she snuggled back down in bed with his soft, husky voice in her ear, she somehow felt safer than she had in a very long time and the words just came tumbling out. "When the phone rang, I thought it was him, and I was furious that I was scared. I'm just so tired of being scared."

"It's been a long time, hasn't it?"

"As long as I can remember," she replied simply. "When I was a little girl, my mother would go out drinking at night and leave me at home by myself."

"My God, how old were you?"

She shrugged. "Six or seven."

"You must have been terrified!"

"I was."

"And your mother didn't care?"

"She didn't care about anything when she was thirsty," she said flatly. Nothing had mattered except where the next bottle of rum was coming from. Not even the men she'd brought home with her. Especially the men. She'd taken up with ex-cons and thugs when she'd had to, and on more than one occasion, the cost of a drink had been a beating or rough sex. She hadn't cared. The next night, she'd gone out and done it all over again.

Something in her tone must have given her away her thoughts because he said suddenly, "You're thinking about that monster that tried to hurt you, aren't you? Her boyfriend."

"There were always boyfriends," she said, wrinkling her nose in distaste. "A lot of them. I would try to be in bed before she got home. When I was eleven, I started barricading myself in at night."

"Did it help?"

"For a while. Then she took up with Frank."

Dark, ugly memories bombarded her from every side, sickening her, but with Austin on the other end of the line, murmuring reassuringly to her, she was able to tell him things that she'd told only one other person—Meredith. "He was a horrible man," she said, repulsed. "He'd served time for nearly killing his ex-wife, and I think he had a thing for children. He would watch me, and it used to make my skin crawl."

"Did you tell your mother?"

In the dark, Rebecca smiled slightly at the question. He didn't understand what it was like to grow up with a mother who loved her addiction more than she loved her own child, and she couldn't blame him for that. Most people who'd had a loving, caring mother couldn't comprehend how anyone could put their child in danger, then turn a blind eye to it.

"She just told me to stay out of his way."

"She didn't throw him out?"

"Frank brought her a bottle every day when he came home," she said simply. "She wasn't going to do anything to jeopardize that."

"So you ran away?"

"After he trapped me in the bathroom when I was taking a shower. I knew then I had to get out. I left that night after he and Mom passed out."

"And lived on the street," he said quietly. "You were fourteen, for God's sake! How did you survive?"

That was a question she'd asked herself countless times over the years. Most fourteen-year-olds didn't even do their own laundry, let alone know how to make it on their own in a cold, dark world. She'd just done what she had to do. "I didn't have any choice. Anything was better than going back to Mom...and Frank."

She told him then how she'd panhandled to get money and slept under bushes in the park at night, where no one could see her. And how she'd taken up with a stray dog she'd named Butch, and he'd protected her during the long, lonely summer nights. But then the dogcatcher took Butch away, and once again, she was all alone. Fall, then winter came, and the weather turned bad. After spending a night in the rain and getting sick, she'd felt like she had no choice but to go to a homeless shelter.

"It was a mistake," she confided. "I know that now, but at the time it seemed like the only logical thing to do. My mother had pneumonia once, and I was afraid I was getting it. So I went to the shelter...and nearly got raped again."

"But you weren't raped," he reminded her. "You fought him off and there were people there to help you. I know it had to be a horrible experience for you, but from there, you went to the Hopechest Ranch and met

Meredith. Instead of thinking about the attack, try to think of that.''

"But I'm such an emotional cripple."

She expected him to sympathize with her—instead, he laughed. "Are you kidding? You're the bravest woman I know."

"Yeah, right," she retorted, chuckling. "In case you hadn't noticed, I don't even date!"

"Because you don't like starting a relationship you can't continue," he tossed back. "It takes guts to do that."

"But I'm afraid of men."

"No, you're afraid of intimacy," he corrected her quietly. "There's a difference. If you were afraid of men, there wouldn't be any in your life. But you're friends with Richard—or at least you were until he gave you a reason not to be. And I like to think we're friends. Granted, it's not like I'm a stranger on the street—we have a family connection—but if you were afraid of me, you would have kicked me out of your life the first time I kissed you."

Stunned, Rebecca realized he was exactly right. All this time she'd thought that she had an aversion to men because of Frank and everything else that had happened to her after she ran away from home, but that wasn't the case at all. She *did* like men! She'd enjoyed their company, their sense of humor, everything about them... except intimacy. Why had it taken her so long to see that?

Not sure if she wanted to laugh or cry, she couldn't seem to stop smiling. "Do you know that you're the first person who's ever pointed that out to me? I can't believe I didn't see it myself. Thank you! God, I feel so much better! Maybe there's hope for me, after all."

Wishing she could hug him, she lay in the dark and

talked to him for hours. The next time she looked at the luminous dial of her clock on the nightstand, it was four o'clock in the morning.

"Oh, my God! I can't believe I've kept you talking most of the night. We both have to work tomorrow."

Far from concerned, he only laughed. "You mean today. If we hang up now, you can still catch a couple of hours sleep. Load up on coffee on your way to work, and you'll be fine."

Still smiling, Rebecca wished him good night and hung up, sure she'd never be able to sleep simply because she was feeling so wonderful. But the second she punched her pillow into the right shape and closed her eyes, she realized just how tired she really was. She sighed, and within minutes she was asleep and dreaming of Austin.

Two hours later, Rebecca stood in front of the mirror on her bedroom door and surveyed herself critically. Dressed in a pale yellow summer suit with a white blouse, she looked cool and professional, and that was no accident. She'd deliberately chosen the most sedate outfit she had so Richard couldn't accuse her of wearing something flirty to encourage him.

Her stomach knotting just at the thought of facing him, she would have given anything to call in sick. But she wouldn't stay home and cower in her apartment like she had something to be ashamed of. She hadn't done anything except trust the wrong man.

That wasn't a mistake she would make again.

Still, walking into the school fifteen minutes later was one of the hardest things she'd ever done. Invariably, Richard usually stood right outside his office in the hall, greeting students and teachers alike as they walked into the building. Braced for a cold, unpleasant scene, she dragged in a calming breath and stepped inside…only to discover that he was nowhere in sight.

Relieved, she let out her breath in a rush, but she didn't fool herself into thinking that the reprieve she'd been granted was anything but temporary. Richard was there somewhere—as long as she'd known him, he'd never missed a day of work—and she would have to deal with him sometime before the day was over. Grimacing at the thought, she headed for the teachers' lounge for a cup of coffee that she would take with her to her first class.

Normally at that time of the morning, everyone was getting ready for their first class, and few people lingered in the lounge. The minute Rebecca stepped inside, however, she stopped in surprise. Half the staff was there.

"Hey," Penny Taylor greeted her when she saw her at the door. "Have you heard the news?"

"What news? What's going on?"

"Tricky Dick is retiring."

The news caught Rebecca completely by surprise, and she almost laughed aloud in triumph. Yes! She wouldn't have to deal with him after all, she thought happily. Then she realized that Penny had to be talking about next May, since the new term had just started at the beginning of July.

Frowning, she said, "So that's the big deal? I knew that months ago. I thought everyone did."

"But you couldn't have," Penny replied, confused. "He just found out yesterday when he went to the doctor."

"The doctor? For what? What are you talking about?"

"His heart," the other woman retorted, as confused as she. "Can we start this conversation over? I feel like I just stepped into the middle of an Abbott and Costello routine. How did you know Richard was retiring today when his doctor only recommended it yesterday?''

Stunned, Rebecca felt like she'd been hit between the eyes with a brick. Grabbing Penny's arm, she pulled her over to a corner where they could speak in relative privacy. ''What do you mean *today?* The last I heard, he was thinking about quitting at the end of the term.''

''That's what we all thought,'' Penny said. ''But you know how stressed he's been over his divorce. Apparently, his blood pressure's been up for some time now, but for some reason, it went through the roof last night and he had to be rushed to the hospital.''

''Is he okay?''

She shrugged. ''He didn't have to be admitted to the hospital, so I guess so. But his doctor advised him to quit work or risk having a stroke. So he took the rest of the week off and put in for early retirement. He won't even be back for a farewell party.''

He'd quit, Rebecca thought, reeling. He'd actually quit, and she had to believe it was because of what had happened between them yesterday afternoon in his office. Knowing him, he'd probably gone home and convinced himself she was going to turn him in to the school board for his attack on her, and he'd worked himself into a panic worrying about his image.

Maybe she should have felt guilty about that, but in spite of the fact that she considered herself a charitable person, she couldn't summon any sympathy for him. They would never be friends again, but the least he could have done was call to apologize for his outrageous behavior.

''Are you sure about this?'' she asked Penny. ''You know how rumors are around here. Nobody ever stops to ask the source.''

''This time it came straight from the horse's mouth,''

she said with a smug smile. "He called Christina from the hospital last night and told her everything. She'll take over his duties until the school board appoints another principal."

Christina Lopez was the assistant principal and one of Penny's best friends. She also had a reputation for being as honest as the day was long. If the story came from her, it could be counted on to be the gospel.

Which meant Rebecca never had to worry about working with Richard again.

Thrilled, she was so relieved, she didn't know if she wanted to laugh or cry. What she wanted to do more than anything, though, was call Austin. She couldn't, wouldn't, tell the other teachers about yesterday—what happened between her and Richard was none of their business—but Austin would understand. Especially after all they'd shared last night. But a quick glance at the clock told her that she'd have to wait until later to talk to him. School started in ten minutes, and she had to get to her classroom.

It was one of those days when nothing went right, which was to be expected after only two hours sleep the night before. And although Austin silently acknowledged that he wasn't operating on all cylinders mentally, that had nothing to do with his mood. He could have been fully rested, with a solid eight hours of sleep under his belt, and he still would have hated the day and everything that it held. Because on this day nine years ago, his wife and unborn daughter had died in childbirth.

Every year, long before the painful anniversary arrived, he told himself he wasn't going to mark the day on his calendar. He'd just go about his business and let it pass without acknowledgment. His head told him it really could be that simple. Ignore the pain, the loss, and the year would finally come when the day would come and go and he'd never notice.

But even though he knew that was probably the only way he would ever get past their deaths, his heart wouldn't let him ignore the day. Because to do so was to deny their very existence and his love for them, and he couldn't do that. So he'd crawled out of bed that morning with a heavy heart, and from there, the day had only gone from bad to worse. Just as he'd known it would.

He shouldn't have worked. It wasn't as if one day off would make a difference one way or the other—the investigation wasn't going anywhere fast anyway. But he needed a distraction, something to take his mind off the sense of loss that squeezed his heart, and he still hadn't finished questioning everyone who'd had access to the ranch the day of the party. So with nothing better to do, he went in search of the last possible witnesses to the shooting.

By noon, he'd tracked down and interviewed all six people left on his list. Not surprisingly, none of them could tell him anything of importance. He'd talked to everyone who had been at the ranch the day of the shooting, and he had a list of suspects that included at least half of the entire guest list. The only thing he knew for sure was that all of them hadn't tried to kill Joe.

His mood darker than ever, he headed for Ruby's Café, where he grabbed a booth at the back, ordered coffee and a turkey sandwich he didn't really want, and considered his options. There weren't many. He could start over, do what the police were doing and focus on immediate family and close friends, or give Joe back the money he had advanced him as partial payment for the job and concede defeat.

The problem was, neither option appealed to him. He'd

never liked playing the odds in an investigation. He knew why the police did it—they were underpaid and overworked and the faster they named a suspect and had him in custody, the quicker they could proceed to the next case. But the odds didn't always play out, and he didn't like dismissing anyone as a suspect just because he or she didn't happen to be a close friend or family member.

And he sure as hell didn't like the idea of admitting to Joe or anyone else that he'd been outsmarted by the shooter. He wasn't a quitter. Over the course of his entire career, there were only two cases he'd given up on, and that was only when he'd exhausted all leads and hadn't had a single suspect to show for it. That wasn't the case here. The problem wasn't that there were no suspects, but too many. Narrowing it down was turning out to be much more difficult than he'd anticipated.

Brooding, he stirred his coffee absently, and still didn't know what he was going to do when his cell phone rang. Reaching for it, he frowned when he saw the call was from Coker Elementary, where Rebecca worked. "Rebecca? What's wrong?" he asked the second she came on the line. "Are you okay? Foster hasn't been bothering you, has he?"

"No," she said, chuckling. "I know I shouldn't be so happy—I just found out this morning that he has a serious blood pressure problem I didn't know anything about—but it's just so perfect. He's taken an early retirement. Can you believe it? I won't ever have to deal with him again. He quit."

"You're kidding! When?"

"This morning. I don't know if his conscience was bothering him or what, but his blood pressure skyrocketed last night and he had to be rushed to the hospital. His doctor recommended early retirement, and he took it. He didn't even put in an appearance this morning.''

She chattered happily about how great it was that things had worked out so easily, and Austin didn't have the heart to tell her that it wasn't just dumb luck. If Foster really did have high blood pressure—and he found it odd that Rebecca was only just now hearing about it—Austin doubted it was that that had caused him to put in for early retirement. More likely, it was due to the little visit Austin himself had paid him last night. Foster had realized he'd screwed up and it was only a matter of time before others knew it, too, and he hadn't been able to face that. So, like a coward, he'd cut and run.

And for Rebecca's sake, he was glad. She'd been through enough. ''That's great, honey. I was wondering how your day was going. I knew you were dreading seeing him again.''

''Oh, I was! My stomach was in knots. Then when I found out he was gone for good, I was thrilled. Not that I would ever want him to be sick,'' she quickly added. ''I would never wish that on anyone.''

''Of course you wouldn't. Anyone who knows you knows that.''

''I hope so. I was just so relieved, I had a hard time hiding it.'' Her news now told, she said brightly, ''Enough about me. What about you? How's the investigation going?''

''I finally wrapped up the last of the interviews, so at least that's finished. Where the investigation goes from here is still up for grabs, but I'll figure something out.''

He would have sworn that his tone was positive and disguised his low mood, but Rebecca was more discerning than most. ''Is something wrong?'' she asked worriedly. ''You sound down.''

"I'm just frustrated," he said with a shrug, skirting the whole truth.

"Maybe it would help if you reenacted the shooting," she suggested. "I know you have it all drawn on paper, but actually seeing where everyone was standing, who might have had an opportunity to fire a gun without anyone else seeing, might give you some real insight. If nothing else, it should help narrow down the list of suspects."

The idea was so simple, Austin wondered why he hadn't thought of it himself. Grinning for the first time all day, he teased, "Are you sure you were never a P.I.? That's a terrific idea. I'll call Joe and set it up for this afternoon. You're going to help me with this, aren't you?"

"I wouldn't miss it for the world," she assured him with a chuckle. "I'll meet you at the ranch after school."

She hung up soon after that—she had to get back to class—and had no idea what her call had done for him. His mood lighter, he reached for his sandwich. Maybe he'd eat, after all.

Eight

When the call came at two o'clock that afternoon, Patsy was just on her way out the door to go shopping for a new dress to wear to the Governor's Ball. It was the social event of the summer and still a month away, but it took time to find just the right dress. Maybe she'd make a quick trip to Beverly Hills. She was bound to find something there that would be perfect for her and outrageously expensive. Smiling at the thought, her brown eyes gleamed with malice. She did so love spending Joe's money.

"Wait, Miss Meredith," Inez called before she could slip out the front door to where her Mercedes waited in the drive. "There's a call for you."

"Take a message," she said coldly, not sparing her so much as a glance. "I'm going shopping."

"But it's the police! That nice Detective Law."

Dread striking her heart, Patsy stopped in her tracks. Every instinct she had urged her to run, to pretend that she'd already left before the call came in, but it would be just like that bitch Inez to tell that awful Thaddeus Law that she refused to talk to him. Then he'd start to wonder why.

Sick with fear at the thought, she shot Inez a murderous look. "I'll take it in my sitting room," she snarled, and stormed upstairs to the intimate room at the back of her bedroom. Furious, she would have liked nothing more than to snatch up the phone and demand to know what Thaddeus Law thought he was doing, harassing her the way he was. Damn him, didn't he know who she was? She could have him fired. She knew the right people. All she had to do was make one phone call. One stinking phone call!

For a moment, a cunning smile curled her mouth. But even as she toyed with the idea, she knew she couldn't. The man was already too suspicious of her as it was. She had to handle him with kid gloves, or everything was going to come tumbling down around her ears, and that scared the hell out of her.

"You can't screw this up," she said fiercely. "Just remember who you are—Mrs. Joe Colton—and no one can touch you."

But pretending to be sweet, syrupy Meredith wasn't nearly as easy as she'd have liked when she picked up the phone and greeted the man who wanted to bring her down. "Goodness, Detective, you almost missed me. I was just on my way out the door to buy a dress for the Governor's Ball. What can I do for you?"

"Actually, Mrs. Colton, I need to speak to you about the shooting," he said smoothly. "Since you're on your way out, anyway, why don't you stop by the station before you go shopping? Do you think you can be here in fifteen minutes?"

Trapped, fury flashing in her eyes, Patsy just barely resisted the urge to tell him to go to hell. What kind of idiot did he think she was? She wasn't going anywhere near him or the police station!

Then he'll just come after you, a snide voice in her head taunted, *and lock you up. Is that what you want?*

No! She didn't even have to think twice about that. She broke out in a cold sweat just at the thought of being caged again like an animal. "Fifteen minutes should be more than enough time," she said in a voice that wasn't nearly as steady and confident as she would have liked. "I'll see you then."

With barely controlled rage, she hung up the phone, then lightning quick, hurled it across the room. "Cocky son of a bitch!" She would come in, all right, she fumed. Then she'd go straight to the police commissioner, who was a good friend of Joe's, and tell him exactly what she thought of the oh-so-irritating Detective Law. Then they'd see who had the last laugh.

But even as she imagined herself taking advantage of Joe's connections, she knew she couldn't. Not without casting suspicion on herself. She could just hear Thaddeus Law now. If she was innocent of any wrongdoing, why would she object to answering a few questions? Didn't she want to help the police catch the man who had tried to kill her husband?

"Bastard!" she raged. They were all bastards—Joe, the police, Austin McGrath. And they all wanted to bring her down, especially Joe. He'd never forgiven her for getting pregnant with Teddy. Oh, he'd stuck by their bargain—in public, he gave her all the attention and respect due his wife, and he raised Teddy as his own even though they both knew he wasn't—but he despised her and their sham of a marriage. He was just waiting for the day she left him.

"Not till hell freezes over," she vowed grimly. She'd see him dead first.

That thought brought her back to the police. Glancing at her watch, she blanched. Time was running out. Panic clawed at her from the inside out, tying her stomach in knots, and she could feel herself start to come undone. Horrified, she snatched up her purse. "Oh, God, oh, God, oh, God." Where were her pills? She needed her pills to settle her nerves!

She found them almost immediately, but her hands were shaking so badly that it was several long, agonizing minutes before she could get the child safety lid off. Frantic by then, she poured four into her hand and popped them hurriedly into her mouth, swallowing them dry.

"Calm down," she told herself, pacing the length of the room restlessly. "Everything's going to be fine. Just wait for the pills to kick in and you can handle that bully Law with one hand tied behind your back."

She'd skipped lunch and hadn't had anything but toast for breakfast, so it didn't take long for the sedative to hit her bloodstream. Almost immediately, her panic subsided and she started to smile. That was more like it.

The flashback came out of nowhere. One second she was in her sitting room, plotting how she was going to outsmart Law, and the next, she was back in that flea-bitten motel room where she'd given birth to her daughter, Jewel, and Ellis Mayfair was lying dead at her feet. Horrified, she took a step back and bumped into her restoration French desk. In her mind, however, it was the cheap particle-board dresser at the Wayside Inn that cut into the back of her thighs.

"No!" she whispered. This couldn't be happening. She'd just taken too many pills.

The illusion, however, wouldn't go away, and suddenly, the police were swarming that long-ago hotel room and roughly dragging her from the dresser. Only hours before, she'd had a baby, her darling baby girl who had been stolen from her by Ellis, and the cops had treated her like *she* was the criminal! They'd clamped handcuffs on her wrists, read her her rights and bullied her when she refused to confess. And all the while, Meredith stood silently by and never said a word in her defense. Not then, and not later at the trial, when she could have lied and claimed she herself killed Ellis when she walked in and found him trying to hurt her sister.

"Bitch." She'd always been the favored one, Saint Meredith, the one who could do no wrong, and she hadn't lifted a finger to help her. Right then, Patsy had started plotting her revenge.

The grandfather clock in the foyer struck the hour, jerking her drug-hazed mind back to the present. She had to get to the police station! A drink. She needed a drink to clear her head. Rushing to her private stash, she poured a stiff scotch.

She had it halfway to her mouth when she suddenly froze. Dear God, had she lost her mind? What was she doing? She had to be at the police station in fifteen minutes! What was she going to do? Stroll in there with liquor on her breath?

Muttering a curse, she slammed the glass back down, uncaring that she'd splashed the expensive liquor all over her hand. She had to get control of herself or she was going to blow this and end up in jail again! One misstep, one slip of the tongue, and Law would know she'd put poison in Joe's champagne....

Breaking out into a sweat at the thought, she stumbled toward the door. She had to sober herself up and get to the police station. "Inez!" she yelled harshly. "I need some coffee. Now!"

By the time she reached the police station, she'd downed an entire pot of coffee. It hadn't helped. Regardless of how hard she tried, she couldn't shake the image of Ellis's dead body from her mind. If the cops were somehow able to connect that murder committed by Patsy Portman to Joe Colton's wife, Meredith, it would be all over but the crying. She almost threw up in the parking lot just thinking about it.

"Don't go there," she mumbled as she staggered from her Mercedes and smoothed the material of her black silk shift over her hips. She had to concentrate on Meredith. *She* was the one the police were interested in, not Patsy. All she had to do was convince that awful detective that she was Joe's faithful, loving wife, and no one would ever suspect that she had already killed one man and wanted another one dead.

Hanging on to that nasty little secret, she started up the stone steps to the front entrance, thankful that there was a balustrade to grab. Without it, she would have fallen flat on her face. She liked to think, however, that she hid it well. With her head held at a proud angle, she glided up the steps and walked into the station as if she owned the place. Adopting the same superior look that she'd seen Graham's wife, Cynthia, adopt countless times, she looked down her nose at the cops and criminals alike who littered the foyer and let them know without saying a word that she was someone to be reckoned with. After all, she was Mrs. Joe Colton, dammit! She didn't belong here.

"May I help you, ma'am?"

Her head starting to throb and bile rising in her throat, Patsy looked down at the policewoman at the desk who'd finally noticed her and snapped, "It's about time! I'm here to see Detective Law."

"Have a seat," she said dryly, nodding to the benches that lined the walls on either side of the entry. "He'll be with you in a minute."

Irritated that the stiff-necked woman actually expected her to wait, Patsy took one look at the grimy benches and the even grimier people sitting on them and sniffed disdainfully. "I don't think so."

"Suit yourself," the woman retorted and immediately turned her attention to the next person who walked in the door.

Tapping her foot impatiently, Patsy told herself she was giving Law five minutes, and not one second more. If he didn't put in an appearance by then, she was walking out the door. If he didn't like it, too damn bad. She wasn't standing around with the dregs of Prosperino while he sat on his butt upstairs eating doughnuts and drinking stale coffee. Her time was valuable, even if his wasn't.

One minute passed, then another, and with every tick of the clock, Patsy found it more and more difficult to focus on the anger that was the only thing holding her in the present. Clouds of images from the past swirled in her head like gathering thunderheads, threatening to break over her at any moment and drag her down into a living nightmare. Saliva pooling in her mouth, she swallowed, but it didn't help. She needed some air. Whirling, she took a step toward the entrance.

"Mrs. Colton?"

Her stomach reeling, she almost didn't stop. But then Thaddeus Law was standing directly in front of her, blocking her path, and she had no choice. He was a bear of a man, six-two if he was an inch, with the muscled chest and broad shoulders of a linebacker, and nothing short of a backhoe was going to budge him when he didn't want to budge.

Neatly cornered, she fought back her nausea and lifted a delicate, disdaining hand to her mouth. "If you don't mind, Detective, I was going outside for some fresh air. The stench in here is abominable."

"Police work is a dirty business," he said wryly. "Criminals carry their own special odor. Why don't we go upstairs? It's not so bad up there."

The last thing she wanted to do was step farther into the bowels of the police station, where the flashbacks to her interrogation after Ellis's murder would no doubt be worse than ever, but what else could she do? Law was already suspicious of her. His piercing blue eyes were as dark as midnight and seemed to see to her very soul. With one look, he struck fear in her.

She didn't, however, dare look away or let him see just how shaken she was. He would eat that up with a spoon, and she'd be damned if she'd give him the satisfaction. "Anywhere is better than here," she said coolly, with her nose in the air. "Lead the way."

For a moment she caught the gleam of something in his eyes—speculation or amusement, she wasn't sure which—then he led her to the elevator. When the doors slid shut on them and a half dozen other people, she felt like the walls of a cell were closing in on her. Perspiration beaded on her brow.

"Are you all right, Mrs. Colton? You look a little pale."

He would notice, damn him. Staring straight ahead at the doors, she said stiffly, "I don't like elevators, Detective."

The doors opened then, thankfully, but her ordeal was only just beginning. "This way," Law said, and motioned her into what she immediately recognized as an interrogation room.

Horrified, Patsy stopped at the doorway and said sharply, "What's the meaning of this? I thought you just wanted to ask me a few questions about the party. You didn't say this was an interrogation!"

The second the words were out of her mouth, Patsy wanted to kick herself. Dammit all, she didn't want to give the jackass any reason to be suspicious of her, but that was exactly what she'd done. Any second now he was going to ask her why she was afraid of being interrogated. Did she have something to hide?

But instead of putting her on the spot, he only said, "Detectives Jones and Shoemaker are joining us, and my office isn't much bigger than the elevator. I thought you'd be more comfortable in here."

It was a plausible excuse, but Patsy trusted cops about as much as she did a snake poised to strike. Still, if he could play games, so could she. Dredging up a self-deprecating smile, she said, "I guess I put my foot in it then, didn't I? Sorry about that."

"Maybe some coffee would help," he suggested. "Have a seat. I'll be right back."

He was gone before she could tell him that she'd already drunk enough coffee to float a battleship, and she was left with no choice but to take a chair at the table in the middle of the room. Hiding her distaste, she didn't dare look at the mirror hanging on the wall opposite her. She wasn't a fool—she knew it was a two-way mirror and that even now someone was watching her. Let them look. If they thought she was going to give herself away by doing something stupid, they were in for a rude awakening.

The door opened then and in walked Law, along with his two cronies, Jones and Shoemaker. All three of them had talked to her the night of the shooting, and every day since. They always used the excuse that they just needed some clarification about some of the guests, who was standing where, who hated whom, who came late or left early, but Patsy wasn't a fool. She knew what they were doing. They hadn't ruled her out as a suspect, and until they did, they intended to keep an eye on her and see if they could make her sweat—hence this little visit to the station to "talk."

And it was working. They just didn't know how well. Every time she inadvertently glanced at the mirror on the wall, images from the last interrogation she endured swam before her eyes. With shaking fingers, she took the coffee Thaddeus Law handed her and took a sip, only to nearly choke. "My God, what is this?"

"Some folks call it battery acid," David Jones said with a chuckle. "If you put enough cream and sugar in it, it almost tastes like coffee."

"Of course, it's nothing like that fancy gourmet stuff you had at your husband's party," Mark Shoemaker said easily. "That was the best coffee I ever tasted."

Flashing him Meredith's simpering smile, Patsy silently congratulated herself on the way she'd kept her wits about her after the shooting. Playing the worried, tearful wife and concerned hostess to the hilt, she'd hovered over everyone like a mother hen, making sure the cops were well fed and supplied with all the coffee they could drink as they worked long into the night investigating the scene and talking to all the guests. It had been one of the best performances of her life.

"I'm glad you enjoyed it," she said graciously. "It's my husband's favorite blend."

"Speaking of your husband," Thad said with a frown, bringing the conversation back to her reason for being there, "why were you standing at his left when the toasts started? Just moments before, hadn't you been standing on his right? Why did you move?"

He threw the questions at her like darts, one after another, not giving her time to answer one before he thought of another, and every one hit its mark. Outraged, she almost told him to go to hell, but she never had to say a word. Before she could open her mouth, David Jones scowled at him and said, "Whoa, Thad, you're coming on a little strong, aren't you? She already told us why she moved. She had to instruct the caterers to make sure everyone had a glass of champagne for the toasts, and by the time she made her way back to where Joe was on the bandstand, everybody had gathered around him and she just squeezed in on the left."

"There was nothing sinister about it," she said in her own defense. "There was no place else for me to go."

It was a logical excuse—and nothing but the truth, thank God, Patsy thought smugly. No one had to know that while she was gone, she'd slipped the poison in Joe's champagne glass.

Pleased with herself, she saw that Jones and Shoemaker accepted her story without so much as blinking, but Law wasn't nearly as easily satisfied. "All right, I'll give you that," he growled, "but that doesn't explain why you were so nervous all evening. A number of people commented on the fact that you were fidgety and ill at ease all night. Why was that, Mrs. Colton? What were you so antsy about?"

"I had three hundred guests in my home, Detective,"

she retorted haughtily. "Not to mention a band, dozens of wait staff, and security. Of course I was nervous. My husband was really looking forward to this party, and it was important to me that everyone enjoyed themselves. If you'd had that much responsibility on your shoulders, I'm sure you would have been more than a little nervous, too."

Her tone was belligerent, and she didn't give a damn. Yes, she'd been a nervous wreck at the party. And she'd had every right to be. She'd planned to kill her husband, for heaven's sake! She could have been spared all that if she'd just known someone else was going to try to kill him, too!

"Please don't be offended by Detective Law," Mark Shoemaker said when she glared at the other man. "He's new to the department, and sometimes he gets a little overzealous. He means well, though. We all want the same thing—the name of the shooter."

They may have all had the same goal, but it was obvious that Jones and Shoemaker didn't share Law's suspicions of her. Taking over the questioning, they focused on Joe's enemies and how someone not invited to the party might have gotten access to the ranch. And there was nothing Law could do but stew.

Delighted, it was all Patsy could do not to laugh. Let him suspect whatever he liked. No one was going to take him seriously. He was the new kid on the block and his opinion didn't count for squat.

Ruthlessly fighting a smile, she patiently answered the other men's questions and made sure she didn't tell them anything that could be used against her. She was good. Damn good. By the time they finally thanked her for her help and announced that she was free to go, she'd convinced them she was as saintly as her precious sister.

All but Thaddeus Law, she corrected herself as she left the interrogation room and headed for the elevator. She didn't spare him a glance, but she could feel his midnight-blue eyes piercing her back. And she knew she hadn't heard the last from Detective Law.

Standing on the patio at the ranch with Joe and Rebecca, Austin finally felt like he was getting somewhere. It was about time! He had elaborate diagrams of where the band was, the buffet tables, and every guest that could be accounted for. But it wasn't until he stood in the exact spot where Joe had been standing when the toasts began that he could actually see how the shooting played out. He still didn't know who the shooter was, but he was slowly getting there.

"All right, Joe, you were standing here," he said as he took a position where the bandstand had been set up for the party. "And you were looking...where? Straight ahead? At someone in the crowd off to your left or right? Where?"

"Straight ahead," Joe said promptly. "I was waiting for everyone to fill their glasses, and there was this red-headed hippie waiter who was moving slower than Christmas—"

"A redheaded waiter?" Austin cut in with a frown, checking his notes. "Man or woman?"

"Man," Rebecca answered for him. "I remember him now. He was tall and geeky, with stringy red hair he wore scraped back into a ponytail. He did look like a hippie—he even had an earring. And Joe's right. He moved like a turtle stuck in molasses."

"But who is this guy? I interviewed the wait staff. There was no redheaded hippie!"

Austin was positive he hadn't talked to such a person,

but they were just as positive the man had been there. Which meant he had missed him somehow. And if he'd missed one, how many others had slipped through the cracks without him even being aware of it?

"Damn!" he swore. "The caterer assured me the list he gave me was a complete list of everyone he'd hired for the night."

"Maybe it was," Rebecca said.

"Then how—"

"It was a large party—the caterer had to hire college kids to supplement his staff," she explained. "And you know how they are. Something comes up or they decide they can't work, they send someone in their place. The caterer probably didn't even know the switch had been made. He was just glad he had a body to serve drinks."

"Then how the hell is Austin going to find this guy?" Joe asked with a scowl. "He's got no name, nothing to go on."

That was a good question, one Austin didn't have an answer for. "I don't know," he said grimly, "but I'll track him down somehow. I have to. If he was standing where you both say he was, he might have seen the shooter. Do you remember where he was standing when the shot rang out?"

His dark brows knit together in a scowl, Joe stared at the spot where the waiter had been standing just minutes before the first toast. "It seems like he was at the back and a little bit to the right of center. I was waiting for him to finish serving everyone, but then Meredith came up on stage—"

"I thought she was standing right beside you?"

"She was, but she got called away for a few minutes. I don't remember why…" Replaying images of the party in his head, he said, "Oh, that's right. She had special champagne glasses for the two of us and had to get them from the bar. As soon as she returned, I lifted my glass for the toast, and the next thing I knew, a bullet grazed my cheek, and all hell broke loose.''

"And the waiter? Where was he? Could he have been the shooter? Maybe he wasn't a college student at all, but a hired gun. Did you see him after the shooting? Did he stick around or walk away before the police got there?''

"I don't know,'' he admitted. "Everyone was screaming, then the paramedics were there and the police, and it was a madhouse.''

"Everyone was so concerned about Joe that they were all rushing the bandstand,'' Rebecca added. "I don't remember seeing the waiter again, but that doesn't mean he wasn't there. It's all just kind of a blur.''

Unobtrusively standing in the shadow of the open door that opened onto the patio, listening to every word, Patsy wanted to scream. After all she'd endured at the police station, this was too much! This was her home—*hers!*—and there would be no secret meetings behind her back. She wouldn't allow it. She couldn't. Not with Austin. He was too sharp, too much like Thaddeus Law. Austin didn't miss much, and with all the time he was spending at the ranch, it was only a matter of time before he discovered her and Joe's marriage was nothing but a sham. From there, it was a simple step to conclude that she had everything to gain from Joe's death and nothing to lose.

Sick at the thought of being discovered, she stepped boldly out onto the patio. She had to do something, had to stop Austin from getting too close to the truth, had to distract him and Joe and Rebecca from suspecting her. Playing the wounded wife, she cried, "How could you do this to me?''

Startled, Joe whirled and only just then caught sight of

her. Confused, he frowned. ''Do what to you? What are you talking about?''

''Don't play innocent. You know very well what I'm talking about. From the very beginning, you thought I was the one responsible for the shooting, and now you're trying to make Rebecca and Austin think the same way!''

''Oh, no, Meredith!'' Rebecca said, horrified. ''He wasn't doing any such thing. We were just reenacting the shooting—''

''So I would walk in and hopefully give myself away,'' she cut in shrilly. ''Can't you see what a setup this is? He planned this so he could catch me off guard. He hates me!''

''I do not!'' Joe retorted, stung. ''If you'll just settle down and listen…''

But she'd worked herself up into a fine state and she had no intention of giving up center stage anytime soon. She had everyone's attention and if she played this right, she'd make Joe—and Austin—feel so guilty for suspecting her that they'd never again consider her a suspect.

''Yes, you do,'' she said tearfully, taking advantage of a talent she'd had for crying on demand since she was little more than a toddler. ''Do you think I haven't noticed the way you've been looking at me since the shooting? You know I wasn't the one who pulled the trigger—I couldn't since I was standing right next to you!—but you still think I had something to do with it.''

''That's ridiculous!''

Even to his own ears, Joe knew his denial sounded more than a little weak, but the truth was, he *had* wondered if she was somehow involved with the shooting. And every time he found himself thinking that way, he felt guilty as hell.

She was his wife. His Meredith. The woman he'd loved

almost from the moment he'd met her. They'd shared everything, all their hopes and dreams, all the joy and sadness and triumphs life had to offer. She would never do anything to hurt him. Would she?

It was that doubt that was tearing him apart. There'd been a time when he thought he could trust her implicitly. But the woman he would have sworn he knew inside and out would have never betrayed him with another man. She would have never gotten pregnant, then cold-bloodedly mocked his sterility and tried to pass that child off as his. Not the woman he married. She just wasn't capable of such a thing.

He readily admitted, though, that this Meredith was a far different woman than the one he had fallen in love with so long ago. She had changed, ever since the accident nine years ago. He couldn't quite bring himself to trust her as he once had.

Still, she was his wife, and he owed her his loyalty and protection. And that wasn't hard to give when he thought of all those years of their marriage, before she changed, when they were happy. "I don't believe for a second that you would ever do anything to hurt me or anyone else," he said, irritated that she'd put him on the spot in front of Austin and Rebecca. "You could never be that ruthless. Why do you think I hired Austin? It was obvious the police were focusing the investigation on family and friends, and I couldn't just stand by and let that happen. Tell her, Austin."

"That's exactly right," Austin replied when she turned tear-filled eyes on him. "He was afraid that Law and his buddies would be so busy looking at the wrong people that the real shooter would get away—or find a way to finish the job. That's why he brought me down here. To make sure that no stone was left unturned in looking for the bastard.''

"No one suspects you, Meredith," Rebecca assured her. "Especially Joe."

"Then why is everyone asking me so many questions?" she sniffed, playing the injured party to the hilt. "First Austin, and now the police—"

"The police?" Joe cut in, scowling. "You were questioned by the police? When? Why didn't you say something?"

"Because you weren't here and that awful Detective Law insisted that I come down to the station. That's where I've been all afternoon, sitting in a smelly interrogation room while they grilled me!"

She knew Joe would be outraged, and he reacted just the way she expected him to. Cursing, he pulled out his cell phone and quickly punched in the number of the police department. "I'll take care of this right now," he said grimly. "My family is *not* going to be harassed by the cops!"

Pleased as punch that she knew just how to push his buttons, Patsy had to bite her lip to keep from smiling. The old boy might hate her for the way she'd screwed things up when she got pregnant with Teddy, but she was still his wife, for better or worse. And that meant he stood by her and protected her. Hopefully, he'd be so busy doing that, he wouldn't have time to notice that she was guilty as hell.

Caught up in her reflections, she didn't notice that Austin was still watching her until he said, "What kind of questions did Law ask you in the interrogation? What was he looking for?"

Her heart lurching in her breast, she reminded herself it was too soon to get cocky. Just because she'd easily distracted Joe didn't mean she could do the same with Austin. He'd been a cop and still thought like one.

Summoning very real indignation, she said, "He tried to imply that I knew the shot was going to come from Joe's right, so I deliberately moved to his left before the toasts started so I wouldn't get shot myself. As if I would have been anywhere near the spot where I thought a bullet was coming," she added, rolling her eyes. "Nobody in their right mind would do that."

Austin's lips twitched. "True. If I remember correctly, you told me you went to get champagne for you and Joe before the toasts started. Right?"

"That's right," she agreed, and wanted to kick herself for bringing up the toast in the first place. If he thought to ask her why she didn't just have one of the waiters bring them each a glass, she'd have to think of something fast. "I also wanted to make sure there was enough champagne to go around and the waiters were doing their job. I did a quick check and got back just in time for the first toast. And the shooting," she added with a shudder. "It was awful."

She gave him the same story she'd given the police ad infinitum and wasn't surprised when he didn't ask her any more questions, but, instead, turned his attention back to Joe and what he'd seen right before the shooting. From the moment she'd first been asked about the shooting, she'd made sure her story never wavered, so Austin had already heard everything she had to say.

He wasn't the one she had to worry about, anyway, she silently acknowledged. Granted, he made her damn nervous and so did Thaddeus Law, but there was really only one person who could bring down her house of cards and that was Emily Blair Colton.

Nine years, Patsy thought, grimly. It had been nine

years since she'd run Meredith off the road and switched lives with her, and to this day, that little bitch Emily still remembered the moment right after the accident when she'd hit her head and saw two mommies. Oh, her memories of that day were still fuzzy, but Patsy didn't fool herself into thinking that Emily's images of the accident wouldn't one day snap into focus. And when they did, Emily would figure out that there were really two Merediths. Patsy wasn't waiting for that day. She already had the name of a man who would eliminate the little bitch for her. It was time to set up a meeting with him.

Nine

"**W**hat do you mean, there was no redheaded waiter at Mr. Colton's party?" Austin demanded, outraged. "Then who was the hippie with the earring serving drinks?"

Not the least bothered by his anger, the snooty assistant to John Roberts, the caterer, simply looked down her nose at him and said airily, "I neither know nor care. Perhaps he was one of the guests. Whoever he was, he wasn't employed by Mr. Roberts. He doesn't hire hippies."

"He did for the Colton party," he snapped, wishing he'd brought Rebecca with him. She might have known how to appeal to this little snob. But he hadn't known how long the search would take and she'd had papers to grade. "Look, lady, I've got witnesses that this jerk worked the party. Not," he added with a scowl, "that I have to prove anything to you. You're just the receptionist, right? You answer the phone. Where's Mr. Roberts? I need to talk to him."

"I'm afraid that's impossible," she said without a smidgen of regret. "He's in L.A. doing a party for the American Film Institute."

"Then let me talk to somebody else. Who's Mr. Roberts's assistant? Maybe he can help me."

Her mouth pursed in disapproval, she just stared at him like he was a bug who'd landed in her soup. Finally, just when he thought she was going to turn him down flat, she scrawled an address on a slip of paper and pushed it across her desk at him. "His name's Sean O'Connor. He's working a wedding tonight. Don't be surprised if he doesn't have time to talk to you."

He could take time, Austin vowed as he checked the address and strode out. He just needed the name of the redheaded waiter and an explanation of why he hadn't been included in the list of other employees who'd worked the party. How long could that take? Five minutes? Big deal.

But when Austin arrived at the hall where the wedding reception was being held later that evening, O'Connor was as cool as the receptionist. "You can't be serious," he growled when Austin identified himself and asked for a few moments of his time. "Do you have any idea who is getting married tonight, Mr. McGrath? Congressman Hart's daughter! So, you can see, this is a very *big* reception, and I still have a million things to do. Surely you don't really think I'm going to drop everything so I can talk to you?"

Austin liked to think he was a reasonable man. If O'Connor hadn't copped an attitude, he would have been happy to make arrangements to meet with him the following day. But there was something about his superior attitude—and the way the caterer looked down his thin nose at him—that rubbed him the wrong way. If the jackass wanted to drop names, he'd be more than happy to do the same.

"You know, you're right. I'm sorry, man. I wasn't thinking. Go back to what you were doing. I'll just call former Senator Colton and tell him that you didn't have time to help me because you had bigger fish to fry tonight. Uncle Joe will understand…I hope."

O'Connor, to his credit, wasn't stupid. He knew who Joe Colton was and that one negative comment from him could do irreparable harm to the reputation of Roberts Catering. Not that Joe would do that, but this little worm didn't know that. He paled and immediately began to try to make amends.

"Wait!" he said quickly when Austin half turned to walk away. "Maybe I was a little hasty. I can spare a few minutes. Who did you say you were looking for? A red-headed waiter?"

Satisfied he'd gotten his attention, Austin nodded. "He must have been someone who was brought in at the last minute. He wasn't included in the list of employees who worked the party that night. Mr. Colton and his foster daughter both remember the man. He was tall and lanky, with long red hair and a ponytail."

Frowning, O'Connor said, "I was in charge of the staff for that party—John handled the food—and it was a nightmare. There was some kind of stomach virus going around, and we had people calling in sick just hours before the party was scheduled to begin. Normally in a situation like that, we call our competitors—we all help each other out—but they were having the same problem we were."

"So what did you do?"

"Got on the phone and started calling every restaurant in town until we found one that would give us the names of some of their waiters who weren't scheduled to work that night. That must have been where your guy came from. There's certainly no one on our regular payroll that fits that description.''

''You don't remember him personally? Surely he checked in with you before the party started.''

''That party was so hectic, I doubt that I would have remembered seeing my own mother that night. Mrs. Colton was—''

Suddenly remembering who he was talking to, he immediately snapped his mouth shut, but it was too late. ''Mrs. Colton what?'' Austin prompted. ''What were you going to say? You can tell me, O'Connor. I may be a family member, but I was hired to do a job, and whatever you tell me is confidential.''

Still, the other man hesitated. ''She was impossibly demanding,'' he finally admitted. ''I've worked with her in the past, but I've never seen her so…manic. She insisted that everything be perfect, and was constantly rushing into the kitchen, giving orders and throwing everyone into chaos. It was very nerve-racking.''

''It was a big party,'' Austin said. ''It was obviously very important to her that Joe's sixtieth birthday was memorable.''

''True,'' he agreed. ''As it turned out, it was anyway. I don't imagine he or anyone else will ever forget it.''

That, unfortunately, was only too true. ''Back to our redheaded waiter. What restaurants did you call that day for help?''

''The Irish Tavern and the Baja Steakhouse,'' he replied promptly. ''Try the Irish Tavern first—ask for Susan LeCoke. She's the manager and was very helpful.''

He'd given him more information than Austin had expected—even though he'd had to threaten him to get it—

and he was appreciative. Thanking him for his help, he hurried outside to his rental car and headed across town to the Irish Tavern. If Susan LeCoke was as cooperative as Sean O'Connor, he just might have the name of the shooter by nightfall.

The dinner crowd was already starting to gather, but Susan LeCoke was, thankfully, happy to take a few minutes to talk to Austin in her small office right off the kitchen. Pleasant and easygoing, she made a list of the employees she knew had helped with Joe's party, but when it came to the redheaded waiter, there wasn't, unfortunately, much more she could tell him than his name.

"He was employed here until he didn't show up for work last week," she said when he described the waiter. "His name's Bryan Walker, but good luck finding him. When I tried to call him to see if he was coming into work, his phone had been disconnected. I don't think he's very responsible when it comes to paying his bills."

Great! Austin thought in disgust. If he wasn't paying his phone bill, he probably hadn't paid his rent either. "Do you know where I can find him? It's very important."

Flipping through her employee records, she pulled out Walker's file. "Let's see, the only address I have is 1908 Johnson Street. You might try there. Just because the phone was disconnected doesn't mean he moved."

Austin appreciated her optimism, but considering the way the investigation had led him on one goose chase after another, he wasn't holding his breath. "Thanks," he said. "At least I've got a name now. And these," he added, holding up the list of the names and phone numbers of six of her waiters who'd helped with Joe's party. "That's a start."

Just to humor himself, Austin drove by 1908 Johnson Street and wasn't surprised to find the small house empty and deserted. Just as he'd feared, Bryan Walker had cleared out his stuff and moved on, and it was too late to track him down tonight. He'd pick up the trail again tomorrow. There had to be someone, somewhere, who knew where he'd gone.

In the meantime, he was tired and disgusted and it had been a very long day. His defenses were down, and as twilight pushed in on him, he could no longer hold memories from the past at bay. With no effort whatsoever, he found himself going back in time to that moment when the doctor had told him that he'd lost not only the baby, but Jenny, as well. He could still hear the animal cry that had ripped from his throat.

Dear God, would he ever forget the pain of that moment? he wondered as he drove away from the restaurant. In the awful silence of two lost heartbeats, his whole life had changed forever.

With time, he'd learned to deal with the loneliness of his own existence. He never forgot the anniversary of the day he'd lost Jenny, but he had managed to let go of most of the hurt. Or so he had thought—until today. For some reason, it was worse this year and he didn't know why.

He needed a drink.

It was, he tried to tell himself, the logical solution. He should go back to the hotel, order a bottle of whiskey from room service, and get plastered. He'd wake up in the morning with the mother of all hangovers, but at least he'd be able to get through the rest of the night without thinking.

But instead of doing the smart thing and driving back to his hotel, he found himself heading for the one place he knew he would find comfort and the last place he should have gone. Rebecca's.

In the middle of cooking supper, Rebecca couldn't stop her heart from lurching in her breast when the doorbell rang. In spite of the fact that she was thrilled that Richard had resigned, deep down inside, she'd been half expecting to hear from him all day.

"Oh, God," she whispered, setting down the wooden spoon she'd used to stir the homemade spaghetti sauce she was making. That had to be him. Now what did she do? It would be horrible of her not to accept his apology if he'd come to offer one, but she started to tremble just at the thought of letting him into her apartment.

So don't answer the door, her common sense retorted. You're under no obligation to talk to him or anyone else if you don't want to. Ignore him.

For all of ten seconds, she considered it. Then when the doorbell rang again and she realized she was standing there in her own apartment letting him terrorize her just by ringing her doorbell, she was furious. Damn him, she would not let him or any other man ever frighten her again!

Storming to the front door, she jerked it open without even checking the peephole. "How dare you— Austin!"

As surprised as she, he started to grin. "Why do I have the feeling you were expecting someone else?"

"I thought you were Richard," she admitted sheepishly.

"Ahh," he said, understanding. "I guess it's lucky for him I wasn't. You looked like you were ready to take his head off."

"I was," she said simply, and didn't apologize for it. Suddenly realizing she hadn't invited him inside, she pulled the door wide. "I didn't mean to leave you standing on the doorstep. Come in. I was just cooking supper. Did you find the redheaded waiter?"

"I was able to get his name and where he used to live," he replied as he followed her into the kitchen. "Tomorrow I'll track down his former landlord and see if he knows anything."

"Oh, Austin, that's great! Maybe this is just the break you've been looking for."

"Time will tell," he said with a shrug. Taking a seat at the breakfast bar, he sniffed the air. "Are you making spaghetti sauce from scratch?"

Smiling, she nodded. "And meatballs, too. You'll stay to eat, won't you? I made enough for an army. It's hard to make just a little spaghetti sauce."

He should have said no. In spite of the fact that everything smelled delicious, he didn't have much of an appetite. His mood was lousy, and he wouldn't be very good company. But he didn't want to be alone. Not tonight, of all nights. "Sure," he said huskily. "Thanks."

He set the table for her, and within minutes, it was time to eat. Sitting across from her, Austin served himself from the steaming bowl in the middle of the table, sure he wouldn't eat much. Then he took a bite, and the flavors exploded on his tongue. Surprised, he said, "My God, this is fantastic! Where'd you learn to cook like this?" But even as he asked, he knew. "Inez!"

She grinned. "When I was a kid, my mother's idea of home cooking was to open a can of Spaghetti-Os. I didn't realize you could even make it from scratch until I went to live at the ranch."

"So what else did Inez teach you to cook? She didn't give you the recipe to her chocolate cake, did she?"

"She doesn't give that to anyone," she laughed. "I

know. I've tried to get it out of her more times than I can remember.''

Lost in her memories, she happily reminisced about all the successes and disasters she'd had in the kitchen with Inez. She'd burnt cookies and set off the smoke alarm, made cakes that never rose, and to this day, had yet to live down the dried-out chicken breasts she'd baked too long in a too-hot oven. And she'd had a wonderful time doing it.

"The first time I made gravy that wasn't lumpy, Inez baked a chocolate cake just for me. I ate the whole thing."

"You didn't!"

"I did, too. It was just a little cake, hardly bigger than a saucer, but the whole family teased me about it for weeks."

Austin could see her now, stuffing her face with cake like a three-year-old. And just that easily, his thoughts slipped to the baby he'd lost, a daughter who would be eight now. What would she be like if she'd lived? Would she have Jenny's smile? Her laughing blue eyes? Her joy of living? Sadly, he would never know.

"Austin? What is it? Suddenly you seem very far away. Is something wrong?"

It was several long seconds before he heard her, and when he did, he jerked himself back to the present with a smile that was dredged in sadness. "It's nothing," he said with a shrug. "My mind just drifted for a moment. Sorry about that."

"Don't apologize. You just looked so unhappy."

That didn't begin to describe what he was feeling, but he hated to burden her with the weight of his past. "It's been one of those days," he said simply. "Tomorrow will be better." Deliberately, he changed the subject, steering it back to her. "So is there any news on who the new principal's going to be? How long do you think it'll take the school board to make an appointment?''

Rebecca knew what he was doing, but she graciously allowed him to guide the conversation away from himself. He would talk when he was ready. ''No one knows yet. Most of the teachers hope they'll promote Christina Lopez, the assistant principal. She gets along with everyone, and she's very fair. The students like her, too.''

Happy to distract him from whatever was bothering him, she talked about school and her students and even the house she one day hoped to buy, but the shadow of pain continued to linger in his eyes. To his credit, though, he tried not to let it show. As they lingered over the meal, he asked questions in all the right places, kept the mood light, and even went out of his way to make her laugh. But he never smiled himself, and when she suggested that he stay for a while after the meal and watch a movie with her, he seemed to accept almost in relief.

They settled at opposite ends of her small couch in front of the TV, and up until the first commercial break, Rebecca would have sworn that Austin was as caught up in the story as she was. His eyes directed on the screen, he seemed totally focused. The only problem was...the movie was a comedy and quite funny, and he never laughed. In fact, Rebecca doubted he heard a single word of it. He just sat there, staring unseeingly at the TV.

Worried, she shifted to face him and said quietly, ''I've been told I'm a good listener.'' When he just looked at her blankly, she said, ''Something's obviously bothering you. It might help if you talked about it.''

For a moment she thought he was going to offer another excuse and change the subject, just as he had during dinner. He glanced back at the TV, and for a long time he didn't say a word. Then he said huskily, "Today's the anniversary of Jenny and the baby's death."

Stricken, she gasped, "Oh, Austin, I'm so sorry! I should have remembered."

"It was a long time ago. People forget."

"No," she said, impulsively reaching across the short distance between the two of them to give his hand a squeeze. "Please don't think that. I may have forgotten the date, but I could never forget Jenny and the baby, and neither could the rest of the family. Everyone knows losing them was horrible for you. If no one talks about it, it's only because they don't want to hurt you by bringing it up."

"I know," he said thickly, "but it hurts, anyway."

His hand holding hers as if he would never let her go, he told her then about Jenny and how happy they'd been when they'd discovered they were going to have a baby. "She wasn't even born yet, and we'd already made all these plans for her. She was going to be smart and pretty, of course, and sweet, like Jenny. She'd take ballet lessons and love Winnie-the-Pooh and books. We were already planning a trip to Disneyland—"

His voice cracked, and Rebecca's heart broke at the sight of the silent tears trailing down his face. "Oh, Austin, I'm so sorry."

She moved then because she couldn't stop herself. He was hurting, and her heart ached for him. With a murmur, she wrapped her arms around him and just held him. "It's okay," she choked, tears welling in her own eyes. "I know it hurts. Go ahead and cry."

It had been nine years, and he'd never cried. At the time he'd felt nothing but anger when the shock wore off. He'd stood dry-eyed at the funeral as he watched his wife and baby daughter lowered into the ground in the same casket, so furious with God he could barely speak. Then when the anger finally faded, he'd ruthlessly refused to let himself cry. Because he'd been afraid if he ever started, he'd never be able to stop.

But with Rebecca holding him, he didn't worry about any of that. Emotions that had been building up for years washed over him like a tidal wave, dragging him down until all he could feel was pain. Endless, agonizing pain. And he couldn't fight it anymore. He just didn't have the strength. Burying his face against her neck, he cried and cried and cried.

Spent, Rebecca couldn't have said how long they held each other after his tears ended. With the TV a soft murmur in the background, she lay with her head against Austin's chest and listened to the steady, reassuring beat of his heart. Her eyes closed on a sigh. A heartbeat later, she was asleep.

It was the sound of an ambulance racing by on the street outside her apartment that finally brought her awake. Groggy, she blinked sleepily, only to gasp softly when she realized she was lying in Austin's arms on the couch. How…?

Confused, she should have distracted herself immediately, before he woke up and the situation became awkward. But even as she recognized the wisdom of that, she couldn't bring herself to move. Not yet. She'd never wakened up in a man's arms before and had no idea how fascinating it could be. He was so close, so…touchable.

He was an incredibly attractive man—she'd always thought so, but never more so than now. He didn't often let his guard down, but with his chestnut hair falling over his brow, his thick lashes dark against his chiseled cheeks, and his lips slightly parted in sleep, just looking at him stole her breath. Her fingers trembling slightly, she lifted her hand to his hair.

Later, she couldn't have said when she realized he was awake. One second, she was stroking his hair and the next, she was looking him right in the eye. "Oh!" Her fingers stopped in midstroke at his temple. "I didn't mean to wake you."

"You didn't," he rasped. Lifting his own hand to her hair, he arched a brow at her. "May I?"

Enchanted, she could only nod, unable to deny either of them this innocent intimacy she'd never shared with another man. Slowly, with infinite care, he stroked her hair, then the curve of her cheek, as if she was the most precious thing in the world to him. And just that easily, he made her float.

Tears of joy misted her eyes, but she didn't have to worry that he would misunderstand. He smiled softly and trailed a finger slowly down to her mouth. "Do you know how long I've wanted to touch you?" he asked in a hushed voice that set her nerve endings humming. "Since the first day I arrived in town and you sat across from me during dinner at Joe's."

Surprised, she stared up at him in wonder. "That long? But that was over a month ago! We barely knew each other."

"I knew all I needed to know when I looked into your eyes," he murmured. "I want to kiss you, sweetheart. You know that, don't you?"

His honesty nearly destroyed her. "Oh, Austin, I want that, too! I never thought I could lie here like this with you. It's wonderful! But I'm not sure how I would react to a kiss."

"I won't rush you," he said roughly. "This is your call. If you get nervous or scared, all you have to do is say the word and I'll stop. Okay? There's nothing to be afraid of.''

Touched, she wanted to tell him that she already knew that. Over the last few weeks, she'd come to trust him so much. He was a good man, a caring man, and she only had to look into his eyes to know that he meant every word. Needing to show him how much that meant to her, she leaned over and pressed her mouth to his in a kiss that was whisper soft. And he kissed her back.

Magic. There was no other way to describe the wonder of the moment. One tender kiss gave way to another, then another, and although he didn't try to hold her, he never stopped touching her. From her hair, his hand moved to her cheek, cupping it, then his fingers skimmed down the side of her neck, warming her blood until her body was sparkling like a new star in the night sky.

And she loved it. Delighted, she melted against him and touched him as he touched her, slowly trailing her hands over him, stroking the rugged lines of his face, the breadth of his shoulders, the hard wall of his chest. And with every touch, every kiss, the need coiling deep inside her tightened.

She should have drawn back then, before her fears unexpectedly rose up to ruin the wonder of the moment. But then his hands moved to the buttons of her blouse just as hers moved to his shirt, and her thoughts clouded. The pounding of her heart drowned out the quiet words of caution whispered by her common sense, and all she wanted to do was curl into his arms and give in to the ache he stirred in her so effortlessly. Murmuring his name, she kissed him hungrily, wanting, needing, something she couldn't put a name to.

''Oh, honey,'' he groaned. ''Does this feel as good to you as it does to me?''

"I never knew it could be like this," she murmured, and pulled him to her for another desperate kiss.

Lost in the taste and feel and fire of her, he would have liked nothing better than to sweep her up in his arms and carry her off to bed, where he would spend the rest of the night making love to her. It was what he wanted, what he ached for, what he'd dreamed of for weeks. But even as his arms tightened around her and he took the kiss deeper, he knew the exact moment her fear started to creep back between them. She stiffened ever so slightly, but he still felt it.

"It's okay," he said quietly, immediately loosening his arms around her. "Everything's fine, sweetheart. There's no reason to be alarmed."

He kept his voice low and soothing as he stroked her with gentle hands, calming her before her fear could get out of hand, but for a moment, he was afraid she didn't even hear him. Stiff as a board in his loose hold, she lay with her eyes squeezed shut, hardly daring to breathe.

Hurting for her, hating the men who had tried to push themselves on her over the years, he brushed a butterfly kiss to her cheek and acted as if nothing was wrong. "You are so sweet," he told her huskily. "So pretty. There's nothing to worry about. We're going to be just fine."

Never taking his eyes from hers, he buttoned her blouse with steady fingers, talking all the while, until he finally felt the tension slowly drain out of her. He started to smile reassuringly at her, then he saw the tears. "Oh, honey, don't cry. It's okay. The time will come when everything's right for us."

Too late, he realized the last thing he should have done was show her sympathy. The tears filling her eyes spilled over her lashes, and with a whimper of hurt, she threw herself into his arms. "No, it won't! How can it? Look at me. I can't even let you touch me."

"What are you talking about?" he said with a confused frown. "You were wonderful!"

"But I panicked again."

"Not at first," he pointed out. "You were doing great until things really heated up between us. Don't you see how encouraging that is? You're making real progress."

Her eyes searching his, Rebecca wanted desperately to believe him. Could he be right? Was she finally getting past the hangups that had destroyed every other friendship she'd ever had with a man? It hadn't felt like it when she'd stiffened in his arms just moments before, but now that the fear had faded and she could remember every touch, every kiss clearly, hope bloomed in her heart like a rose in the desert.

"I wanted to make love to you," she said, amazed. "I still do. I just can't—"

"You don't have to make excuses," he cut in quietly. "I understand. Building trust takes time, and this is a huge step for you. We're going to take it one day at a time."

Tears stung her eyes again, but this time, they were tears of joy rather than disappointment. She'd touched him and kissed him, and his hair was dishevelled because *she*, Rebecca Powell, like a virgin mistress, had done that! And she was damn proud of herself. She'd loved the feel of his hands on her—and hers on him. When his arms had closed around her right before the panic had set in and he'd kissed her like there was no tomorrow, she'd known what it was like to be truly desired by a man.

And for no other reason than that, she could have loved him. He had no idea how much courage he'd inspired in her just with his patience and understanding.

"I'm going to find a way to get past this," she promised him and herself. "I don't know how or when, but I'm going to work at it. And one day soon, I'm going to make love with you the way I long to."

"I'll be waiting," he replied huskily as he rose and held out his hands to help her to her feet. "Because I want that as much as you do. In the meantime, though, I think you'd better walk me to the door. It's getting late and I need to get out of here before I forget my good intentions."

He wouldn't do that—she knew that now—but it was getting late and she did have to work tomorrow. So she walked him to the door, and this time when he kissed her good night, it wasn't on the cheek. And when her heart started to flutter, it wasn't with anything close to fear. And long after he left and the front door closed behind him, she stood there smiling, feeling like she'd just won the lottery.

"I've decided I need a vacation."

Seated at the breakfast table across from his wife, Joe glanced up from his morning paper at her announcement and frowned. "Do you think that's wise? The police—"

That was as far as he got. In the process of taking a sip of her coffee, she set her cup down with a snap and screeched, "I'm sick and tired of worrying about the police and the damn shooting! That's all anyone's been talking about for weeks. 'We need to talk to you down at the station, Mrs. Colton. Where were you when the shot was fired? Why don't you know who the shooter was? Weren't you involved?'" she mimicked.

"No one said that," he said, shocked.

"They didn't have to. Do you think I don't know what they're thinking? I'm not an idiot. I'm tired of the questions, tired of the suspicious looks, tired of everything."

When her shoulders slumped and tears glistened in her eyes, Joe found himself almost feeling sorry for her. There'd been a time in their marriage when he would have stepped around the table and taken her into his arms at the first sign of tears from her, but not anymore. He'd been stung too many times by her sharp tongue over the last nine years to risk that again.

Instead, he stayed where he was and lifted a dark brow at her. "So where are you going?"

With a flip of an invisible switch, her mood brightened. "Palm Springs," she said promptly. "Carly Templeton told me about a wonderful new spa that just opened two weeks ago, and I thought I would try it out."

Carly Templeton was the wife of a California congressman and the most shallow woman Joe had ever met. And she and Meredith were thick as thieves. Normally, he had little good to say about her, but if she was the one who'd given Meredith the idea for this sudden trip, he'd have to be nice to her the next time he saw her. He needed some time to himself.

Immediately feeling guilty at the thought, he said quietly, "When are you leaving?"

"In a few moments," she retorted. "I've already told the boys goodbye and had Marco put my bags in the car."

Not surprised that he was the last to know, Joe would have laughed if the situation hadn't have been so pitiful. And he was feeling guilty? Like hell! "Have a good time," he growled, gathering his paper and rising to his feet. "I'll see you when you get back."

Oh, she was going to have a good time, all right, Patsy thought with a wicked gleam in her eyes as he walked out. She was going to be sinfully pampered at the spa for an ungodly amount of his money. But first she had to stop in L.A. for a meeting. She'd arranged with the hitman who would take care of dear, precious Emily once and for all. By the time she came home, she, at least, would no longer be a problem.

Grinning, she grabbed her purse and keys, and within moments, she was behind the wheel of her newest present to herself, a sporty little BMW, and on her way to Palm Springs. She hadn't felt this good in a long time.

An hour later, wearing a curly black wig and a pair of dark sunglasses, Patsy drove into one of the seediest neighborhoods in L.A. The place looked like a war zone. Windows were broken out of vacant, run-down buildings, trash littered the streets, and hopelessness and bitterness permeated the area.

Checking the address she'd written down on a small piece of paper that she intended to burn later, she smiled in satisfaction. This was the place. Now all she had to do was find her man. It wouldn't be difficult. She had his name, but only an idiot would ask for Silas "Snake Eyes" Pike by name. He was a hitman, for God's sake. A man like that didn't advertise his identity. She didn't need anyone to point him out anyway. The description she had of him was very clear. Medium height, long brown hair, mustache and goatee, mean eyes. He wouldn't be easy to miss.

And neither would she, especially in a bar in this part of town. With its windows painted black and a front door that had two dead bolts, the place was dark and dangerous looking and obviously didn't cater to a high class of clientele. Checking her image in her rearview mirrors, she noted the cheap cubic zirconium in her ears and grinned. She wasn't stupid enough to wear the good stuff to a joint where she was likely to get knocked over the head, but no one inside would know that. Pike would see the flash and sparkle and think she had the dough to pay for services rendered. And hopefully, he'd be so busy looking at the jewelry and the money she intended to flash around that he'd never take a good look at her face. The last thing she wanted was for him or anyone else to identify her later. Satisfied that that wasn't going to happen, she adjusted her wig, grabbed her purse and strolled inside.

When she'd set up the meeting, she'd hoped the bar would be fairly deserted at eleven o'clock in the morning. It wasn't. A rough-looking group sat at the bar, and they all looked up at her entrance. Swearing under her breath, she prayed none of them could see through her disguise, then glanced around for her man.

As arranged, he was seated at a table by himself in the far corner. He wasn't quite what she'd expected—although he had a wiry build, he also had a pronounced beer belly—but she didn't need brawn for this job, she needed ruthlessness. And Silas "Snake Eyes" Pike seemed to have that in spades.

He wasn't handsome—not by a long shot. The top of his head was bald in spite of the long, sandy-brown ponytail that hung down his back, and the Fu-Manchu style mustache and goatee he wore were hardly flattering. There was Native American blood somewhere in his heritage— it was stamped all over the strong lines of his face—but it was his nearly black, close-set eyes that convinced Patsy he was just the man she needed for the job. He looked as mean as she'd been told he was. And in his eyes, she recognized him for what he was. An ex-con. She'd seen that look too many times during her own time behind bars not to know it when she saw it.

Sensing a kindred spirit, she sauntered over to him and took a seat next to him, greeting him with the prearranged passwords that would identify her to him. "Hey, stranger, can I buy you a drink?"

His dark eyes narrowed speculatively, he looked her over for all of two seconds, then nodded curtly. "You look like you can afford it."

"Oh, I can," she purred, tossing the curly strands of her wig back so he could catch the glitter of the fake diamonds in her ears. "Bartender, bring him another and I'll have the same."

Waiting until their drinks were set before them and the bartender walked away, she lifted a delicately arched brow. "So when'd you get out?"

He didn't pretend to misunderstand what she was asking. "Six months. So what's the job you've got for me?"

Patsy hadn't wanted to chance talking about it on the phone, but she'd been assured by the contact that had set her up with Pike that he would do anything if the price was right.

"Murder," she said quietly. "I've heard you've done it before."

Silas almost snorted at that. So she thought he was a hit man. Yeah he could do that. Puffing out his chest, he lied like he'd been doing all his life. "You're damn straight. Who do you think the Giovanni family called on to take out Big Eddy Jones down in San Diego? They knew I could do it clean and their name would never come into it."

"You did a hit for the mob? And did time for it?"

"I'm not that stupid," he growled. "I told you I did it clean. That was six years ago and the cops still don't have a clue who knocked off Big Eddy. It was my old lady who sent me to the pen. She was mad and turned me in for car theft and armed robbery."

It was his own ineptitude that landed him in prison, but

that was nobody's business but his own. If the rich bitch didn't have the sense to check him out and get her facts straight, that was her problem. "So what's this job pay?"

Opening her purse, she gave a glimpse of the ten thousand dollars stuffed in there. "That's just the down payment. You get the rest when the job's done."

Patsy knew she was taking a risk, showing him the money before he'd agreed to do the job, but this was an experienced hit man, for God's sake! He wasn't going to agree to commit murder for her without knowing for sure she had the money to pay.

"So," she asked, "are you interested or not?"

"It depends," he retorted. "You're not a cop, are you?"

Alarm bells clanged in Patsy's head. What kind of Einstein was he? If she'd been a cop working some kind of sting operation, she certainly wouldn't have admitted it! Doubts pulled at her, and for a second, she considered backing out. But she was anxious to conclude her business so she could get out of there and enjoy her vacation in Palm Springs, and she wanted Emily taken care of, dammit! He was just the type of man she'd hoped to find for the job—cold and experienced and willing to do anything for a price. If he wasn't very bright, so what. All he had to know was how to pull the trigger of a gun.

"Of course I'm not a cop. Do I look like one of those slimy bastards? I just need someone to do a job for me and it's not something I can put an ad in the paper for."

"Then it looks like I'm your man. Who you want whacked?"

Just that easily, they had a deal. Thrilled, Patsy moved her chair closer to his. "Her name's Emily Blair...."

Ten

Damn, she was good!

Soaking in the hot tub on her private patio at the spa, Patsy leaned her head back against the rim of the tub and sipped at her champagne, satisfaction oozing from every pore of her body. She and Snakes Eyes had worked out a plan to knock off that irritating little bitch, Emily. She didn't want to know the details, just that the only person who could link her to the accident when she'd switched lives with Meredith had finally been eliminated.

She would be safe then, she thought with a sigh of relief. Even Snake Eyes wouldn't be a threat to her. Once he'd done his job, she'd pay him the balance she owed him and be done with him.

Delighted with herself, she downed her champagne and poured herself another. She'd covered all her bases. She was home free. Only Meredith herself could destroy her now, and the odds on that happening after all this time were slim to none. If her memory hadn't come back after nine years, it wasn't going to.

Still, Patsy knew better than to leave anything to chance, which was why she'd hired Ed Garrison, a private investigator from L.A., to track down her sister. She hadn't told him the truth, of course. How could she? All he'd needed to know was her *sister,* Patsy Portman, had once been confined at the St. James Clinic for Mental Health in Monterey, and she—the real Meredith, she assured herself—had lost touch with her after her release.

All she'd wanted him to do was find *Patsy,* that was all. It was a simple enough request. Or so she'd thought. But she'd hired him over a year ago and still had nothing to show for it. Dammit, what the hell was the man doing? Sitting on his hands in his office, while she paid him a fortune to do nothing? Her sister was out there somewhere. Why the hell hadn't he found her?

Frustrated, she wanted to kick herself for leaving so early that morning. Ed's progress report should have come in the afternoon mail. If she'd just waited…

So call him, a voice in her head urged. You're paying him. You don't have to wait for a damn report to find out what's going on. Call him.

Crawling out of the tub, she wrapped one of the spa's thick, luxurious towels around herself and retrieved her small address book from her purse. Ten seconds later she had Ed on the phone and wasted little time with a greeting. "This is Meredith Colton. Have you found my sister?"

"Oh, Mrs. Colton! Didn't you get my report?"

"I'm in Palm Springs," she said shortly. "Give it to me on the phone. You didn't find her, did you?"

"It's not for lack of trying," he said defensively. "You have to remember, it's been years. This is a very old trail, people that might have known Ms. Portman may have moved away or even died. It's like trying to grab a shadow.''

"That's not my problem,'' she said silkily. "I'm paying you an ungodly amount of money to find my sister. If you value your license, you'll damn well quit making excuses and do your job.''

She wasn't a woman who made idle threats, and Edward Garrison was well aware of that. "I warned you that there were no guarantees,'' he said stiffly. "I'm making arrangements to go to Mississippi and check out the address you gave me, but I wanted to run down a few leads I had here before I left.''

"Leads? What leads? You just said the trail was cold.''

"I thought it was. The clinic is very protective of its patients' privacy. The staff wouldn't even admit that Patsy had been a patient there at one time. And that's made my job very difficult. I didn't know when she was released, who her doctors were, if she was transferred to another mental health facility, or what. So I started digging around and finally came across an old newspaper article about Dr. Michael Harper, the director of the St. James Clinic.''

"But what good is that? He's the director, for God's sake. He's not going to tell you any more than the rest of the staff.''

"He *was* the director,'' he corrected her. "He retired back in 1995. I figured he had to know something about your sister, but he moved around the country in a motor home after he retired, and discovering where he landed hasn't been easy. I finally located him in Albuquerque, and it turns out that he was more than willing to talk about Patsy. She was quite an interesting case, and he'd always wondered what happened to her since she was still suffering from amnesia when she was released from the clinic.''

''And?'' she demanded, impatient with the self-serving P.I.

''Dr. Harper was quite amazed, as were the other doctors. When she was first transferred to the clinic from prison, she was suffering from anxiety and depression, not to mention extreme mood swings and psychotic behavior. I don't know if you know it or not, but patients with those kind of mental problems don't usually recover. But not only did your sister recover in a remarkably short time, she didn't need medication to stabilize her condition. That's unheard of.''

The last thing Patsy wanted to hear was praise about Meredith. Hadn't it always been like that? she thought bitterly. Meredith was so smart, so pretty, so *sweet*. Even when she was living *her* life, she did it better than she did. God, she hated her!

''I don't care about any of that,'' she said angrily. ''All I care about is finding her.''

''I understand that, Mrs. Colton,'' Ed said. ''But the news isn't all bad. Even though your sister was still suffering from amnesia when she left the clinic, Dr. Harper was very encouraged that she would eventually recover her full memory. She was already having vivid dreams and flashbacks. Her mind is just waiting for something to trigger the rest. It's just a matter of time till she remembers who she is. Perhaps then she'll come looking for you.''

He only meant to reassure her—deep down inside, Patsy knew that—but that did little to quell the panic that seized her by the throat. Dear God, what if she'd already remembered? What if right this minute, Meredith was making her way back to Prosperino to reclaim her life and destroy everything she, Patsy, had worked for all these years? She would lose Joe, Jr. and Teddy...and go back to prison.

No! she cried silently. She wasn't going to stand by and let that happen. This was *her* life, not Meredith's, dammit, and she wasn't letting her have it back. She'd kill her first. And this time she wouldn't chicken out because she was her oh-so-sweet twin sister. After all, it wasn't as if she'd never killed before. She'd taken care of Ellis, hadn't she, when he'd taken something from her that wasn't his to take? And then there was Joe. Ever since she'd messed up with Graham and gotten pregnant, he'd only tolerated her, and she knew it was only a matter of time before he found a way to get rid of her. So she'd planned to do it first. If he'd just taken a sip of his champagne first....

"Mrs. Colton? Are you still there? You do still want me to go to Mississippi, don't you?"

Jerked back from her drifting thoughts, she said coldly, "Of course. Just keep a low profile. If Patsy's there and hears someone is looking for her, she's going to take off like a scared rabbit and we may never find her again."

"Then I'll make arrangements to leave tomorrow," he replied. "I'll keep you apprised of my progress in my reports."

"You'd better damn well call me the second you discover her whereabouts, Garrison. I don't want to hear about it in any stupid report."

"As you wish," he said curtly, and hung up without another word.

Patsy didn't care. She'd gotten her point across to the jackass—he would do things her way or he'd be out of a job! Not that that gave her much satisfaction. Meredith was still out there somewhere, walking around loose like a time bomb that could go off at any second. If she re-

covered her memory before Patsy could find her and eliminate her, she would destroy everything.

Enraged at the thought, Patsy whirled and threw the
phone across the room, uncaring that it slammed into a
Waterford vase and shattered it. Dammit, she fumed,
where the hell was her sister?

Just as Dr. Harper had recommended all those years
ago when she'd walked away from the St. James Clinic
without a backward glance, Louise had found a way to
let go of the past she didn't remember. She was going on
with her life. Her days had settled into a comfortable,
pleasant sameness, and although she couldn't say she was
wildly happy, she was content. She loved her job, and at
the end of the day, she went home to her house and her
garden and Sparrow, her tabby Persian cat.

That didn't, however, mean she wasn't lonely. She was
still having bad dreams, and at the suggestion of Dr.
Wilkes, she'd accepted a date with Lucas Koffman, one
of the teachers at the university, in the hope that another
step forward in her life might help her get past the tragedy
of her nightmares. Tonight was the big night. They were
going out to dinner, and as she hurried home from school
to change into something more appropriate for a dinner
date, she didn't mind admitting she was nervous. It had
been a long time since she'd been out with anyone. Maybe
one day she'd know just how long.

"Hi, girl," she said, greeting Sparrow with a quick
scratch behind one of her scarred ears. "I don't have time
to stay and talk today—tonight's a big night—but I've got
something special for your dinner. Hang on and I'll get
it." Louise dumped the contents of the can into her bowl.

Her heart pounding at the thought of her own dinner,
she hurried upstairs to take a quick shower, then slipped

into a black-and-white dress that was perfect for a night
out at a romantic restaurant. She didn't know where Lucas
was taking her, but she didn't doubt that there would be
candlelight and soft music. That was just the kind of man
Lucas was. He had been asking her out for some time,
without success, and now that she was giving him a
chance, he would make the most of it.

And that was all right, she told herself as she dabbed
her favorite perfume at her pulse points. She'd been alone
for so long. Dr. Wilkes was right. It was time she took a
step away from the past and into the future. She'd been
dreaming of having someone in her life for a long time.
Maybe Lucas was that man.

When her doorbell rang ten minutes later, her heart
jumped in her breast, but her smile was open and friendly
as she opened the door to him. "Hi! You're right on
time."

"I didn't want to give you an excuse for backing out
if I was late," he said with a grin. "You look beautiful."

A blush tinged her cheeks. She couldn't be sure, but
she didn't think she had ever been a woman who spent a
lot of time in front of the mirror. Still, she appreciated the
compliment. "Thank you," she said softly. "I wasn't sure
what to wear. You didn't say where we were going."

"The Black Swan," he said, naming one of the most
romantic restaurants in Jackson. "I thought I'd give it my
best shot."

He was so honest, she had to laugh. "You're off to a
good start, but you really don't have to wine and dine me
like I'm some kind of princess, Lucas. I'd be just as happy
with a hamburger."

"So we'll go to McDonald's on our second date," he
replied, winking at her. "Tomorrow night."

That set the tone for the evening. The Black Swan was

everything that Louise had heard it was, but in spite of the fact that the restaurant couldn't have been more romantic, the atmosphere was really wasted on the two of them. Instead of gazing into each other's eyes and softly sharing confidences, they talked about friends at work, politics, movies they had both seen. Anyone seeing them together would have thought they'd known each other forever.

And that was exactly how Louise felt...like he was an old friend she was comfortable with. Nothing more, nothing less. She thoroughly enjoyed his company and truly did like him. But to her surprise, she discovered that she really wasn't interested in getting romantically involved with him or anyone else. And she didn't have a clue why.

"So," Lucas said as they finished their dessert and each had another cup of coffee, "what time should I pick you up tomorrow night? We can go to the McDonald's over on James Street."

Louise smiled. She had to give him credit. If she'd been the slightest bit attracted to him as a man, instead of a friend, he would have had her right then. "That was really smooth," she said with twinkling eyes.

"I try."

"Oh, I'm aware of that," she said dryly. "And you're really good at it. But unless you're just looking for a buddy to share a Big Mac with, you might want to ask another woman."

Truly surprised, he blinked. "But why? Aren't you having a good time?"

He looked so wounded that she felt like a heel. "Are you kidding? I can't remember the last time I had so much fun. And that's the problem."

"I beg your pardon?"

She hadn't told anyone at school about her amnesia,

but she could trust him to protect her privacy. Her smile fading, she said quietly, "I can't remember anything about my past, Lucas. My doctors diagnosed it as trauma-induced amnesia, though no one knows what trauma I suffered."

Somber, he didn't try to hide his surprise. "You don't remember *anything?*"

"Only what my doctors have told me. I turned up at a clinic in California where I was recognized, and the staff was able to tell me something about my past. It wasn't pretty."

"My God, that must have been hell! When was this?"

"Nine years ago." He didn't, thankfully, push her for any more details, and she could have kissed him for that. "And you're right—it was hell. Sometimes it still is. I don't know who I am, who I was. And even though I can give you the background information the hospital had on me, that woman was a stranger to me. She did some horrible things, things I can't imagine doing. I can't ask a man to be a part of my life when I don't even know just how bad a person I was. For all I know, I could be married! So until I can remember, I've got to be alone."

"And that's the hardest part of all, isn't it?" he guessed, his blue eyes dark with sympathy. "Being alone. You don't even remember your mother or father, do you? You must feel like you're totally alone in the world."

"I have to be, don't you think?" she replied, her shoulders slumping in despair. "Surely, if there was anyone out there who cared for me at all, they would have found a way to find me by now."

"Don't give up hope," he said, reaching across the table to give her hand a squeeze. "Life is full of twists and turns. Just because your family hasn't found you yet doesn't mean they're not looking. Right this minute, they could be worried to death about you, wondering where you are.''

Tears glistening in her eyes, she gave him a watery smile. ''Thanks. I hate to be a crybaby but sometimes it just gets to me.''

''Of course it does,'' he said gruffly. ''If I was in your shoes, I don't know what I'd do. We all like to think we're independent and self-sufficient. But the truth of the matter is that without that sense of belonging that family gives us, we'd probably all be wandering around in the dark like a bunch of scared kids jumping at their own shadows.''

He understood! Just knowing that someone besides her therapist understood how rudderless she felt lifted a huge weight from her shoulders. ''Yes! That's exactly how I feel sometimes, like I'm caught up in a nightmare and the bogey man is after me, and there's nowhere to run because nobody cares.''

He gave her hand another squeeze, and there was nothing the least bit romantic about it. It was just a reassuring gesture between friends. ''I care, Louise. And I'll bet there are others out there who do, too—friends and family, people who miss you as much as you must miss them. Don't give up hope. You'll find them one day.''

She wanted desperately to believe him. But later, after he'd taken her home and wished her good-night with a kiss on the cheek, the loneliness of her own existence closed around her, just as it always did, and all she wanted to do was cry. In the silence of the night, a pervasive sense of loss filled her, overwhelming her. There was a pain in her heart that wouldn't go away, the kind that only came from missing someone you love.

And that was when she realized Lucas was right. She did belong to someone—a husband, family, people who cared about her—because even though she couldn't remember anyone from her past, she did recall the sense of loving and being loved. In the dark, hidden recesses of her lost memory, there was a warmth, an ache for the feel of familiar arms around her, that she desperately missed. She loved someone, she had to, or she couldn't be missing him now!

And with that silent admission, she didn't know if she wanted to laugh with joy or bury her head in her pillow and sob. Because her loved ones were out there somewhere in the world, possibly right there in Jackson, for all she knew, and they were still as lost to her as ever. She could pass them on the street and wouldn't know them.

The pain of that haunted her all night. She fell asleep with tears on her cheeks, and not surprisingly, she found little peace in her dreams. Once again, the nightmare that had stalked her in her sleep for nearly ten years was back, more horrifying than ever. Trapped in a thick, cold fog, there was evil about—she could sense it, feel it. And somewhere in the night, she could hear someone calling for her, someone who needed her as badly as she needed them. But she couldn't reach them. Whimpering, she woke with a startled cry, calling out in her sleep for someone whose name she couldn't remember.

She didn't sleep for hours after that. She couldn't, not without taking a chance that the nightmare would come back. Knowing she needed help, she reached for the phone to call her therapist, Dr. Martha Wilkes, who had begun hypnotizing her weeks ago to discover the origin of her nightmares and the debilitating migraines that attacked her without warning. The second she started to punch in Martha's home number, however, she remembered that she was in Chicago at a convention and wouldn't be back until Monday. Until then, Louise realized with a feeling of stark despair, she was on her own. Left with no recourse but to deal with the problem the only way she knew how, she switched on all the lights in the house and began cleaning the kitchen from top to bottom.

Armed with Bryan Walker's former address, his landlord's name and address, not to mention the names of his co-workers from the Irish Tavern who had also worked Joe's party, Austin figured it would take all of an hour or two to track down the redheaded waiter and get a few answers out of him. But three days later, he still hadn't found him, and he was starting to get ticked. Were Walker's friends protecting him by sending Austin all over town on a wild-goose chase, or was it just dumb luck that the hippie always managed to stay one step ahead of him?

"I don't know where he went," his former landlord grumbled. "He said something about moving in with his girlfriend. Go ask her."

But the girlfriend, one of the waitresses at the Irish Tavern, would hardly give Austin the time of day. "We broke up two weeks ago. Talk to Jimmy." And without explaining who Jimmy was, she slammed the door in his face.

Frustrated, Austin wasted a whole day trying to track down Jimmy before he finally figured out that Jimmy was Bongo Jim, an eccentric musician who lived in Walker's former apartment building. He didn't play the bongos, but rather steel oil drums that he set up on the beach and played for anyone who cared to listen.

As much of a hippie as Walker, and fifty if he was a day, Jimmy merely arched a brow at Austin when he approached him and asked about Bryan. ''You one of those bill collectors always calling and knocking on the door?''

Surprised, Austin hesitated, not sure if he should admit who he really was. Jimmy was obviously protective of his friend if he was shielding him from collection agencies. He might shut up like a clam if he told him he was investigating an attempted murder. Then again, he reasoned, studying him, the man had a sharp eye and didn't look like anybody's fool. He'd see through a lie in a heartbeat.

In the end, he decided to take a chance on honesty. He had a feeling Bongo Jim was the kind of man who would appreciate it. ''Actually, I'm a private investigator,'' he said bluntly. ''I need to talk to your friend about a shooting he may have witnessed at a party he worked last month. I was told that you might know where he is.''

''I might,'' he said with a shrug, not committing himself either way. ''That boy's got itchy feet—he doesn't stay anywhere too long. And that's his problem. I told him he's never going to get very far as long as he keeps moving around, but he gets bored or in trouble and thinks things'll be better somewhere else.''

''What do you mean he gets in trouble?'' Austin asked sharply. ''Is he in trouble? Is that why no one's seen him? He's lying low for a while?''

Jimmy chuckled. ''He's not hiding out from the cops, if that's what you mean. It's the bank. He's behind on his car loan, and he's been turned in to collections. He left town for awhile so he won't lose his Honda.''

''Do you know where he went?''

''Yep, I do.''

When he didn't volunteer anything else, Austin had to bite back a smile. ''Would you mind sharing that information with me?''

Tilting his head, the older man considered him for a

minute with a frown. "The boy's not under any kind of suspicion, is he? If you're thinking he was involved, you're barking up the wrong tree. He's a free spirit, not a murderer."

From what Austin had heard of Bryan Walker, Bongo Jim was right—he didn't have the temperament of a killer. "He's not a suspect. But he may have seen the shooter and not even realized it. That's why I need to talk to him. He may be the only person who can break this case wide open."

Considering that for a long moment, he finally nodded, satisfied. "He's at Big Bear. A friend of his has a cabin up there. He's going to stay there the rest of the summer and work the resorts. They've got big tippers up there, and he's going to need that if he's going to catch up on his payments with the bank."

It was too much to hope that Jimmy might know the address of the cabin where Walker was staying, but Austin wasn't worried about that. Big Bear wasn't that big. He didn't have to know where the cabin was to find Walker. There were only so many resorts in the lake area. He'd just check them all.

"Thanks, man," he said, tossing ten bucks into the basket he'd set out on the sand for tips. "I owe you."

With a nod of thanks, the older man grinned and went back to playing his drums.

Austin knew he probably should have headed to Big Bear immediately, but the day was already half gone, and by the time he got there, it would be too late to do anything. He wouldn't be able to do anything until tomorrow anyway, so he might as well wait until in the morning to leave. And since tomorrow was Saturday, he could invite Rebecca to go with him.

Grinning at the thought as he drove back to his hotel, he knew alarm bells should have been going off in his head. They'd spent just about every evening together over the course of the last week, working on the case, talking things out, just enjoying each other's company. And he wanted more. More of her time, more of her company, more of her.

That alone should have sent him running for Portland and his nice, safe, lonely life there. He was talking about the future, he thought, amazed. He wanted a future with her. And instead of running, that only made him more eager to see her. She'd gotten past his guard, and although he'd never thought he'd ever want to have feelings for another woman after Jenny died, he thanked God he did.

"You're losing it, man," he said wryly. "You're in over your head and you don't even have the sense to realize you're drowning."

But did he care? Hell, no. The second he reached his hotel room, he went straight to the phone and called her. "Hi, sweetheart," he said the second she came on the line. "What have you got planned for tomorrow?"

"Nothing much. I need to clean the apartment and do a little grocery shopping, but that's not anything that can't wait. Why? What've you got in mind?"

"I've got to go to Big Bear tomorrow—that's where Walker seems to have gone to ground—and I thought you might want to go with me."

"Yes."

That was it, just yes. She didn't need any more details than that, and she didn't have a clue what that did to him. She could change her plans at the drop of a hat and go off with him to God knows where, and she didn't have to ask how long they would be gone or when they would be back or what she needed to take. Wherever he was going, she wanted to be with him, and that was all that mattered.

Touched, he grinned. "You know something? You're amazing."

"I am?" she said, puzzled. "Why? Because I'm going with you to Big Bear?"

"Yeah," he chuckled. "I'm supposed to be working and you just make it so much fun. I'll pick you up in the morning at eight, okay? We'll stop on the road somewhere and grab something for breakfast."

Her heart thumping crazily at the thought of spending the whole day with him, Rebecca hung up and couldn't stop smiling. Ever since that night he'd cried in her arms over Jenny and the baby's death, everything had changed. Although he hadn't kissed her again except on the cheek when he left her each evening to return to the hotel, they had grown so much closer. They'd talked about everything, including sex, and they'd both agreed that trying to force the issue would only make her problem worse. They had to be patient.

But patience wasn't nearly as easy for her as it had once been, and she wanted to laugh aloud with the wonder and excitement of it. Who would have thought that *she*, Rebecca Powell, would be frustrated and actually ache for a man to make love to her? He had changed everything for her, and she was falling in love with him. Of course she'd go to Big Bear with him! He only had to ask, and she'd go halfway around the world with him.

Saturday turned out to be one of those perfect days. Oh, there were more than a few clouds in the sky and traffic was standard California fare—bumper to bumper at fifty miles an hour—but neither Austin nor Rebecca noticed. With an old Dean Martin tape playing softly on the cassette player, they laughed and talked and the miles flew by.

It had been years since Rebecca had been to Big Bear, but it was still just as beautiful as ever. Given the chance, she would have liked nothing better than to spend the day exploring the lake and woods, but they had to save that for another time. For now, they had work to do.

Evidently thinking the same thing, Austin frowned as they drove around the lake. "Where would a redheaded hippie waiter looking for good tips go first?"

Rebecca didn't hesitate. "The Golden Eagle Lodge. It's where the old money goes. It's been here forever."

"Then we'll start there," he replied, and headed for the other side of the lake.

The Golden Eagle had always been Rebecca's favorite resort on the lake. Built of log and native stone at the turn of the century, it looked like the kind of place Teddy Roosevelt would have come with his Rough Riders. Other fancier places, with hot tubs and big-screen TVs, had sprung up around the lake, but the Golden Eagle remained the same. There was no fancy electronic equipment in the rooms, there weren't even any TVs. Tea was served in the afternoons, guests were expected to dress for dinner, and no music more current than 1949 was played at the Saturday night dances.

In the modern world, it was an anachronism that should have closed its doors years ago. It was stuffy, old-fashioned, snobbish. But the rich and famous flocked there, not only for the peace and quiet, but the tradition. It fairly wallowed in understated class.

And on a Saturday afternoon in the summer, the place was a beehive of activity. Every tennis court was in use, swimmers and boaters laughed and splashed in the water, and the older guests either played croquet on the lawn or sat on the veranda or on the tree-shaded patio, enjoying tea and the lodge's famous butter cookies.

Squeezing his rental car into the public lot rather than letting the lodge's valet take care of the parking, Austin came around the car to open the door for Rebecca. Already searching for Bryan Walker, he studied the lodge and its landscaped grounds with a frown. "Walker may have come here looking for work, but I doubt that he was hired. He's just not the right type."

"How can you say that?" she asked as they started up the stone walkway to the lodge entrance. "You've never seen him."

"No, but you have, and according to you, he's got long red hair and an earring." Nodding toward the side veranda, where white-coated waiters were solicitously serving afternoon tea, he said, "There's not a hippie in sight."

Rebecca's gaze followed his, and she had to admit, he had a point. Both the waiters and the guests all wore their hair conservatively cut. Regardless of how good a waiter he was, Bryan Walker would never fit in at the Golden Eagle. "Okay, maybe we need to rethink this."

Not one to leave any stone unturned, Austin still checked with the restaurant manager to make sure no one fitting Bryan Walker's description had been hired recently. He wasn't surprised when he learned that Walker had inquired about a job, but had been turned away.

"Well, at least we know he's here, just like Bongo Jim said. Now all we've got to do is find him."

That turned out to be more time-consuming than either Austin or Rebecca had anticipated. Because of its proximity to the city, Big Bear was a very popular weekend getaway for the L.A. crowd, and there were a number of large resorts in the area that employed a surprising number of people. Trying to find one lone redheaded waiter was like trying to find the proverbial needle in a haystack.

Frustrated, Austin was about to pull his hair out when he and Rebecca walked into the restaurant at the Redwood Inn and there he was. Stopping dead in his tracks, he said, "My God, it's him. It's gotta be. Look at that hair."

"Where?" Her gaze following his across the restaurant, Rebecca sighed in relief at the sight of the tall, thin young man taking an order at a table for six. Bright red hair, confined in a ponytail, trailed down his back. "Thank God! I was beginning to wonder if I'd imagined him."

"You gave a hell of a good description of him," he said with a grin. "He does look like a hippie. All he needs is a tie-dyed T-shirt and sandals, and he'd look like he just stepped out of a commune. C'mon. Let's go see what he knows."

Eleven

Unfortunately, there wasn't a lot that Bryan Walker could tell them. "Yeah, man, I worked that party. It was radical. I got combat pay!"

"But did you see where the shot came from?" Austin urged, suppressing a smile. Young and brash, Walker didn't seem to take much in life seriously. "You were seen at the back of the crowd, serving champagne right before the toasts began. Did you see anyone acting suspicious or angry? Was there anyone who looked like they weren't in the partying mood?"

Bryan gave the question serious consideration, only to shrug. "You gotta remember there were a lot of people there. And that Roberts dude, the caterer, he really cracked the whip on us waiters. At the end, right before the toasts, he was all over our backs to get the champagne out, so all I was really looking for was people with empty glasses."

"What about before then?" Rebecca asked quietly. "Earlier in the evening? Did you notice anyone who looked moody or mad? Anyone who didn't mingle with the other guests and just stuck to themselves?"

His brow wrinkled in a frown, he thought back. "I don't know. Maybe. There were a lot of people that didn't look like they were thrilled to be there. I remember this one tall dude—he sort of favored the old man—didn't look like he was very happy about something. And some people didn't want to join in the toast. But maybe they just didn't like champagne. And then there was Mrs. Colton. Geez, she was nearly as bad as Roberts, hounding us to make sure everybody's glass was full for the toast. That bunch doesn't lighten up much, do they?"

"I wasn't there that night," Austin said, "but it sounds like it was a pretty tense party. After the shooting, did you notice anyone rushing to leave?"

"Yeah," he retorted with a crooked grin. "Everybody. Can you blame them? There was a nut running around with a gun and no one knew who it was. If the cops hadn't come when they had, the whole crowd would have run out and I'd have been right behind them."

Austin had to smile at the image of three hundred people running out of Joe's house with Walker right on their tail. "That would have been something to see."

The grandfather clock in the foyer of the inn struck the hour, signalling the end of the younger man's break. Grimacing, he said, "Sorry I couldn't be much help, but that's all I know."

"No problem," Austin said, offering him his hand. "Thanks."

"Well, at least it wasn't a complete bust," Rebecca said as the younger man hurried back to work. "Who do you think the tall man was he mentioned? He said he looked like Joe. Do you think he was talking about some-one in the family?''

''Maybe. Maybe not. There were a lot of people there that night. It could have been anyone from Rand to Jackson to one of the guests who just happened to have the same coloring and build. And just because somebody didn't look very happy doesn't mean they were the shooter. From what everyone's said, Meredith didn't have a good night that night, but we know she wasn't the shooter.''

So once again they were at a dead end. Austin didn't exactly say that, but Rebecca could see that frustrated look in his eyes, and she couldn't blame him. He'd worked so hard over the last few weeks, tracking down every lead, and he had little to show for it.

''Why don't we forget the investigation for now and get something to eat?'' she suggested. ''It's been a long time since breakfast.''

They had, in fact, skipped lunch because they hadn't wanted to take the time to eat until after they found Walker. They hadn't realized the search was going to take most of the afternoon. ''There's a great seafood place down the road,'' she said as they stepped out on the front porch of the inn. ''Or we could get a hamburger some-where. What sounds good to you?''

The words were hardly out of her mouth when there was a sudden crack of thunder from above. Startled, they both looked up and realized that while they'd been hunting all over Big Bear for Bryan Walker, the weather had taken a turn for the worse. The wind had shifted, bringing in storm clouds that had been gathering overhead all af-ternoon, and suddenly, the day had turned dark and om-inous. A cold wind slapped them in the face, and an instant later, the skies opened up. In the time it took to blink, it was pouring.

"Well, I guess that answers that question," Austin said wryly, over another rumble of thunder. "Looks like we're eating here."

Turning, they hurried back inside to the inn restaurant, and within minutes, found themselves seated at a window table that overlooked the lake. When Bryan Walker waited on them, they couldn't help but laugh over the ironies of fate. They should have come there for lunch and they wouldn't have had to spend the whole afternoon looking for him.

Casting an eye at the dark, stormy skies, Austin frowned as streetlights came on outside. It wasn't that late, but evening was already upon them. "It looks like it's going to be a nasty night."

"It's just a summer storm," Rebecca replied, watching the wind whip through the trees. "It'll probably blow itself out while we're eating."

That sounded good, but as Bryan brought the ribeye Austin had ordered and Rebecca's blackened walleye, the storm showed no sign of lessening. If anything, it worsened. Lightning streaked across the dark sky, while the rain came down in blowing sheets. Once or twice, the lights even flickered.

His face grim, Austin finished his steak and scowled out at the wild night. "I'm not looking forward to driving in this."

Rebecca could well understand that. They had to take a narrow, winding road down the side of a mountain to get back home. She didn't relish the idea of making that drive in a thunderstorm, herself.

"We could stay the night," she suggested, "and go back in the morning. Joe's got a cabin here and as far as

I know, no one's using it this weekend. He wouldn't mind if we spent the night.''

''Won't it be locked?''

''There's a key under a rock by the back door,'' she replied. ''I haven't been there in years, but I think I can find it—if I can remember where the cabin is.''

''*If?*''

Grinning, she said, ''I think it's over somewhere by the fire department. I'll know it when I see it.''

He groaned at that, but they really didn't have much choice. All the lake resorts were booked solid for the weekend, and there wouldn't be any hotel rooms available in the nearby towns, not when the weather was so bad. If they couldn't find the cabin, they'd have to drive all the way home in the storm.

''Then I guess we'd better go look for it before it gets any later,'' he said, reaching for the check. ''We may still have to drive home.''

The storm was fiercer than ever when they ran to the car a few minutes later. Thunder boomed overhead like exploding bombs, and any second, Rebecca expected to be struck dead by lightning. Still, she couldn't help but laugh as she and Austin ran through puddles in the parking lot, splashing water up to their knees, while the rain pelted down on them. She felt like a six-year-old.

''Silly,'' he said fondly, ruffling her dripping hair as they finally tumbled into his rental car. ''This is crazy!''

''But it's a fun crazy,'' she laughed. ''Who would have thought when we left town this morning that we'd be running in the rain this evening?''

''Not me,'' he said with a grin, starting the car with a flick of his wrist. ''Otherwise, I'd have brought some dry clothes to put on. I hope Joe has something at the cabin I can wear."

"If we can find the cabin." Her eyes twinkling in the glare of a brilliant flash of lightning, she said, "Turn right...I think."

She wasn't kidding when she'd said she wasn't exactly sure where the cabin was. She'd only been there a couple of times, and the last was years ago. She had a vague recollection of the place being near the water and surrounded by trees, but what cabin on the lake wasn't?

"Okay," she said after they'd made three wrong turns and ended up in the driveways of three different houses that didn't look anything like the small log cabin she remembered, "just sit here a second and let me think. The sun sets across the lake from the cabin."

"Then we're on the right side of the lake, at least," Austin said, checking the compass directly over the car's rearview mirrors. "You must have gone swimming when you were here. Could you see the marina from the shore?"

"Yes, you could!" she said excitedly, only just remembering. "It was to the right!"

"Now, we're getting somewhere," Austin said, and turned at the next corner.

With the windshield wipers beating out a steady rhythm and the rain pounding on the roof, they slowly drove down the winding streets, searching in the darkness for the right cabin. Set back on its lot and surrounded by trees, they would have missed it completely if lightning hadn't chosen that exact moment to light up the sky.

"That's it!"

"Where?"

Pointing to the trees off to the right ahead of them, she

said, "There. I remember now. There's a big rock by the driveway. See it?"

The headlights picked the large boulder out of the darkness, and just beyond it was the narrow drive that wound through the trees to where the dark cabin sat huddled in the rainy night. "Thank God," Rebecca sighed. "I was beginning to think we'd never find it."

It may have taken a few wrong turns to find the place, but she wasn't mistaken about the key. Dodging raindrops, she sprinted around to the back porch and quickly found the rock at the foot of the steps. It was right where she remembered it had been, and the key was safely tucked underneath it.

"Ta-da!" she crowed, holding up the key for Austin to see in the flash of lightning overhead. "Told you."

If they hadn't both been soaking wet and chilled, Austin would have liked nothing more than to grab her and kiss her. Her hair was dripping in her eyes, her clothes were plastered to her body, and her makeup had worn off hours ago. But she was still the most beautiful woman he'd ever seen in his life. And she didn't even know it. That never ceased to amaze him.

"Yes, you did," he said, grinning, and found that he couldn't resist her, after all. Leaning over, he kissed her full on the mouth and caught her completely off guard. She sighed softly and leaned into him and the kiss. In the next instant, he had the key. "Last one in gets to carry in the firewood." And before she could get her wits about her, he turned and bolted up the stairs to the back door.

"Hey, that's not fair!" she cried, laughing as she ran after him. "You didn't say ready, set, go."

"Ready, set, go," he rattled off quickly as he unlocked the door and flipped on the lights in the kitchen.

They were both still laughing when thunder boomed overhead and the lights went out.

"Oh!"

In the dark, Austin immediately found her hand and tangled his fingers with hers. "It's okay," he said huskily. "Lightning must have hit the transformer. Do you know where Joe and Meredith keep the candles?"

"Not here, no. But at home, they keep them in the drawer next to the refrigerator."

"Then they probably do the same thing here," he said. "Let's look."

Outside, lightning flashed again, lighting their way to the cabinet next to the refrigerator. "All right," he said in satisfaction as his fingers closed on not only candles, but matches as well. "Let's shed a little light on the subject." And with a strike of a match, they once again had light, albeit a small one.

Over the flickering flame, Rebecca's dancing eyes met his. "My hero."

"Just call me Superman," he chuckled. "You can call me Super for short, if you like."

Grinning, Rebecca knew it was crazy—they were both cold and wet and looked like a couple of drowned rats—but she couldn't remember the last time she'd been so happy. "C'mon, Super, I'll give you a candlelit tour."

The cabin consisted of two bedrooms, a living room, and kitchen, and was furnished with sturdy furniture that had withstood time and the Colton clan. There'd been a time when Joe and Meredith had loved to come there to fish and relax and just get away from the pressures of life, but that was years ago, when they were younger and both happier. Finding their old fishing clothes hanging in the closet, Rebecca couldn't help but be saddened by that.

"Hey, why the long face?" Austin said when her smile

faded. "It's not the Hilton, but the roof doesn't leak and there's a stack of dry wood by the fireplace in the living room that should last us all night. We've got it made."

"I know," she said, forcing a smile. "Don't pay any attention to me. I was just thinking about Joe and Meredith and the way things were when I first came to live at the ranch."

"They were closer."

She nodded. "They've grown so far apart, and I just think that's so sad. What happened?"

"It's just life," he said with a shrug. "People change as they get older. That doesn't mean they don't love each other. They just have different interests than they once did, and sometimes that takes them in opposite directions for a while. Give them some time. They'll find their way back to each other."

She hoped so, but it just seemed like they'd been unhappy for so long. "I'm afraid it's too late."

Outside, the wind howled around the house, sending chill bumps racing over Rebecca's bare arms. Seeing her shiver, Austin frowned. "Why don't you change out of those wet clothes while I light a fire? You're freezing."

She couldn't deny it. Suddenly, she was practically shaking with cold. "While I'm at it, I think I'll take a hot bath."

"Good idea. Let me put a couple of candles in there for you."

Within seconds, he had the bathroom all ready for her. Two squat candles sat on the vanity, their twin flames emitting a soft glow that filled the room with just enough light, while hot, steaming water filled the tub. Sending up a silent prayer of thanks that the hot water heater was gas and not electric, Rebecca grabbed some clothes from Meredith's closet, thanked Austin for his help, and shut the bathroom door in his face. Within seconds, she was up to her neck in hot water.

How long she lay there just like that, she couldn't have said. It could have been minutes or hours. Austin checked on her once, knocking on the door to make sure she hadn't fallen asleep in the tub, then left her alone to relax. It was wonderful. By the time the water started to lose its warmth and she finally stepped from the tub, she felt like a new woman. And Meredith's clothes, while not an exact fit, were warm and comfortable and infinitely better than her own wet ones.

Spreading everything out to dry, she carefully picked up the two candles and went in search of Austin. Not surprisingly, she found him in the living room in front of the fireplace, adding another log to the fire.

Stopping at the entrance to the living room, she couldn't help but appreciate the cozy scene. He'd set out a dozen candles around the room to chase away the darkness, then gathered a couple of old quilts and pillows from the bedroom and spread them out on the floor between the hearth and the old couch positioned in front of the fireplace. Just that easily, he'd made the room warm, romantic and intimate.

It was Austin, however, she couldn't take her eyes from. He, too, had changed. And even though the old jeans and denim shirt he wore were a size too large, he looked incredibly handsome. His chestnut hair had dried, and in the firelight, it glistened with gold. Watching him as he tended the fire with a poker, she suddenly ached to touch him.

She didn't make a sound, but he looked up suddenly and smiled at the sight of her, and just that easily, he melted her heart. "Wow!" he said, whistling softly. "You look fantastic!"

With the heat of the fire reflected in his emerald green eyes, he let his gaze roam over her and had no idea what he did to her with just a look. Color climbing into her cheeks, she adjusted the collar of her blue plaid shirt and smiled shyly. "So do you. I feel like a kid playing dressup in my mother's clothes. Did you ever do that?"

"What?" he teased as she joined him in front of the fire. "Wear my mother's clothes?"

"No, silly! Play dressup. Or is that a girl thing?"

Grinning, he settled on the floor next to her and leaned back against the couch. "It seems to me I remember stomping around in my father's boots and thinking I could wear his overcoat when I was about five. I think that's when I tripped and fell and broke my nose."

"Oh, no!"

"Oh, yes!" he chuckled. "Trust me, I never did that again. I walked around with two black eyes for a week."

"You poor baby. But look at your nose today. It looks great!" When he just gave her a wry look, she giggled and impulsively leaned over and kissed him on the nose.

And just that quickly, everything changed.

Outside, the storm continued to rage, but all she saw was the surprise that flared in Austin's eyes...and a need that matched her own. That was when she realized she'd been wanting to kiss him all day.

Her heart thumping crazily in her breast, she lifted fingers that weren't quite steady to the chiseled line of his jaw. "Do you mind?" she asked softly. "I really want to kiss you."

"I'd be disappointed if you didn't," he said in a voice as rough as sandpaper. "You can kiss me whenever you like, wherever you like."

Where she liked was the side of his neck. Leaning closer, she pressed a featherlight kiss there and felt his start of surprise. Smiling, she lingered there for just a second, drawing in the intoxicating scent of him. She could smell the rain on him and the fresh scent of the pine trees that surrounded the cabin, and with a quiet murmur, she pressed another kiss to the side of his neck just below his ear.

"Rebecca...honey..."

Afraid he was going to tell her to stop, she pulled back slightly, but only so she could change positions and cover his mouth with hers. Nibbling on his bottom lip, she felt a groan rip through him and loved the idea that she could do that to him. With a soft sigh of pleasure, she slipped her arms around his neck and gave in to the need to tangle her tongue with his.

Heat flared deep inside her, fireworks exploded behind her closed eyelids, and Rebecca couldn't think of anything but Austin and the way he made her feel. When they stretched out on the quilts in front of the fire, she couldn't have said. It just seemed so natural. She was in his arms and lying down with him, and *she wasn't afraid!* It was wonderful, fantastic. And she loved it.

Holding him close, not wanting to ever let him go, she dragged his hand to her breast. "Touch me," she whispered against his mouth. "I need you to touch me."

"Are you sure? Honey, I don't want to do anything to frighten you."

"You won't," she assured him. "You couldn't. Austin, please..."

He couldn't have denied her for all the money in Switzerland. Not tonight. Not when she kissed him without restrictions, as if she couldn't get through the night without one more soul-destroying kiss. His thoughts blurring, he covered her mouth with his and gave in to the need that burned low and hot in his belly.

One soft, hungry kiss blended into another while the fire crackled in the fireplace and the candles burned low, and quiet intimacy settled over them. Their clothes seemed to melt away piece by piece and they discovered what made each other sigh, shudder, cry out in pleasure. Then, with their mouths they retraced the paths their hands had made.

Caught up in the taste and heat and wonder of her, Austin forgot his own name. There was only Rebecca. Sweet, giving, incredibly, surprisingly sexy Rebecca. With a touch, she stole his breath; with a slow, languid kiss, she made him want her more than any other woman ever had. And when she whispered his name in the dark of the night, she made him hers.

"Oh, honey," he groaned, kissing her fiercely. "You don't know what you do to me. I want you so much."

"Then make love to me," she whispered, and pulled him on top of her.

With that, he lost any chance of keeping his head. Shadows danced on the walls, but all he saw was Rebecca—her face, the flush of desire that turned her soft skin pink, the desire that darkened her eyes to midnight blue—as he slowly, carefully entered her. In the glow of the firelight, she was stunningly beautiful...and his. Murmuring her name, he linked his fingers with hers and began to move.

After that, there was no time to think of anything but each other and the emotions that swamped them from all sides. Need, desire, love. The fierceness of the storm moved inside, and within seconds they were caught up in its wild energy. Their hearts pounded and their breath tore through their lungs. The fierceness of the night was in their blood, driving them on and on. Just when they couldn't stand the wonder of it another second, lightning flashed and thunder roared. And with a startled shout, they both shattered.

Cradling Rebecca close, Austin knew that for the first time since Jenny had died he hadn't just had sex—he'd actually made love. When had he fallen in love with her? he wondered, shaken. How? He'd been so sure that it wasn't possible for him to ever love anyone, not after the way he'd loved Jenny. But then again, he'd never met anyone quite like Rebecca.

Dear God, he loved her! Just thinking about her made him smile. And when he held her, kissed her, the pain of the past faded and all was right with his world. She made him feel whole again. How could he not love her?

The words trembling on his tongue, he almost told her right then and there. Love was meant to be shared, and he needed to tell her. But before he could say anything, she stirred in his arms and suddenly hugged him fiercely. "Oh, Austin, that was wonderful! I never knew…never expected…"

Words failed her and when she drew back just far enough to see his face, he grinned. "I know. That was pretty damn special."

"And I wasn't scared! Did you notice? I didn't get the shakes or anything, even when you held me tight. We made love and I was right there with you every step of the way. I still can't believe it!"

She was bubbling with excitement and happier than he had ever seen her, and that, he realized, was why he couldn't tell her he loved her. She'd never done this before, never thought she *could* do it, and if he told her how he felt now, it would be all too easy for her to confuse her own feelings for love.

That was the last thing he wanted. He'd waited years

for her. She was the most precious thing in the world to him, and he wasn't going to blow this. When he told her he loved her, he wanted to make sure she was clearheaded and there was no chance that she would mistake sex for love.

The words would come later, he promised himself. But that didn't mean he couldn't show her how he felt now. Especially when she was so beautifully, gloriously naked, and she didn't even seem to realize it. Grinning, he reached for her. "Believe it," he growled, and kissed her again.

Over the course of the next twenty-four hours, Rebecca lost track of how many times they made love. Sated, she slept in Austin's arms, only to wake hours later and make love all over again. It was wonderful, fantastic, incredible, like something out of a fantasy that she didn't want to ever end.

But they couldn't hide away in the cabin forever. Sunday seemed to fly by, and before Rebecca was ready for it, it was time to return to the real world.

"Hey, don't look so down," Austin teased as they left the lake behind and began the long drive home. Taking her hand, he linked his fingers with hers on the center console and gave her a reassuring squeeze. "We'll come back someday. Joe won't mind."

She desperately wanted to believe him, but as they drew closer to town, she felt more and more unsure of where she stood with him. Over the course of the last two days, he'd made no mention of how he felt about her or of the future. Had the weekend and their lovemaking meant anything to him? Did he care that once he discovered who tried to kill Joe, he would return to Portland and they wouldn't, in all likelihood, see each other again except at rare family functions? Had he thought that far ahead at all? Or had the weekend just been about sex for him?

Confused and hurt, she wanted to ask, but she couldn't. Not without sounding like a sixteen-year-old making a fool of herself over the first boy who'd kissed her. She wouldn't do that to herself or him. She loved him, more than she'd ever thought it was possible to love anyone. She should have been laughing with joy and dancing in the rain. Finally, she knew what it was like to love a man! Instead, she'd never been so low in her life. If he loved her, wouldn't he have said so?

Fighting tears, she stared blindly out the passenger window and said, "I guess it's just the weather. Rainy Sundays always depress me."

"Let's put on some music then," he said, switching on the radio, only to wince when nothing but static poured from the speakers. "See if you can find something decent."

Thankful to have something to do, she fiddled with the dials until she was finally able to tune in a jazz station. But it did little to improve her mood. By the time they finally reached Prosperino and Austin drove her home, all she wanted to do was go inside, throw herself on her bed and cry her eyes out.

And she couldn't hide it. The minute she turned to him and told him that he didn't have to escort her to her front door in the rain, he got a good look at her face and knew something was wrong. "What is it? What's wrong? This is a lot more than just the rain. Do you want to talk about it?"

Yes! she wanted to cry, but it was too late for that. When she'd accepted his invitation to Big Bear, she'd never dreamed she'd be gone all weekend. She had clothes she needed to wash for work tomorrow, not to mention lesson plans to prepare for the week. It would take what was left of the night just to do that.

"I can't," she said. "Maybe another time."

He wanted to argue, but she looked so fragile, he was afraid she'd shatter if he pushed her. Still, he had no intention of sitting in the car like some kind of fool while she walked herself to her door. "C'mon," he said gruffly. "I'll walk you to the door."

She didn't, thankfully, give him a hard time about that, and seconds later, he unlocked her front door and handed her the key. "I'll call you later," he said, frowning down at her. "Are you sure you're okay?"

"I'm fine," she assured him. "Stop worrying."

He wanted to believe her, but as they'd drawn closer and closer to Prosperino, all the joy from last night had gradually faded from her eyes. And he didn't mind admitting that had him worried. Something had definitely upset her, but she wasn't ready to talk about it, and until she was, there was nothing he could do.

Frustrated, he forced a smile. "Okay. But if you need to talk, call me. I don't care what time it is."

He kissed her then because he hated to see her so sad. Because he loved her and couldn't stop himself. Because he didn't want to leave her. And if she'd said one word, just one—stay—he would have. But she didn't.

And that hurt. Left with no choice, he said, "I'll call you later." Kissing her on the cheek, he turned and walked away.

He truly meant to call her. He could think of nothing but her all the way back to the hotel. But when he got back to his room, there were ten messages on his phone from Nate Thompson, an old friend in Portland. Surprised, he listened to one message after another and could make little sense of them except that Nate's business partner had run off with half the company's assets.

Scowling, he immediately punched in Nate's number. "What the hell's going on?" he greeted his friend. "What's this about Dennis embezzling money? Are you sure? The guy's a wienie. He wouldn't have the guts to take a nickel that didn't belong to him."

"Don't kid yourself," Nate said bitterly. "The bastard was stringing us along, wanting everyone to think he was a numbers cruncher who was afraid of his own shadow. But it was just an act. He's been draining me dry for the last two months, taking everything that wasn't nailed down, then setting it up to look like I did it! Dammit, I was arrested yesterday!"

Austin swore and grabbed pen and paper. "Give me the details."

Twenty minutes later, he had everything he needed…and enough work to keep him busy the rest of the night. "I'll do what I can, man," he assured Nate. "I'll call you in the morning."

"My butt's toast if you don't track down the money trail, Austin," he said somberly. "He had all the access codes, everything he needed to take whatever he wanted. If you can't find where he hid the money, I'm going to jail."

"It's not going to come to that," Austin replied. "I know it's hard, but try not to panic. I'm not going to let anything happen to you."

Confident of his ability, Austin meant every word. Nate was one of his oldest friends, and Austin didn't stand by with his hands in his pockets when someone he cared about was in trouble. He'd do whatever he could to help. He booted up his laptop and began the tedious task of trying to track down money that Dennis LeRue had squirreled away God only knew where, he found himself chasing shadows. He worked long into the night, and as one hour gave way to another, then another, it became increasingly obvious that this wasn't something he was going to be able to do from a distance. He had to go back to Portland.

Twelve

He didn't want to leave Rebecca.

The thought nagged at him the rest of the night, making it impossible to work, to sleep, to do anything but restlessly pace his hotel room. When he'd first made arrangements to come to California, he'd known it was only for a limited time, and he'd been fine with that. He'd do his duty by the family, find whoever was trying to kill Joe, then head back to Portland where he belonged.

It had all sounded so simple. But that was before he'd known that Joe had more enemies than a con man. And before he found himself falling in love with Rebecca.

Dammit, he fumed, what was he supposed to do now? His life, his friends, his business, were all in Portland. And Rebecca was here. This was where she felt safe, where her roots were, where Joe and Meredith and the rest of her foster family was. How could he ask her to

leave that and go to another state, another city, where she
would know no one?

Frustrated, he almost called her in the middle of the
night. They needed to talk. But even as he reached for the
phone, he knew this was a conversation they needed to
have face-to-face. But first he had to talk to Joe. He'd
made him a promise he'd find the man who tried to kill
him, and now he was going to have to renege on that
promise. The least he owed him was an explanation.

It was barely seven when Austin showed up at the
ranch, but he wasn't surprised to find Joe already at breakfast. His uncle was one of those type A personalities who
had too much energy to lie in bed in the morning like a
slug. For as long as Austin could remember, the family
had teased Joe about making his first million before most
people were even out of bed in the morning. If he ever
slept in, it was time to call the doctor.

Seeing him now, Austin could believe it. In the process
of taking his first sip of coffee of the day, Joe smiled
broadly at the sight of him. "Hey, what are you doing
here so bright and early on a Monday morning?" With a
nod of his head, he motioned to the buffet, where Inez
had set out a tempting array of rolls, muffins and danishes.
"Grab something to eat and some coffee and sit down
and tell me what's going on. I hope you've got some news
for me."

He had news, all right, but Austin doubted that he
would see it as good. "Finish eating. This can wait," he
told him as he stepped over to the buffet and poured a
cup of coffee. "Where's Meredith? Sleeping in?"

"No, she took the boys to school," he replied. "She
spent the weekend in Palm Springs, so she felt like she
needed to give them a little extra attention this morning."

"No kidding? What was she doing in Palm Springs?"

"Pampering herself at a new spa. She said she needed a break because of the shooting."

That was one way to deal with stress, though not the way Austin would have chosen, but he couldn't blame her for needing a break. "She was standing right next to you when the shot was fired. That's got to haunt her. Not only did she see you almost get killed, but she must be wondering what would have happened if the shooter's aim had been off. She could be dead right now."

Startled, Joe nearly choked on his coffee. "Do you think the shooter was after her instead of me?"

Taking a seat at the table, Austin shrugged. "Whenever you've got bullets flying around, you've got to consider the possibility that they could be meant for anyone. Meredith doesn't have any enemies, though—at least not that anyone's mentioned—so I doubt she was the target. You, on the other hand," he added dryly, "have any number of friends and acquaintances who would like to blow your head off."

Grinning, Joe didn't deny it. "People shouldn't be so damn sensitive. Everybody takes everything so personally nowadays. They don't understand that business is business."

Austin just rolled his eyes. "It's that kind of arrogance that probably almost got you killed. You need to make peace with some of these people, Joe. You know it's the right thing to do."

"The only peace some of them want is a piece of me. But I'm trying," he added when Austin gave him a hard look. "Rebecca suggested I might need sensitivity classes. So how are the two of you doing? I noticed she's been helping you a lot with the case."

Austin knew what he was asking—just how close were

they getting?—but he had no intention of going there. Until he'd had time to talk to Rebecca and find out if she loved him as much as he loved her, he wasn't discussing their relationship with anyone.

"She's been very helpful," he said easily.

Waiting for him to go on, Joe prompted, "And?"

"And nothing."

Irritated, Joe scowled. "Is that all you can say? I was hoping—"

Suddenly realizing what he was saying, he snapped his mouth shut, but it was too late. Austin was on to him. Giving him a narrow-eyed look that had made more than one guilty party squirm in his seat over the years, he said silkily, "Don't stop there, uncle. Just what exactly were you hoping?"

"Nothing," he said innocently. "Nothing at all." Abruptly changing the subject, he nodded at the oversized envelope Austin had brought with him. "What's that?"

Austin knew exactly what he was doing, but he was just as thankful for the distraction as Joe. "It's my report on the investigation."

Surprised, Joe reached for it eagerly. "You've finished?"

"Not exactly, but I've been called back to Portland on an emergency." Quickly telling him about Nate and the money his partner had embezzled from him, he said, "Nate's an old friend, and I can't turn my back on him when he needs help. And to be perfectly honest, I'm not any closer to solving the case than I was the day I came to town."

He hated like hell to admit that, but there was no getting around it. "I've got a list of suspects a mile long, some more suspicious than others, but nobody stands out in the crowd. And that irritates me. You called me down here to do a job for you, and I haven't done it. I'm sorry about that.''

"Don't be ridiculous,'' Joe said with a scowl. "The police have had a whole team of detectives on the case for weeks, and they haven't been able to solve it, either. So don't you dare apologize. We may never know who the shooter was. Unless he tries again.''

Austin wanted to tell him that wasn't going to happen, but they both knew it could. "Thanks for understanding,'' he said gruffly. "I want you to know that just because I have to leave doesn't mean I'm giving up on the case. I just have to put it aside for a while.''

"Don't worry about it,'' Joe said as they both rose from the table and shook hands. "Nothing's going to happen fast around here, so go ahead and help your friend find his money before that bastard partner of his buries it in the Caymans and it's lost to him forever. He needs you right now more than I do. And who knows? The police may turn up something while you're gone.''

The front door slammed then, and they both turned to see Meredith walk in from taking the boys to school. Dressed in a simple cotton dress and sandals, she looked rested and almost like the old Meredith Austin remembered from his childhood. Then she saw him and she immediately stiffened. "You're an early bird this morning. What's going on?''

She made no attempt to hide the hostility she felt for him, but Austin didn't take it personally. If he'd been in her shoes, he probably would have felt just as hostile. Someone had tried to kill her husband, and all the detectives investigating the case could talk about were their suspicions of her and the rest of the family.

"Austin just came by to give me a report on the case

and say goodbye,'' Joe replied before he could say anything. "He's going back to Portland."

"Goodbye?" she repeated, turning to Austin with widened eyes. "Did something happen while I was in Palm Springs? I didn't realize you'd found the shooter."

"I haven't," he said, "but something's come up in Portland that I've got to take care of, and I'm not sure when I'll be able to work on the case again."

"I was just thanking him for all his help and wishing him a safe trip home," Joe added. "The case will still be here when he gets back."

"But what about the shooter?" she asked worriedly. "He's still walking around. What if he tries something again?"

"If someone's going to kill me, they're going to do it whether Austin's here or not," he retorted. "That's just a chance we'll have to take."

"I don't think you have anything to worry about," Austin told them both. "Whoever the shooter is, he's not an idiot. He knows the police are still on the case. You can bet he's not going to do anything until things quiet down again, and that could take months."

"So don't get your nerves in a twist," Joe told Meredith pointedly. "You don't need to run off to Palm Springs again. Everything's fine."

At any other time, Patsy would have sent him a murderous glare, but not today. Oh, no, not when she was feeling so good. Let him have his condescending attitude, she would have the last laugh. Austin was giving up! He might claim he had an emergency, but he wasn't fooling her. He was running back to Portland with his tail between his legs because he didn't have a clue who the shooter was and knew he never would.

If she wouldn't be giving herself away, Patsy would

have laughed right in his and Joe's faces. They'd both thought they were so smart. Joe had gone on and on about Austin and what a terrific detective he was—he was smarter than the police. He'd find the shooter. Yeah, right. He hadn't done squat! And she was thrilled. Now if the police would just drop the case, too, she'd be home free.

Not that she was worried, she assured herself smugly. Thaddeus Law was an idiot—she didn't have to worry about him or those bumbling jackasses he worked with. They didn't suspect a thing about the poison—or who she really was—and she was going to make sure things stayed that way. Her new friend, Mr. Pike, would take care of that sniveling little brat, Emily, and then there'd be only one person left in the entire world who could ruin things for her.

Meredith.

Sweet, wonderful Meredith, she thought bitterly. Everyone had always thought she was such a little angel, so kind and giving and loving. They'd never seen her for what she really was—a selfish bitch who didn't care about anyone but herself.

Fifteen years, she raged silently. She'd lost fifteen years of her life, her baby daughter, Jewel, and the childhood she hadn't been able to share with her, and any chance for happiness in the future. All because of Meredith. And now, God only knew where her sainted sister was. If there was any kind of justice in the world, she'd gone completely batty after she'd been released from the St. James clinic and was now living on the street out of a shopping cart.

Stark images flashed before her mind's eye at the thought, and it was all Patsy could do not to laugh in triumph. Revenge really was a wonderful thing. And she wasn't through with her dear sister yet. Oh, no. Not by a long shot. It might take him awhile, but Edward Garrison would find Meredith for her. And when he did, she'd have another little *job* for Mr. Pike to take care of for her. Then she would finally be safe and no one would ever be able to hurt her again.

That's the day she would celebrate with the finest bottle of champagne in Joe's wine cellar. In the meantime, she hugged the thought to herself and once again played the role of sweet, loving, concerned Meredith. If she nearly choked on the part, no one had to know that but her.

"It isn't that my nerves are in a twist. I just don't like the idea of a nutcase walking around with a gun. But if Austin's not concerned, then I don't need to be, either. After all, he's the expert."

Pasting a deliberately cheerful smile on her face, she gave Austin a hug that didn't hold an ounce of true affection. "Well, I've got to go—I've got a hair appointment. Have a safe trip home, and make sure you call when you come back to town. Joe sleeps better when he knows everything that's going on with the investigation."

And so did she. But for completely different reasons than Joe. She didn't like surprises. But now that Austin was definitely leaving, there wouldn't be much chance of that. Feeling like she'd just won the lottery and didn't have to share it with anyone, she wished Austin a safe trip home and sailed out to her hair appointment, laughing all the way.

"Martha, thank God you're back!" Rushing into the therapist's office, Louise hugged her and found herself on the verge of tears. "I've been frantic to talk to you!"

"So I've heard," she said, returning her embrace. "The minute I came in this morning, Julie told me you'd called to move up your appointment. What's going on? We were going to meet at your house on Friday, weren't we? What's happened?''

Not surprised that Martha had jumped to the conclusion that something was wrong—very little had gone right over their last few months of therapy—she smiled tremulously, her brown eyes shining. ''Nothing's wrong. At least I don't think there is. I just went out with Lucas and...''

''What? It was a success? A disaster? What?''

''I remembered him.''

Thanks to all their sessions, Martha didn't have to ask who. In all the times she'd been Louise's therapist, there had always been only one ''him.'' Without a word, she shut the door to her office so they could talk undisturbed, then waited for Louise to take a seat on the chaise lounge that often helped patients relax. ''Tell me,'' she said quietly.

Louise needed little more encouragement than that. It seemed like she'd waited a month instead of just the weekend for Martha to return from Chicago, and the second she sat down, the words just came tumbling out. ''There's no name. No face. I know that must sound silly to you, and I can't tell you any more about him than I did the last time we discussed him.''

''But you can tell me more about you, can't you?'' Martha said with a small, understanding smile. ''That's why you're so excited. You don't know the details, but you've remembered another piece of the puzzle, haven't you? You remembered more of who you are?''

Just that easily, she described exactly what Louise was feeling. ''Yes! I knew you would understand. If I'd known where you were staying in Chicago, I would have called you immediately. It was wonderful and terrifying and so incredibly sad. He's out there somewhere, Martha. I can feel him.''

Her gaze drifted to the window, where the slanted blinds allowed a glimpse of the bright summer morning that seemed so alive with promise. "I don't know how to describe it," she said softly. "It's like an ache in my heart that won't go away. If I close my eyes, I can almost feel his arms around me, holding me tight against him, as if he'd never let me go."

Blinking back sudden tears, she turned her gaze back to her friend and therapist and choked, "But he did let me go, and I don't know why. Do you have any idea what that feels like? It's tearing me apart. Did he let me go, or did I just walk away? Why would I do such a thing when all these years later, I still miss him so much? Help me, Martha. Help me find him again. I don't know how we lost each other or why, but I know I have to get him back. I need him. I need what I had before. I can't take this any more."

Martha couldn't have agreed more. In all their sessions together over the years, as Louise struggled to find herself and her past, one of the things that had been the most difficult to watch was her loneliness. She was a kind, caring woman who shouldn't have been going through life alone. She had to belong to someone, somewhere. The question was, who? The answer was locked away in her own mind, and until she was ready to face her past, it would remain there.

Settling back in her own chair, she studied Louise through calm, steady eyes. "How are the nightmares?"

With a single shrug, Louise said more than she could have with a dozen words. The nightmares that haunted her nights continued to be a problem. "But I still think it's time to try hypnosis again," Louise said earnestly. "Once I remember everything, the nightmares will go away."

She was, in all likelihood, right, but it was the migraines, more than the bad dreams, that worried Martha the most. There was no doubt that there was a direct correlation between the increased severity of Louise's headaches and the recent progress she'd made under hypnosis. She was barely able to tolerate the pain now, even with medication. And it was for that very reason that Martha had stopped the hypnosis in the first place. Louise had been through so much, all of it painful. How could she possibly endure more without chancing a complete mental breakdown?

"You know my reservations on this," she replied quietly. "I can't put you at risk."

"But I already am at risk," she argued. "Can't you see that? I'm at risk every time I close my eyes at night and the dreams start. I'm at risk every time I hear a child laugh and I look around for one that looks like me. And what about when I step into my house at night and I'm met by the aching loneliness for a man I can't remember? Do you know what that does to me? How it rips me apart and threatens to destroy my soul? I can't go on this way, Martha. I have to remember...even if it kills me."

Martha liked to think that as a therapist, she was ruled by her head, not her heart. It was that mental clarity that gave her an edge with her patients and the distance she needed to do her job well. It had never been that easy with Louise, however. Right from the beginning, there'd just been something about her that had touched Martha's heart. As much as she continued to try, she couldn't keep her emotions at bay when she was dealing with a friend.

"I just don't want to put you in jeopardy," she told her, a worried frown sitting heavily on her forehead. "Not when your memory may return on its own eventually, if we're patient."

"But it's already been nearly *ten* years! How long am I supposed to be patient, Martha? How much longer am I supposed to live without my family? How much longer are they supposed to live without me? This has to end."

Put that way, Martha had no choice but to agree. If she'd been in Louise's shoes, she'd never had been able to wait this long, not without going quietly out of her mind. "Close your eyes and relax," she said quietly. "Breathe easily and think of the fountain in your garden. You can hear the water. So calm. So peaceful. Just the sound of it takes you back to another garden that you love."

"I can smell the ocean. I forgot how much I loved that." Her eyes closed and a soft smile curling the corners of her mouth, Louise breathed quietly for a few minutes, then took over the session from there. "He's here, sitting in the sun, watching me tend my flowers. I can feel him smiling."

Taking notes, Martha stiffened slightly with excitement. In all the sessions that they'd had, Louise had spoken of "him" before, but she'd never come close to describing him. Would today be the day that she finally saw his face? Martha wanted to ask, but she'd learned in the past not to be too eager. The memories would come at Louise's pace, not her own.

"And you're smiling, too," she said gently. "You're happy to have him there with you."

"Oh, yes," she sighed, content. "From the moment we first met, we just clicked. We weren't like other married couples who grew tired of each other over the years. We grew closer. We just had so much in common. There were the children and the foundation and business, of course…"

Suddenly realizing what she was saying, she frowned

and pressed a trembling hand to her temple. "M-my head h-hurts. I must have hit it. I don't remember. Why can't I remember?"

Agitated, her happy memories now gone, she shifted in her seat and Martha could almost see fear overtaking her. Hurriedly, she moved to soothe her and bring her out of the trance. They'd gone as far as they could today. "Listen to the fountain," she said softly, gently. "You are relaxed and comfortable and in a safe place. Nothing can harm you. Take a deep breath and slowly release it. That's right. You're safe, Louise. When I count to three, you will open your eyes and there will be no fear, no tension, nothing to be afraid of."

On the count of three, Louise slowly opened her eyes, and for a second, she was as calm and at peace as Martha had hoped. Then memories of the session came flooding back. Horrified, she lifted stricken eyes to Martha. "I have a husband. We have children. And I can't remember any of them. What kind of wife and mother am I?"

That, unfortunately, was a question neither she nor Martha could answer.

From the ranch, Austin drove straight to Rebecca's school, telling himself all the while that he was making a mistake. This wasn't the time to talk to her. She was working, and he had to catch a ten-thirty flight to Portland. He had all of thirty minutes to spare before he left for the airport, and a man needed a hell of a lot more time than that to tell a woman he loved her. At least, he did. Especially when the woman was Rebecca. She deserved candlelight and roses and all the romance he could give her, not a quick, "Luv you, honey," as he was running for a plane.

So what the hell was he doing? he asked himself with

a scowl as he pulled into the school parking lot. What did he hope to accomplish in thirty minutes?

The answer eluded him, but he didn't care. He just knew he couldn't leave town without telling her he loved her—even if he had to say it in front of a whole classroom full of third-graders.

Grinning at the thought, he strode into the school and stopped at the office to check in. If Richard Foster had still been working there, Austin didn't doubt that he'd have refused to let him go anywhere near Rebecca. The older woman who was temporarily in charge while the school district searched for a new principal, however, seemed happy that Rebecca had a visitor.

"She's in the middle of a literature class right now, but I'm sure she can talk to you for a few minutes," she told him with a smile. "She's in the last room at the end of the hall on the right. You can't miss her."

His footsteps echoing as he walked down the hall, Austin had to smile at the older woman's words. She didn't know how right she was. From the moment he'd sat down to dinner with her at the ranch his first night back in Prosperino, there'd never been any chance of him missing Rebecca. She'd been in his thoughts every time he turned around. And even when he was grieving for Jenny and what might have been, it was Rebecca he'd turned to. It was Rebecca he dreamed of, Rebecca he laughed with, Rebecca he loved. And if everything worked out the way he hoped, it was Rebecca he would share his future with.

Not too long ago, the very idea of that had scared the hell out of him. Now, he couldn't imagine his life without her. Smiling at how quickly things had changed, he stopped in front of her closed classroom door and knocked softly. The future started today.

* * *

He was the last person Rebecca expected to find standing at her classroom door. "Austin!" Her heart expanding at the sight of him, she wanted to step into his arms and kiss him, but twenty pairs of very young eyes watched her every move. "What are you doing here?" she asked in a low voice that wouldn't carry to curious ears. "Is something wrong?"

"I need to talk to you about something. Can you take a few minutes?"

Surprised, she nodded. "Give me just a second." Shutting the door, she turned back to her students and wasn't surprised to see Suzie Harper madly waving her hand. In another life, she surely must have been an investigative reporter. "Yes, Suzie?"

"Is that your boyfriend, Miss Powell? He's cute!"

"He's a friend, Suzie," she said, not daring to crack a smile. "And we have something very important to discuss. So while we're doing that, I'd like all of you to start reading chapter three in Harry Potter."

Thankfully, the third Harry Potter book was everyone's favorite, including Suzie's, so they were all willing to be distracted. Rebecca, however, didn't fool herself into thinking that she'd escaped all of Suzie's questions. There would be more later.

In the meantime, however, everyone hurriedly dug out their Harry Potter books, and with a sigh of relief, Rebecca slipped out into the hall and quietly shut the door behind her. "Okay," she said with a smile, "all clear. So what are you doing here? I was going to call you after work to see if you wanted to come to dinner tonight."

"I'd love to," he replied, "but I can't. I'm catching a plane for Portland this morning."

After everything they'd shared over the weekend, that

was the last thing Rebecca had expected him to say. Stricken, she could do nothing to hide the hurt that flashed in her eyes. "You're leaving?"

"Not because I want to," he assured her quickly. "But I got a call from a friend in Portland who needs my help, so I have to go back. I couldn't leave, though, without talking to you first."

Hurt still squeezing her heart, Rebecca sternly ordered herself not to cry. If a friend needed his help, he had to leave, of course. And it wasn't as if there was any kind of commitment between them. They'd made love, but there'd been no mention of the future. Just because he'd changed her life and she'd fallen head over heels in love with him didn't mean he felt the same way about her.

"I appreciate that," she said huskily. "When do you think you'll be back? You are coming back, aren't you?" she asked with a frown as it suddenly hit her that the reason he might have wanted to talk to her was to tell her goodbye. "Joe—"

"I'm not abandoning him," he said. "But this has turned out to be a lot more complicated than anyone anticipated. It's not going to be solved anytime soon. So, yes, I'll be back, but not just for the case."

Her eyes searching his, she wanted to believe that he meant he was coming back for her, but she was afraid to hope, afraid to have that hope shot down. After all these years, she'd finally found a man she could trust enough to love. If he didn't love her the same way she loved him, she didn't think she could stand to know. Not yet. Not without falling apart in front of him, and that was something she was determined not to do.

"I see," she said quietly, but didn't see anything at all. Still, she couldn't take a chance and ask him what he meant. Instead, she twined her hands together and forced a smile. "I'm sure Joe was happy to hear you'll be back. He has a lot of faith in you. So does the rest of the family. Knowing there's someone in the family working on the case, helps."

"And what about you?" he asked, studying her with shrewd eyes. "Are you happy I'm coming back?"

Sure he must have guessed how she felt about him, she cursed the hot color that spilled into her cheeks. "Of course," she said with a shrug. "Joe needs you."

"And what about you?" he asked again.

She didn't pretend to misunderstand him. He wasn't really asking if she needed him, but rather, if she loved him. And if she'd been smart, she would have turned the question around on him and insisted that he tell her how he felt about her before she said a word. But suddenly the words she thought she couldn't say were right there on her tongue, and it didn't matter that she was the one who said them first. What mattered was that she loved him, and it was time he knew that.

Her heart in her eyes, she smiled tremulously and took the biggest chance of her life. "I need you, too," she said softly. "More than you can possibly know. I love you."

With nothing more than those three little words, she brought Austin to his knees. Her love wrapped around his heart like sunshine on a rainy day, and he wondered how he'd ever thought just knowing that she loved him would be enough for him. "I love you, too," he said huskily, reaching for her. "So much it scares me. I don't want to lose you."

He didn't have to tell her he was thinking of Jenny and the baby. He could see the understanding in her eyes as she lifted her hand to his mouth and gently shushed him. "That's not going to happen again. Fate couldn't be so cruel."

Just to make sure, he wasn't taking any chances. "I want to marry you. You know that, don't you? I can't leave you without knowing that you'll be waiting for me when I come back. Will you marry me?"

"Yes."

Just that simply, with no questions asked, she laid all his fears to rest. He only had to look into her eyes to know that nothing was ever going to take her away from him. She would be there when he got back from Portland. And years from now, when they were both old and gray and surrounded by their children and grandchildren, she would still be looking at him with that same love in her eyes. A man couldn't ask for more than that.

Groaning, he pulled her close against his heart and kissed her, telling her all over again how much he loved her, how much he would always love her—and he never said a word.

Look for more of
THE COLTONS
in August 2001 with Sharon De Vita's
I MARRIED A SHEIK

One

"**I** want you," he said simply, slipping an arm around her slender waist to draw her closer. He couldn't bear to have her so near and yet so far. "You want me. It is not a complicated thing. Do not be afraid of what you feel, of what is between us. It is the most natural thing in the world."

"No." She shook her head, and even though her legs were shaking, she stepped out of his embrace. She wasn't afraid of what was between them—she was terrified of it to the tips of her soul.

"I *don't* want you," she lied, raising her chin and letting her gaze defiantly meet his.

He looked at her long and hard for a moment. "Your mouth tells lies your body denies, Faith." A small, sad smile touched his lips. "Who is lying now, Faith?" he asked quietly. "Who is lying now?"

Ashamed that he'd turned the tables on her, she shook

her head. Desire was still roaring restlessly through her. She wanted nothing more than to walk back into his arms, to hold him.

Which was precisely why she knew she couldn't ever go back to that place she'd just visited.

Not ever. It was far too dangerous.

"I'm not lying." She wished her voice was firmer, stronger, more believable. Even to her own ears she sounded weak. It infuriated and shamed her.

"I *don't* want you." Maybe if she kept saying it, it would be so.

"Ah, but I want you." He trailed a finger sensuously down her bare arm, making her body quake, and her blood heat, wanting to prove to her, to force her to see what was between them.

She jerked back, unwilling to admit that just his slightest touch could reduce her to mush. "You can't have me."

She couldn't succumb to passion, couldn't forget all that she'd learned growing up, all the pain and heartache a man like this could bring to a woman's life. To her life.

"Oh, but I will have you, Faith," he whispered confidently, only infuriating her.

"You arrogant…" Her voice trailed off and she caught herself before she said something she knew she'd regret. Her eyes darkened. Anger quickly smothered the passion, making her realize how foolish she'd been. She welcomed the anger, it was familiar, comfortable, something she knew she could handle. "I don't know who you think you are—"

"I thought you knew." His voice had gone soft again, laced with steely determination. "I am Sheik Ali El-Etra—"

"Auggh!" She wanted to smack him. "You're gonna

start with that nonsense again? Tossing your title around like I should bow to you?''

''Nonsense?'' His brows drew together slowly as he tried to comprehend what she'd just said to him. No one had ever dared refer to his title as nonsense. He stiffened, his eyes narrowing dangerously. ''There are those who would bow merely because of my title, Faith.''

Frustrated and fuming, she blew out a breath. The man was insufferable. Arrogant and pigheaded.

''Yeah, well, I'm not one of them. I am *not* one of your beautiful bevy of the brainless. Nor am I interested in a one-night stand, I don't care who you are.'' Eyes shooting sparks, Faith lifted her chin. ''And I have a news flash for you, *Sheik.* You may have had everything you've ever wanted in life up until now, but there's one thing you will *never* have.'' She gave his chest a poke, furious at the smug arrogance shimmering in his eyes. ''Me.''

With that Faith turned on her heel and marched away, leaving Ali standing in the middle of the dance floor, alone, staring after her with a perplexed look on his face.

''Ah, dear Faith, but on this too you are wrong.'' Slipping his hands in his pockets, he watched her sail through the doors into the cool, dark evening with a confident smile. ''I *will* have you.''

THE COLTONS

Silhouette®
Where love comes alive™

If you've enjoyed getting to know **THE COLTONS**,
Silhouette® invites you to come back and
visit the Colton family!

Just collect three (3) proofs of
purchase from the backs of three (3) different
COLTONS titles and receive a free **COLTONS**
book that's not currently available in retail outlets!

Just complete the order form and send it, along with three
(3) proofs of purchase from three (3) different **COLTONS**
titles, to: **THE COLTONS**, P.O. Box 9047, Buffalo, NY
14269-9047, or P.O. Box 613, Fort Erie, Ontario L2A 5X3.

(No cost for shipping and handling.)

- -

Name: _____

Address: _____ City: _____

State/Prov.: _____ Zip/Postal Code: _____

Please specify which title(s) you would like to receive:

❏ 0-373-38716-4 *PROTECTING PEGGY* by Maggie Price
❏ 0-373-38717-2 *SWEET CHILD OF MINE* by Jean Brashear
❏ 0-373-38718-0 *CLOSE PROXIMITY* by Donna Clayton
❏ 0-373-38719-9 *A HASTY WEDDING* by Cara Colter

Remember—for each title selected, you must send three (3)
original proofs of purchase. To receive *all four (4)* titles, just send
in all twelve (12) proofs of purchase.

(Please allow 4-6 weeks for delivery.
Offer good while quantities last.
Offer available in Canada and the U.S. only.)
(The proof of purchase should be cut off the ad.)

THE COLTONS
ONE PROOF OF PURCHASE
COLTPOP-R2

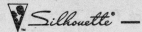

THE COLTONS

If you missed the first exciting story from **THE COLTONS**, here's a chance to order your copy today!

0-373-38704-0   BELOVED WOLF by Kasey Michaels $4.50 U.S.☐ $5.25 CAN.☐

(limited quantities available)

TOTAL AMOUNT	$ _____
POSTAGE & HANDLING	$ _____
($1.00 for one book, 50¢ for each additional)	
APPLICABLE TAXES*	$ _____
TOTAL PAYABLE	$ _____
(check or money order—please do not send cash)	

To order, send the completed form, along with a check or money order for the total above, payable to **THE COLTONS**, to: In the U.S.: 3010 Walden Avenue, P.O. Box 9077, Buffalo, NY 14269-9077; In Canada: P.O. Box 636, Fort Erie, Ontario L2A 5X3.

Name: _____

Address: _____ City: _____

State/Prov.: _____ Zip/Postal Code: _____

Account # (if applicable) : _____ 075 CSAS

*New York residents remit applicable sales taxes.
 Canadian residents remit applicable GST and provincial taxes.